MISSING
from the
LAKE HOUSE

Dan Casey
Rom 8:28

DAN CASEY

⬡ dustjacket

© 2012 by Dan Casey

© 2012 DustJacket Press
Missing from the Lake House/Dan Casey

ISBN: 978-1-937602-48-2

Dust Jacket Press
PO Box 721243
Oklahoma City, OK 73172

www.DustJacket.com
Info@DustJacket.com

Cover and Interior Design by D.E. West at ZAQ Designs
Stock Images: Deposit Photos

Printed in the United States of America

www.dustjacket.com

Dedication

To Sharon, my wife. Thanks for patiently enduring
the hours I "lived in another world."

To James and Daphna Bickerstaff. The use of your
lake house helped inspire me to write.

To Allen Quattlebaum. Your skills as a former Little Rock Police
Officer and a private investigator refined much of my book.

To Barbara Angel. You were an angel for proofreading
my manuscript.

Foreword

Dr. Dan Casey and I have been friends for years. In fact, we have written a book together as well as served in ministry related positions. Therefore, I am delighted to be asked to write the foreword for his book.

As I read the manuscript for the first time, I was reminded that Jesus often used stories and parables to connect with the culture in His day. That's what Missing from the Lake House is all about! It's a parable about everyday life that makes a spiritual application.

I was captivated by its message because my friend Dan shared that his inspiration came while he was on sabbatical and staying in a cabin located on a lake. What a perfect place to be encouraged, inspired and motivated to write a book that is destined to lift the spirits of any person who reads its pages.

The reader will soon discover as they read the book that it is filled with spiritual advice, lessons for life as well as wise counsel. Also, the book brings hope even when the lead character is accused of a crime that he did not commit. Frequently, it reminds us that God is at work even when things seem to be getting worse. In fact, God's faithfulness shines through time and time again as the author reminds us that God uses ordinary things to deliver life impacting answers to his children.

I love great fiction, and this book is just that! It's well written, an easy read and will serve as an inspiration to many readers for years to come. So, grab a cup of coffee and settle into a comfortable chair and enjoy a great book by my lifelong friend, Dan Casey.

-Stan Toler
Bestselling Author
Oklahoma City, Oklahoma

CHAPTER ONE

Ted Black had been around many dead people during his career as a pastor, but this was the most frightened he had ever been. Finding a body floating in a lake was enough to rattle anyone. As soon as he touched the swollen leg of the corpse he had just found floating in the water of Greers Ferry Lake, Ted's fingers began to shake uncontrollably. He tried again and again to stretch a rope around the gruesome remains. His breath was coming in great gulps, partly from the shock of what was happening and partly from a run up the hill to find the rope he was trying to use.

After three or four futile attempts, Ted finally got the rope stretched around the horribly disfigured leg. Tying it into a knot would prove even more difficult. He attempted the task many times, but his fingers were trembling so badly they kept him from pulling the rope tightly enough for the knot to hold.

Silently Ted asked God to help him finish this unexpected challenge. He desperately wanted to tie the body to a tree so he could find a phone and call the police to report what he had found. In the few rational moments he enjoyed as he struggled with his unwelcome assignment, he scolded himself for not getting a new phone charger. His job would have been much easier if he had just driven to the store and purchased a new charger like he should have. Then he could have used his cell phone to call the police to report the tragedy. No rope would be needed, nor would he have to come into contact with the dead body.

Ted nearly jumped into the lake beside the floating body when a husky voice behind him said, "Just stay right where you are, Mister. One wrong move and you'll answer to us." Ted had been so consumed by the challenging task at hand that he had not heard anyone walk up behind him. He dropped the rope he was holding in his shaking hands and twisted his body to see who had spoken.

Staring at him were two men in light green uniforms. They looked like they were ready to subdue him if necessary. It was obvious that one wrong move on his part would cause one or both of them to tackle him in an instant. They were unarmed as far as he could tell, but it was obvious they were strong enough to handle any resistance Ted might offer. He was much older than they were and would be overpowered quickly.

Slowly it dawned on Ted that these men thought he was responsible for the body being in the water. "You've got it all wrong," he said as he slowly stood to his feet and turned to face the two young men.

When he saw the tense faces of his accusers, he realized they were the same two young men he had seen in this very spot a few days before. He had been sitting in a chair by the lake with a book in his hands when they stopped briefly to speak to him about what a great day it was for reading. He had eagerly agreed with them. He even told them a little about the book that held his attention. He had also shown an interest in them by asking about their activities in the area.

"We're inspecting the docks along the lake," the man with the husky voice had said. He looked a little older than his partner and seemed to be the one in charge. His blond hair was brilliant in the sunshine and was complimented by his deep brown eyes. He continued sharing information by saying, "We had a lot of severe storms earlier this spring. The storms damaged many of the docks. We are making sure the owners know what repairs have to be made so they can continue using them."

Ted remembered that Greers Ferry Lake had nearly poured over the dam when torrents of rain had fallen in the area as the state was inundated with storm after storm during the previous spring. Normally the waters of the lake were calm and gently stroked the shore. Boats and jet skis usually filled the lake from mid spring until long after Labor Day. Nestled in the foothills of the Ozark Mountains of North Arkansas, the lake was a favorite vacation spot for people throughout the state. Vacation homes, as well as permanent residences, lined the shoreline around most of the lake.

"How high did the lake get?" Ted had asked the men.

"It was all the way up past those dead trees," one of them had answered. Ted had turned to look at the spot behind him where several six-foot tall evergreens were totally brown in color. They stood in stark contrast to the beautiful green trees just a few feet further up the hillside. His untrained eye had grasped the fact that the lake had risen to an unbelievable height during that time. It was hard to believe that this peaceful lake could be so deep without causing catastrophic damage.

"Many of the docks have taken a beating," the younger of the two men had said, obviously feeling the importance of his position. His auburn hair and hazel eyes were a total contrast to his partner. "We have to inspect them to make sure they are safe for people to use. We sure don't want anyone to get hurt up here at the lake. It's our job to make sure that everyone who comes to the lake stays safe."

Safe! The word shocked Ted back to reality. No one had kept the person he had just found very safe. As he stood face-to-face with these two young game wardens, he noticed how young they looked. They also looked very serious. One wrong move on his part and he probably would "answer to them" just like they had told him. He certainly didn't want to find out since he had done nothing wrong.

"I need to tell you what happened," Ted tried to explain. "I came down here to the lake to read like I was doing a few days ago when you saw me. But this time…"

The older of the two men rudely interrupted him by saying, "You can give your explanation to the police as soon as they arrive. For now, just sit on the ground while I call the sheriff's office and get someone over here to investigate this matter."

As soon as he finished telling Ted what to do, the young man keyed the radio he was carrying. "Jill, this is Bob," he said matter-of-factly. "Call the sheriff and have him come to Lot 53 on the west side of Pigeon Point. There is a body in the water. It appears to be a female. We found some guy untying a rope from her ankle."

He paused for a moment to allow Jill time to respond. Then he said, "Probably some kind of love triangle, I would guess."

With that comment, he ended his conversation and turned toward Ted who had done what he was told. Ted was sitting on the ground about ten feet from where the body was lodged among the plants. He had carefully made sure he kept his back to the disturbing sight. He didn't want to look again at the remains of this person whose life had been so tragically cut short in the water of Greers Ferry Lake.

"It wasn't a love triangle." Ted yelled as he tried again to explain what happened. "I didn't even know the body was a female until you just said so. Besides, that's not what I was doing!" Ted declared. "I wasn't trying to untie the rope. I was trying to tie it around her ankle. I wanted to keep the body from floating away while I went for help."

"Is that right?" the younger man asked as a grin spread across his face. "Why didn't you just use your cell phone?" He glanced suspiciously at the cell phone that was in its leather case on Ted's belt. Ted had left it strapped to his belt out of habit. Carrying it with him was also the easiest way of making sure it was not misplaced like his charger had been.

Ted started to explain that the battery of his cell phone was dead when the older of the two men interrupted him again. "Just tell the police when they get here," he said, refusing to listen to any more of Ted's story.

Ted was anxious for the police to arrive. He figured he would give them an explanation of what had happened and his part in this unwelcome event would be over in a few minutes. He didn't have anything to hide, so he was certain they would believe what he told them.

After waiting for what seemed like hours but was actually just a few minutes, Ted could hear the sirens from the police cars getting louder and louder as they got closer to his location. He sure would be glad when they got there so he could tell his full story.

Things moved at a rapid pace when the police arrived on the scene. The sheriff and two of his deputies hastily made their way down the hillside to where Ted was sitting under the careful surveillance of the two uniformed men. The two deputies started stretching yellow crime scene tape from tree to tree. The sheriff approached Bob, one of the uniformed men, and asked him to follow him to a place where they could talk without Ted hearing the conversation.

From his spot on the ground, Ted could tell that the sheriff was upset about something. The conversation was animated to say the least. Ted noticed that the sheriff was doing most of the talking. The two young men nodded their heads in agreement with whatever they were being told. Sometime during the next few minutes both of them disappeared.

When Sheriff Bill Bixley walked over to him, Ted stood and started his explanation of what had happened by saying, "I've been staying here in the lake house for the last two weeks." He was glad to finally have an opportunity to explain what had happened.

"Yes, Mr. Black. I know who you are and where you have been for the last two weeks," the sheriff responded in a dry tone that made Ted think he was bored with the whole process. "Now, please turn around and put your hands behind your back."

Ted couldn't believe what was happening, but decided he had better do what he had been told. The sheriff didn't look like he was going to put up with any resistance. As Ted turned around, Sheriff Bixley grabbed his arms and slammed hand cuffs on his wrists with so much force that he scratched and bruised them. A few drops of blood oozed from beneath the handcuffs and made a trail into Ted's palms.

"Mr. Black, you have the right to remain silent..." Sheriff Bixley began. As the sheriff spoke, Ted's head began to spin and he nearly fainted. He was being arrested for the death of someone he didn't even know. All kinds of questions rushed through his mind. *How could this be happening? Why did they suspect him? Why wouldn't anyone listen to his explanation? What in the world was going on? Why was God allowing this to happen?*

The sheriff concluded his obviously memorized speech with words that sent chills up Ted's back. Without compassion the sheriff said, "Mr. Black, you are under arrest for the murder of Marla Harris."

Words began to spew from Ted like a geyser, "I had nothing to do with her death, Sheriff. I don't even know who Marla Harris is. I had just come down to the lake to read a book like I have been doing every afternoon. Look! There's my book on the ground beside my chair right over there," Ted said as he tried to point with his chin in the general direction of the vacant chair about twenty feet away.

"Then why were you untying a rope from her leg," the sheriff demanded.

"I wasn't," Ted answered. "I was tying the rope to her leg. I was going to tie the other end to a tree. I didn't want the body to float away while I came to tell you about finding it."

"Why didn't you just call 911?" the sheriff wanted to know.

"I couldn't. My cell phone battery is dead. It quit working last night while I was talking to my wife. And I couldn't find my charger, so I haven't been able to charge my phone enough to make a single call."

"That was real convenient, wasn't it, Mr. Black?" the sheriff asked with a sneer on his face. "How do you explain the rope burn on her ankle if you had not even tied the rope to her leg yet?" he demanded.

"I don't know anything about that," Ted admitted. "I was just trying to do what I thought would be the best thing to do," Ted tried to say, but the sheriff had already walked away to meet the paramedics. Ted could vaguely remember hearing the sirens from the ambulance as it had approached. One of the deputies had apparently called them.

Ted could hear the sheriff as he talked to the paramedic team. "It's Marla Harris," he said. "She's been missing for several days now. She couldn't be a day over twenty-three, but apparently this guy was having an affair with her. His wife probably got suspicious, so he had to get rid of her. It looks like he tried to dispose of the evidence by tying her body to something heavy and throwing it in the lake. The rope must have come untied from the weight. Her body floated to the surface and lodged in those plants. Ironic, isn't it? She came right back to the spot where she must have been before she died. He might have gotten away with it, too, if Bob and Jeff hadn't come along when they did."

"No," Ted screamed. "That's not what happened at all. I had just come here for a few days of rest. I came down to the lake to read, saw the body, and went to investigate. I wasn't having an affair. I love my wife. We've been married for 32 years now. I would never be unfaithful to her. I was just tying the body to a tree so it wouldn't float away while I went to report finding it. Please believe me," Ted begged, but no one was listening.

Sheriff Bixley finished his so-called lakeside investigation and pushed Ted into the back of the police cruiser without taking any of the precautions normally taken to protect a suspect. He quickly jumped into the front seat and started driving toward town at dangerously high speeds. It was obvious that he was irritated by something.

As the car made its way around the curves on its way to the police station, Ted asked God to help him convince the sheriff of the truth. He also reminded God of His promise to be with His people when they were mistreated and falsely accused of things. "God, that's exactly what's happening right now," Ted prayed, "and I can't seem to do anything about it. I need Your help right now more than I ever have. Please help me get out of this mess," Ted begged God as he struggled to keep from being thrown across the back seat by the sheriff's reckless driving.

Ted then asked God to give Carla the strength she needed to deal with the shocking news of his arrest. He knew she wouldn't believe he could actually take someone's life, but he also knew it would break her heart when they told her what they thought he had done. Ted had never given Carla any reason to question his faithfulness, but he was afraid that the news that he was arrested for killing someone to cover up an alleged affair would crush her emotionally.

Ted concluded his time of prayer with a request for God to give his church leaders discerning hearts as well. He knew something like this could cause all kinds of harm to the church if it hit the newspaper. The media seemed to enjoy reporting news about the moral failures of pastors and crimes committed by church leaders. He sure didn't want to hurt the church he loved and to which he had given the last several years of his life.

"God, how could something so wonderful turn into such a nightmare?" Ted questioned God as he thought about how much he had enjoyed his first two weeks at the lake house. He also wondered why no one would listen to him. No one seemed the least bit interested in anything he had to say.

When they arrived at the police station, Ted was read his rights again and then taken to a bare room containing nothing but a table and a few chairs.

"Mr. Black, why don't you just admit your guilt so we can get this whole thing over with?" Sheriff Bixley spoke with obvious irritation in his voice. "We all know what you were doing over there on Pigeon Point. If you would just make a statement confirming your activities, it would make things a lot easier for all of us…especially you. Judge Cox always gives lighter sentences to people who plead guilty than he does to those who make the prosecutor prove they're guilty."

"Sheriff, I can't plead guilty to something I didn't do!" Ted exclaimed. "I told you back at the lake that I didn't do anything but find a body. When those two men found me, I was simply trying to secure the body to a tree so it wouldn't float away while I came to report it to you. Why won't you listen to me? I've been trying to tell you what happened, but you won't listen."

"Mr. Black, I don't like it when people tell me I'm not doing my job like I should. If you keep making accusations, I'll add a few more charges to your case. Now tell me plainly…did you or did you not have an affair with Marla Harris that you tried to cover up by killing her? Didn't you then try to dispose of her body in Greers Ferry Lake?"

"No! I did not! I don't even know Marla Harris. I've been a happily married man for 32 years. I've never been unfaithful to my wife in my entire life. And if I was, I sure wouldn't kill someone. I've been a pastor of churches for 30 years now and would never take anybody's life," Ted informed the sheriff with a note of defiance in his voice.

Sheriff Bixley winced when Ted mentioned being a minister, but he managed to say, "Then why don't you tell the truth? Mr. Black, I'm not much of a religious man, but there's one thing I do know. Preachers are supposed to tell the truth. Why don't you just start doing that so we can get this wrapped up?"

"I am telling the truth, Sheriff." Ted protested. He was becoming irritated by the repeated accusations. Ted grew more and more concerned that he was not going to be able to convince the sheriff of his innocence.

"Don't I get a phone call? Am I not entitled to a lawyer?" Ted asked hoping to show the sheriff that he knew he had some rights that were being overlooked.

"You sure are," Sheriff Bixley replied with a sinister smile on his face. "I've already called Eric Stout. He's the best lawyer in this town. He'll represent you. I told him to drop by tomorrow. You can tell him your story then. And, about that phone call. You can make your phone call when I say so. Now, shut up about it. I'll let you know when the time is right."

"But, Sheriff..." Ted started to object. He wanted to tell the sheriff that he would decide for himself who would represent him. Before he could say anything else, however, Sheriff Bixley left the room. Although he was some distance away, Ted could hear the sheriff tell his deputy to take Ted to the cell. From that comment Ted concluded that the jail only had one cell.

He didn't have to think about it very long, however. An obviously angry deputy arrived and said, "Mr. Black, follow me. And don't cause me any trouble. I've already had enough trouble today because of you. If you try anything, I'll take care of you...and make it look like an accident." With that comment he brushed his hand across his gun. Ted cringed at the sight of the gun and inwardly renewed his commitment to cooperate in every way he could. He also decided he would maintain his innocence no matter what the sheriff, his deputies, or anyone else did to him.

When they arrived at the cell, Ted could see two men already behind bars. The deputy stopped at the doorway and pushed a key into the lock. As the door swung open, he waved his arm toward Ted and then toward the cell, making a mock bow as if escorting royalty into a luxurious room.

Ted walked hesitantly past the deputy and into the small enclosure. He couldn't believe he was actually being put in jail. If he had been arrested for preaching the gospel like the Apostle Paul, he would have considered it an honor. But being charged with murder took any honor away. It left him feeling like he was the victim of circumstances over which he had no control.

As soon as the deputy left the area, the crusty, old man in the back corner of the cell asked, "What're ya' in here for, fella?"

Because he couldn't bring himself to say he was charged with murder, Ted just said, "I've been accused of something I didn't do, so I really don't know why I'm here." He spoke more harshly than he intended, but he really didn't care. He wasn't in the mood for conversation right now. His mind was swirling because of the way he had been treated during the last few hours. Ted wasn't sure he could trust anyone anymore, especially the sheriff and his deputies.

The old man would not be deterred, however. "What did they accuse you of?" he asked.

"They said I killed some woman I don't even know and then tried to dispose of her body in Greers Ferry Lake," Ted answered, trying to keep his answer as brief as possible. He was growing skeptical of everyone he met in this crazy, little town.

"Did you do it?" the old man wanted to know as if he had a right to information others might not be entitled to receive.

"Of course not!" Ted exclaimed. "I wouldn't kill anyone for any reason. I just came to the lake to get a few weeks of rest. When my wife gets here, she'll let them know my story is true." Ted hoped the old man would be satisfied and would stop asking questions, but he didn't.

"Why did they accuse you?" he wanted to know.

"Because I found her body floating in the lake behind the cabin I was staying in. My cell phone was dead, so I was trying to secure her body to keep it from floating away while I came to get the sheriff. Two game wardens came up behind me and accused me of disposing of the body. And the sheriff believed them," Ted exclaimed, not quite sure why he was saying so much to the old man. He couldn't help but wonder if the old man believed anything he was telling him.

The old man must have been satisfied with his answers, however, because he asked no further questions. Ted breathed a sigh of relief as he moved toward an empty bed along one wall. It was one of four narrow, single beds crammed into a small area that was only large enough for two beds. A commode was the only other item in the small cell. Ted suddenly felt tired and wanted to get some rest.

Squashed into a bed that wasn't nearly big enough for a man his size, Ted spent a restless night. Just before he slipped into a fitful sleep, he wondered what Carla would think when he didn't call. He would love to let her know what was going on, but they had taken his phone, and wouldn't let him make a phone call to anyone. All he could do was place her into the hands of the loving God that he trusted in spite of his circumstances. Ted tried to pray, but his mind was too full of confusion. It was a rare thing for Ted to be unable to concentrate enough to pray.

When morning finally came, Ted tried to organize his thoughts. He wanted to make sure he shared all the details he could remember with his lawyer. At noon the younger of the two men in the cell was released. That was okay with Ted since he had not spoken one word since Ted had been put in the cell the evening before. Ted and the crusty old man talked about the weather and other everyday topics, but the young man never said a word. Nothing else was said by either man about why Ted was in jail.

By evening Ted was growing impatient in spite of his efforts to control his emotions. Thoughts of Carla swept through his mind as he stretched out on the cramped cot. He wondered if she had even been notified of his arrest. He would love to call her...to hear her voice...to have her reassure him that everything would be okay. Again Ted tried to pray, but his prayers seemed to evaporate in the air just above his head. Questions about why God had not intervened in his behalf flooded his mind as he drifted into a second, restless night of sleep.

The morning of the next day was filled with more waiting. About two o'clock in the afternoon a deputy came to tell the old man that he was being released. He warned Ted to be quiet while the door that led to the office was open. "People in the front office don't like to be bothered by the criminals back here in the cell," the deputy informed Ted. Ted sank back on his bed as the deputy opened the door. He was happy for the old man, but a little disappointed for himself when the deputy motioned for the old man to follow him.

As the old man and the deputy disappeared, Ted wondered why Mr. Stout, his sheriff-appointed lawyer, had not come to see him. When he still had not come by 3:00 p.m., Ted yelled for the deputy.

The deputy came to find out why he was yelling. It was the same angry man who had threatened him the night before. Ted cringed when he saw who it was, but he was determined to find out where his lawyer was, so he asked the deputy, "Do you know when my lawyer is coming? Have you heard anything from him?"

"Now, how in the world do you think I would know what your lawyer's schedule is?" the deputy asked. "He doesn't check with me before he does stuff! Why don't you just sit back down and stop bothering me? The sheriff will make sure he gets here when he wants him to come."

"Well, I want to see him today! Why don't you just let the sheriff know that I'm expecting him to come by this afternoon? I'm entitled to legal representation, and I expect to get it," Ted stated with more confidence than he felt. He couldn't help but wonder if this was how every prisoner in Highpoint was treated.

"Watch your mouth, boy!" the deputy said with parental authority even though he was obviously younger than Ted. Then he stomped across the floor and disappeared through the door.

CHAPTER TWO

When Carla Black got up Thursday morning, her mind was filled with all kinds of questions. She tried to resist them, but they kept forcing their way into her mind. The morning was sunny and beautiful, but Carla didn't even notice. Her husband, Ted, had not called her before she went to bed the night before and she was concerned.

It was not like Ted to fail to contact her. He had started calling her daily on his very first trip out of town many years before. It was a practice both of them greatly enjoyed whether the visits were lengthy or lasted only a few minutes. It allowed them to keep up with each other's activities while they were separated from one another.

"Maybe he got interested in his book until he thought it was too late to call," she said aloud, as she made her way into the comfortable kitchen of the lovely ranch-style home she shared with Ted. She could not help but wonder if he was having trouble with his cell phone. His phone had gone dead when they talked the previous night, but a dead phone was no excuse she decided. He could have plugged the phone into the charger, charged it for a few minutes, and then made at least one short call even if he had forgotten to charge it earlier in the day.

"At least he could have called to apologize," she said to the empty kitchen.

"Why didn't he call this morning?" Carla asked herself a few minutes later while she was in the master bathroom putting on her makeup. As she glanced into the mirror, she realized that she looked extremely tired and a little pale. Black circles engulfed her eyes. "Maybe I'm the one who needs a break," she thought to herself.

Like bullets from a machine gun, question after question assaulted Carla's brain and threatened her sanity. She was sobered by the more serious questions. *What if something had happened to her wonderful husband? What if he had fallen and broken a bone? What if he had twisted an ankle, or messed up his knee? What if he had been bitten by a snake? What if he had tried to swim in the lake? He was a good swimmer, but something could have gone wrong.*

Visual images of Ted lying seriously injured on the ground in an isolated area near the lake captured her mind and held it enslaved for several minutes. "No one would find him for days if something did happen to him," she muttered to herself, suddenly sobered by the unwelcome thought.

Carla realized that she was getting worked up without a good reason. "Everyone makes mistakes from time to time," she reasoned. Even her wonderful husband was not perfect. He reminded her of that frequently. It was hard to believe, however. Ted was the most thoughtful and considerate man she had ever met. He was always doing something special to show her that he loved her.

For her birthday the previous spring, he surprised her with yellow roses. She smiled as she remembered the first time he had given her these special flowers. They were in a corsage he bought for her while they were dating. From that time forward yellow roses had been one of her favorite gifts from Ted. When he wanted to do something extra special for her, he always bought her yellow roses.

Ted had also made reservations for a special dinner at one of the fanciest restaurants in town for her special day. Carla chuckled to herself briefly as she remembered meeting Ted at the restaurant. He had gone directly there from work and had told her to come as soon as she could. When she got there, three other couples were already there with balloons and gifts. Ted had invited them to share in the celebration without letting her know what was happening. Such happy memories reminded her that she loved him more than anyone else in the world.

As Carla gave thanks for her food that morning, she breathed a prayer for Ted. She asked God to give him a good day and to remind him to call home.

Her spirits had been lifted by her special memories, so Carla ate a quick bite of breakfast, got dressed, and left home to take care of some of the business she had to handle since Ted was out of town.

When Ted did not call Thursday night either, Carla was visibly shaken. She tried to sleep, but could not keep from worrying about Ted. She felt extremely uneasy about him. When she did manage to fall asleep for a few minutes, she was jolted awake by bad dreams. In one dream she found Ted lying at the bottom of a ravine with his leg broken. In another he was struggling to stay afloat in a lake while his boat floated further and further away from shore. After each dream she would sit straight up in bed, gasp for breath, and fight back tears. Her dreams were horrible. They kept invading her sleep over and over causing her to toss and turn throughout the night.

Dawn finally pierced the darkness of the night, but it failed to bring much relief to Carla's despair-filled mind. As soon as she got dressed that morning, she called Tiffany Lee, one of the members of the leadership board at the church where she and Ted served as pastoral leaders.

"Tiffany, I'm worried about Ted," Carla said. Then she broke down and cried in spite of her attempts to maintain her composure. "He hasn't called me for two nights," she sobbed. "That's not like Ted. He calls me every night when he is out of town. I've tried to call him, but all I get is a recording saying, 'the cell phone customer you are calling is not available.' Tiffany, I'm so worried about him... and...and...and I'm scared. Is there any way you could come over for a few minutes?"

"Of course I can, Carla," Tiffany answered. She could tell that Carla was really upset. "I'll be there in fifteen minutes. Why don't you put on a pot of coffee and we'll spend some time together?" As soon as she hung up the phone, Tiffany made a quick call to her boss and told her she would be late for work.

As Tiffany drove toward Carla's house that morning, she asked God to give her the right words to say. She knew she was totally unskilled in these kinds of things. All she knew to do was listen to what Carla had to say. She certainly didn't have any idea why Pastor Ted had not called his wife.

The aroma of freshly brewed coffee swept through the open doorway when Carla responded to Tiffany's knock. As soon as Carla closed the door behind her, Tiffany reached out to hug her. Tears flowed in streams from Carla's eyes. Tiffany noticed that the tissue in Carla's hands was already soaked. She reached for a dry one and forced it into Carla's hand as she held her friend in her arms.

"I'm sorry, Tiffany," Carla apologized. "I just don't know what I would do without Ted. I'm afraid something awful has happened to him." Then she told Tiffany about all the questions that had forced their way through her mind over the last two days. "I know you don't have any answers for those questions, but sometimes it helps a little to share them with someone," Carla said, apologizing again for her lack of control.

"You don't owe me an apology, Carla," Tiffany said. "That's why I'm here. I want to help any way I can…even if all I can do is listen to your questions. I love you, Carla. And I love Pastor Ted, too. Over the last few years, you two have ministered to my family in more ways than you'll ever know. The least I can do is stay with you until you can figure out why Pastor Ted has not called."

Carla smiled at her friend and then said, "How about that cup of coffee now? How do you drink yours?" she asked as she made her way to the kitchen and began pouring two cups of coffee. Carla uncovered a plate of brownies and sat them in the middle of the table. She was grateful she had something on hand to serve her guest.

As the two ladies pulled two chairs from under the table, they each took a brownie and pretended to eat it. Tiffany spoke first, "Now, tell me about some of your recent conversations with Pastor Ted?"

For the next thirty-five minutes Carla told Tiffany about Ted's activities at the lake house. Finally, Carla said, "Tiffany, I'm so sorry. I have taken too much of your time. I'm going to drive up to the lake house this morning to see if I can find out what has happened to Ted. I'll let you know what I find out when I get back."

"Do you want me to go with you?" Tiffany asked. "I think I can make arrangements to be gone from work for the day."

"No, you've done enough already. Just help me pray that Ted is okay," Carla replied.

Tiffany assured Carla that she would be praying for Ted. She also volunteered to pray for Carla's safety as she drove to the lake.

As soon as Tiffany backed out of the driveway, Carla grabbed her keys from the hall table and sprinted toward her car. "Why hadn't I thought of driving up to the lake before now?" she asked herself as she started the car, backed into the street, and headed in the direction of Greers Ferry Lake.

Carla struggled to keep her speed within reason as she made her way toward the lake house, but she frequently caught herself going fifteen or twenty miles per hour over the posted speed limit. In spite of her excessive speed, the trip seemed to take forever. As each mile passed by, Carla grew more and more tense. She knew something was wrong, and she intended to find out exactly what it might be.

A state trooper fell in behind Carla at one point, causing her to shudder and put her foot on her brake. She hurriedly glanced to see how fast she was going, but breathed a sigh of relief when she saw that she was going the speed limit for once. She knew she needed to slow down or she would end up sitting on the side of the road while a stern-faced policeman wrote her a ticket. Keeping her speed under control proved to be a bigger task than Carla expected however. She was so eager to find out what happened to Ted that she kept going faster than she should.

"Let's see now," Carla said aloud even though no one was in the car. "Which way should I go?" She studied the road signs and tried to remember what Ted had said to her about where he would be. She scolded herself for not bringing the directions Ted left on the top of his desk. Neither of them thought she would need them, so she had not paid much attention to what Ted had said when he told her he was leaving her directions to the lake house just in case she needed them. It was just like Ted to make sure everything was taken care of before he left. Unfortunately, her determination to leave quickly had kept her from thinking about his instructions.

Once again she thought about how much she loved that man and how much she needed him. Tears threatened to spill from her swollen eyes again, but Carla forced herself to concentrate on the road. She certainly didn't need to be involved in an accident right now. Ted needed her too much for that.

Finally, Carla saw a sign with a name on it that she remembered Ted mentioning during one of his phone calls. She turned left and hoped she was on the road that led to the lake house. Nothing looked familiar to her since she had not been to the lake house before, but she kept going anyway.

"God, would you please guide me to Ted?" she prayed. "And, please let everything be okay when I get there," she begged. The rest of her prayer was left unspoken.

"I'm sure that's it! That's the house Ted described. It has to be!" Carla screamed the words into the empty car. "It's a pale green, two-story house with an unusual roof and a huge front porch...and it has a fruit and vegetable stand right beside the road just like he said." She recalled Ted telling her about his conversation with the neighbors just before they left to go on vacation. He had described the house as they talked.

"It should only be another mile or so now," Carla verbalized her hopes aloud as she pushed down on the accelerator. Soon she would know what had happened to her beloved Ted. She hoped he was okay, but deep inside she felt an awful sense of fear clutching her heart and holding it in its grip. She squeezed the steering wheel so tightly her fingers turned white and began to ache.

"That's it! It looks just like Ted said it did!" Carla exclaimed when she saw a small, redwood cabin sitting on the side of a hill just off the road. When she caught a glimpse of the lake through the trees, she was certain she had found the right place.

"Thank you, God," Carla said as she turned into the driveway and pulled up behind Ted's car. She honked the car's horn two or three times, but no one responded.

As Carla got out of her car, she hardly noticed a car pass by on the road up the drive from where she stood. She was too anxious to locate Ted. As she walked by Ted's car, she saw his old camping chair sitting down the hillside near the lake. She was sure she could see a book lying on the ground a few feet from the chair. Leaving a book on the ground and a chair out of place were not like Ted at all, she thought.

As her eyes traveled down the hill toward the lake, Carla was startled when she saw some yellow ribbon blowing from a tree. "Oh, no!" she screamed as soon as she recognized it as crime scene tape. "Why is that ribbon there? Something's happened to Ted! I knew it. I knew he would have called if he could have!" she declared.

Carla ran the last few steps across the gravel driveway. She wanted to get to the door of the cabin as quickly as she could. She banged on the rustic-looking door, but no one answered. She tried the knob, but it was locked. She put her hands around her eyes and strained to look through one of the windows near the door. Carla desperately wanted to see what was inside the cabin.

When her eyes adjusted to the change in light, she could see Ted's books scattered on the coffee table. His laptop was sitting on the dining room table. His slippers were in front of the couch. Unused food was on the counter. But there was no sign of Ted. He certainly wasn't in any of the rooms she could see from the window.

Carla was so frightened that she nearly fainted, but she managed to pull herself together. She jumped off the porch of the cabin and ran down the hill. She quickly examined the chair. It was Ted's chair. Of that she was sure. She didn't know if the book belonged to Ted or not, but the title, *Making Sense Out of Nonsense*, sounded like something Ted would enjoy reading.

After running first one way and then the other looking for some sign of Ted, Carla headed back up the hill toward her car. She was breathing heavily when she got back to Ted's car. She stood there a minute trying to catch her breath. Again she failed to take note of a car that made its way slowly past the driveway. Tears began streaming down Carla's face. Where was her beloved partner? She had to find him! Suddenly feeling as if she might fall over, Carla jerked the door of her car open and fell into the seat behind the steering wheel.

Carla's shoulders shook violently as she sobbed and sobbed. The entire car began to vibrate from her convulsive crying. "Why didn't I come up here yesterday?" she asked herself. "He needed me and I wasn't anywhere to be found. I failed him. He would have been okay if I had gotten here yesterday. I just know he would." Over and over she loudly condemned herself and sank further and further into despair.

Finally, she began to pray between her sobs, "Lord, what's happened to Ted? Please let him be okay. I need him, God. I'm not sure I can make it without him. Please help me know what to do." Then she leaned her head against the back of the seat, dried her eyes and tried to calm herself enough to decide what she should do next.

"I know what I'll do," Carla spoke loudly as if someone were in the car with her. "I'll go into town and find the sheriff's office. He'll be able to tell me what has happened. He should know where Ted is. Maybe Ted's in the hospital somewhere. If he is, he's probably wondering where I am." She shuddered again at the thought that her husband might be seriously injured.

Carla turned the key, started the car, and backed slowly out of the driveway. It was difficult to drive because her eyes kept filling with tears. She blinked rapidly to keep them from spilling over. She kept telling herself that she had to keep herself under control. She had to find the sheriff. She had to find out what had happened to Ted.

When Carla reached the highway, she turned in the opposite direction from the way toward home. Driving as fast as she dared, she headed toward the small town of Highpoint. After driving down several streets and around many blocks, she finally found the sheriff's office. It was an extremely plain building that could have been easily overlooked. It was dwarfed by the buildings that surrounded it. She parked her car and made her way anxiously to what looked like the office door.

Carla forced the heavy door open and stepped into a rather small, dimly-lit office. She looked around. There were a couple of deputies in sight, but no one seemed anxious to help her. Carla stopped in front of the paper-laden desk closest to the door and looked intently at the nearby deputy.

The deputy on duty looked up with a sneer on his face. "Can I help you, Lady?" he asked in a way that made Carla feel like he resented being interrupted by someone like her.

Carla was angered by his tone of voice, but decided not to make an issue of it. "Yes," she answered. "My name is Carla Black. My husband is Ted Black. He has been staying at the old cabin on Log Mountain Road over on Pigeon Point for the last two weeks. He hasn't called me for two days, so I came to check on him…but he's not there. I noticed some yellow ribbon stretched along the lake. Do you know if something happened to him? Has he been hurt? Is he in the hospital? Where can I find him?"

"Slow down, Lady," the deputy interrupted harshly. "In the first place, someone has to do more than fail to make a phone call to his wife for us to get involved. I haven't even heard of nobody named Ted Black. And I don't keep track of the patients at the hospital. Maybe he just drove over to Clinton for a change of scenery."

"But his car is there. And his books are on the coffee table in the cabin. And his computer is on the dining room table. What about the yellow ribbon? Where did it come from? It's the kind police use when a crime has been committed or some kind of tragedy has taken place," Carla protested, trying to keep herself from considering what might have happened to Ted during the last two days.

"Look, Lady, I don't know nothing about no car…or no books on no coffee table…or no computer on no dining table. And the police around here don't use no ribbons for nothing. Why don't you head on over to the hospital to see if your husband is there? If he ain't, you might want to think about where he might be. I don't know nothing about him," the deputy said rudely as he turned away and pretended to look through some papers that were on a nearby desk.

While the deputy was speaking, a crusty, old man, escorted by a young deputy, appeared through a doorway at the back of the office. Instinctively Carla glanced in his direction. Their eyes met for a moment and Carla had the strange feeling that the old man wanted to tell her something. The deputy nudged him from behind, so the old man pushed past Carla and made his way out of the same door she had entered. Carla couldn't help but wonder if the old man knew something about Ted. She longed to ask him if he had seen Ted, but resisted the urge to say anything. She felt like she would cause trouble for the old man and for herself as well.

When Carla realized she wasn't going to get anymore information from this hateful deputy, she dared to ask one more question. "Will you please tell me where the hospital is and how to get there?" Carla tried to be as polite as the deputy was nasty.

"It's on Pratt Street. Go down the street out front for two blocks, then turn left on Second Street, then right on Main. In one block, turn left on Pratt. It'll be on your left. You can't miss it," the deputy said as he disappeared through the door in the back of the office. Carla wanted to run after him and give him a piece of her mind, but she knew it wouldn't do any good. Instead she slowly turned away, pushed the door open, and left, feeling alone and very frightened.

The deputy's directions led Carla to the hospital. "At least he got that part right," she said to herself as she parked her car. Almost paralyzed from fear, Carla sat in her car for several long minutes trying to gain her composure. That deputy had really angered her.

As she sat there, she began to pray, "Dear God, I don't know what to do. I'm worried about Ted. I'm afraid I'm going to find him in some kind of horrible condition. I don't know if I can handle that. Please help me to be calm as I face whatever I find in this hospital. And, please, God, please help Ted to still be alive." At that point she started sobbing uncontrollably again.

CHAPTER THREE

Ted sat down on his undersized cot and tried to get comfortable. The feeling that he was being abused by an angry sheriff and his equally angry deputy would not leave his mind. He was beginning to feel alone and totally overwhelmed by what he was going through. As he sat there, the events of the last seventy-five days flashed through his memory at the speed of lightning.

His first thought centered on the meeting he had with the official leadership board of Hillside Community Church where Ted had served as the lead pastor for the last seven years. It had taken place on June 12, just two and a half months ago. He remembered the conversation word for word.

"I've got to have an extended break," Ted told the group of leaders that sat before him with shocked looks on their faces. With passion in his voice, he explained, "I'm so tired and worn out that I'm having trouble remaining positive about what God wants me to do. Some days I even question my ability to lead the church. The demands and expectations of the people are getting to be more than I can handle. There are days when I struggle to put one foot in front of the other," he told this gathering of strong leaders. He had enjoyed working with many of them for the entire time he had given leadership to the church. The pastor's voice cracked a little as he addressed the group.

"Is there any way I can have a few weeks off so I can get some rest and have my heart refreshed?" he asked them. "If I can just have a month or so to myself, maybe I'll be able to go for another thirty years," the pastor said with a chuckle. The church leaders had recently helped him celebrate his thirtieth anniversary in pastoral ministry, so everyone understood his weak attempt at humor.

Sure enough, just like Ted expected, Mr. Jeffries asked, "Where are we going to get the extra money it will cost us to get supply speakers?" Mr. Jeffries had enough money to buy half the city, but he squeezed every penny two or three times before he spent it.

Ted was prepared with an answer, however. "We'll take most of it from the special speaker's budget and the rest from the travel budget," Ted informed the whole group as he glanced at Mr. Jeffries to see if he was satisfied with his answer.

He would not have been at all surprised to hear Mr. Jeffries object. If he did, Ted was prepared to offer to pay the expenses himself. He was desperate. He needed this time away. It wasn't just an ordinary vacation he was seeking. He needed to be alone... to meet with God...to refresh his spirit...to renew his calling into ministry...to regain his sanity.

Mr. Jeffries remained quiet, however, but Mrs. Majors had a question. "Who will call on people when they are in the hospital? And who will contact people when they are absent?" she wanted to know.

Quickly Ted informed the group that he had spoken with Pastor Carson from the church a few blocks away. He had agreed to visit people from both churches when he went to the hospital. He told them that he was sure the follow-up team would agree to add absentee calling to their other responsibilities while he was out of town.

John Ingles, a very astute businessman, posed this question, "Who will handle the routine business affairs of the church?"

"I was hoping maybe this group would oversee the daily operations of the church while I am gone. The secretary of the board could call any necessary meetings. The office secretary could handle the more routine matters. It was obvious that Ted had anticipated the questions that were being asked.

Ted was totally shocked, however, when Joe Hawkins, perhaps the most influential of the lay leaders, rose to his feet and said, "I think an extended leave is a great idea. The pastor has always been willing to go above and beyond what is required of him. I think it would be good for us to go above and beyond what is required of us. We need to give our pastor a chance to get some rest so he can continue to serve as our pastor."

No one dared to oppose Mr. Hawkins by asking any further questions except Stan Tucker, one of the newer members on the board. "How soon can you make arrangements to be gone?" the young business owner wanted to know.

"It would probably take me at least a couple of months to get everything in place," the pastor replied in spite of his own doubts that it could actually be done that quickly.

"I think we should help him make the arrangements," George Barrett said. "I know I am willing to do what I can to help," he volunteered.

"I'll be willing to get some of the ladies to stay in contact with Carla," volunteered Tiffany Lee, one of the ladies on the leadership board. Carla, Pastor Ted's wife, was a strong person herself and knew how to take care of herself without any help. She had conquered any fear of being alone long ago since the pastor was required to be out of town frequently when he attended conferences or was the special speaker at various events. This would be different, however. He would be gone for thirty days. No one knew what might happen during that length of time. Tiffany wanted the church to be ready to give Carla any support she might need while the pastor was out of town.

The leadership team quickly organized itself to oversee the various ministries of the church. They felt confident that they could keep all ministries functioning during the pastor's absence. The pastor and the board agreed that his month away from the church would begin on August 13, two months and one day from their meeting.

After discussing a few more items of business, the group decided to close the meeting by gathering in a circle as they sought God's blessings for both the church and its much-loved pastor. Neither the pastor nor the group of leaders that stood around the table that night had any idea what they were asking when they joined hands and prayed, "Heavenly Father, do something unusual in the life of our pastor during the time he is away from us."

Memories of Ted's meeting with his leadership board dissolved into detailed memories of his arrival at the lake house where he had been staying for the last two weeks.

Ted remembered how his body tingled with excitement as he forced the key into the rusty lock on the door of the old, redwood lake house he had borrowed. As he pushed the door open, he couldn't help but notice how clean the house was. He knew it had been empty for months, but there wasn't a speck of dust anywhere. Everything seemed to be in its rightful place and exceptionally clean. The only indication that his dwelling place for the next month was not used on a regular basis was the musty smell that develops when an old building is closed up for a period of time. Even that smell wasn't as bad as Ted thought it should be. He quickly turned on the ceiling fan, the air conditioner and a dehumidifier he found on the lower level of his temporary abode. Within minutes the musty smell evaporated into the fresh mountain air that surrounded the cabin.

After looking around for a few minutes, Ted headed for the car and grabbed his suitcase. He took it in and went back for several bags of food, his laptop, a box of books and some paperwork that he would look at if he had time. In a few minutes everything was out of the car and piled in the middle of the living room floor of the cozy cabin.

The lake house was actually a nice, two-bedroom structure with a large living room and a glass wall that opened toward Greers Ferry Lake. The lake seemed to glisten in the bright sunshine of the afternoon. The house was on the side of a hill. The lake was several feet down through some hickory and pine trees. Those trees provided a lot of shade from the bright, August sun. The water of the lake was about seventy-five to one hundred yards from the house, but could be seen with little effort. The view was magnificent. As Ted surveyed his surroundings, he realized that it would not be difficult to get down to the lake and back anytime he wanted to go.

"If a guy couldn't relax here, he probably wouldn't be able to relax anywhere," Ted thought to himself as he sat on the deck for a minute and absorbed the beauty of his home away from home for the next thirty days.

As he moved in that day, Ted left behind the demands of his job, the unreasonable expectations people placed on him, and a few disgruntled tyrants who would never be happy no matter what he did or didn't do. Ted deliberately pushed such unpleasant thoughts out of his mind, choosing instead to focus on what was ahead of him. For the next thirty days he didn't have to answer to anyone. He was free from schedules, appointments and all other intrusions into his life. He almost felt guilty about feeling so good about getting away from things.

Ted looked forward to reading at least part of the sizeable stack of books that had been waiting for him to "find some time" to read them. He planned to relax by spending time by the lake. He didn't have a boat, but that was okay. Being near the water would infuse new life into his tired frame. Ted also wanted to go for walks without being interrupted by phone calls and noisy neighbors. In spite of his best effort, he couldn't keep himself from thrusting his hand into the air as he shouted, "Ted Black, you're a free man! You can do whatever you want to do...and no one can stop you!"

Ted had been dreaming of this moment for the last two months. It had completely filled his thoughts since the day his leadership board had granted his request for a month off with pay. Just thinking about the next thirty days lifted his sagging spirit. Arriving at the lake house brought an even greater sense of anticipation.

Deep inside, Ted knew it would take more than simply arriving at an empty house to bring any lasting cure, however. He didn't fully understand how a man who had such strong faith in God could feel so drained and depleted. Oh, well, that didn't matter now. He was here to be refreshed...and he was going to make the best of it.

Quickly Ted piled his clothes in stacks on the spare bed, put his food away, organized his books, set up his computer, and dreamed about what the next few weeks of his life would be like. When he turned his laptop on, he realized that he would not be able to check his e-mail or surf the web since he had no access to the internet. That was fine with him. He wanted to escape from his normal contacts anyway. Not having internet service would excuse him from answering the myriad of questions people would direct his way. His only contact with the outside world would be a daily phone call to his wife.

For two weeks Ted was in paradise. He was an avid reader and soon consumed ten lengthy books. Most of his reading was done down by the lake in a camping chair he had brought from home. For three or four hours every afternoon he would sit by the water and read. When he returned to the house, he would work on his computer and read even more. Ted was careful to make sure he included the Bible in his readings and spent even more time than usual in prayer. He didn't want his relationship with God to suffer while he was away from his regular responsibilities.

A brisk, thirty-minute walk every evening soon became a part of his normal routine. On his very first trek a big, white dog greeted him. The dog appeared to be a Lab mix of some kind. Ted scratched the dog's ears and said, "Well hello, Buddy. How are you doing?" The dog wagged his tail and walked alongside Ted for the rest of his walk.

When the dog accompanied Ted the next day and the day after that, Ted began to look forward to seeing him each day and soon considered the dog a real friend. He petted him briefly and officially dubbed him, Buddy. When he showed up on Ted's deck one rainy afternoon, Buddy totally enjoyed being petted and kept asking for more. When Ted finally went into the house, Buddy laid on the deck for a while longer before trudging off in the gentle rain that was falling.

With Buddy trotting alongside, Ted felt a little safer in his unfamiliar surroundings …especially when he read the sign posted on a tree along his route. It read, "Parents, watch your children closely due to the unusually high number of recent bear sightings in the area." Ted knew it would be highly unlikely that he would ever actually see a bear, since the only wildlife he had seen was a herd of seven deer that bounded across the road in front of him on one of his walks. He was totally captivated by them as they loped through the nearby field and disappeared into the dense woods.

Each night as Ted reflected about what had filled his day, he would get a strange feeling that he was about to get to know his

Creator better. That was something he had wanted to do for a long time, so he embraced the thought with little, if any, anxiety. After all, getting closer to God was one of the goals he had for his retreat to the mountains. Little did he know that his expanded knowledge of God was about to come in a totally unexpected way.

One day Buddy greeted Ted with constant barking instead of just sitting by the road waiting for him to come to where he was like he usually did. Ted couldn't help but notice Buddy's strange behavior. He would bark once or twice and then take a step or two along a narrow path that made its way through some tall grass in the open field beside the road. It was obvious that Buddy wanted Ted to join him on a hike down that path. Since Ted was not dressed for such an excursion, he kept walking along the road leaving his barking friend standing on the grassy trail. Ted's last glimpse of Buddy was a speck of white in the midst of tall green grass. Soon Buddy was out of sight. As he walked along, Ted wondered what Buddy wanted him to see. He did not know it then, but that was to be the last time he would see Buddy for several days.

Finally, vivid memories of the minutes just before his startling discovery pushed their way into his mind. Ted had awakened much later than usual that morning. He had not slept well. During the night he kept having dreams that caused him to sit straight up in bed as they jolted him awake. Ted couldn't remember any of the details from these dreams, but they had disturbed his sleep over and over. When he finally got his eyes open that morning, he had a strange sense of uneasiness about him.

"Oh, well," he said to himself trying to shrug off his restlessness. "It's just another reaction to being alone for so long." Ted was never used to having more than a few hours without interruptions. His life was one of constant activity and interaction with people of all ages and backgrounds. By this time of day he would have usually had two or three encounters with people and enough meetings to satisfy the quota of any time management expert. To be alone caused him to imagine all kinds of things.

Following a hastily prepared lunch meat and cheese sandwich, a few chips and a Coke, Ted grabbed a book and slung his camping chair over his shoulder. He eagerly made his way down the hillside toward his favorite reading site, a shady spot near a little inlet where the water was usually calm and serene. He was familiar with the route by now. He had stepped over the multitude of exposed roots from the trees that swayed overhead. Almost every day for the last two weeks he had stopped to watch tiny frogs, striped lizards with bright blue tails, spiders and a variety of insects as he made his way down the hillside to the lake. His climb down the hill had become as much a part of his ritual as the time he spent reading once he got to his destination.

As soon as Ted settled into his chair that day, he looked to his left to see if he could spot the otter he had seen swimming there the day before. He had totally enjoyed watching it. He couldn't see all the details, but he could tell that the animal was feeding on something in the edge of the water. It would eat for a few minutes and then swim out a few feet, only to swim back to the edge of the water where it would appear to eat some more. Ted stood up and started to move closer so he could see the animal more clearly. Then he realized that his movements would only scare the animal, so he chose to sit back down and let the animal enjoy its usual habitat without being disturbed.

Ted had unconsciously looked to his right toward a clump of plants that grew in the edge of the lake. He couldn't see very well from where he sat in the shade under the hickory trees forty feet or more from the water, but he noticed something large floating among the plants. Whatever it was, it had not been there the day before. He was sure of that. He had watched a bird sit on those very plants and search for food less than twenty-four hours ago.

Ted decided to go investigate. He dropped his book beside his chair and walked cautiously toward the object in the water. As he got closer, he realized that he was looking at a fully clothed body.

With that thought Ted was summoned back to the harsh reality of the moment. As soon as he had spotted the body floating in the water, he had grabbed his cell phone so he could call 911 to report what he had found, but the battery to his phone was dead. Ted remembered that his cell phone battery had gone dead while he was talking with Carla the evening before. He had searched diligently for his phone charger, but could not find it anywhere. He had just used it three days before, but now it was nowhere to be found.

He should have driven into town that morning to try to purchase a new charger, but had postponed his plans until later in the day. "I won't need my phone before I call Carla tonight," Ted had told himself. "I want to read for a while before I make that twenty-minute trip into town."

Since the nearest neighbors were two miles away and were out of town for a week, Ted had decided to tie the body to a tree so it wouldn't float away while he made his way into town to find the sheriff. He wanted to report what he had found as quickly as he could. Ted had run up the hill to the lake house, found a rope, ran back down to the lake, and started trying to tie one end of the rope around the right ankle of the person in the water. That's when the men found him and accused him of killing this woman named Marla Harris, whoever she was.

Ted was snatched back to the present moment by the loudly spoken words of the rotund man who had just barged through the doorway in front of his cell. The man was present and talking before Ted even realized anyone was coming.

"I'm Eric Stout," said the robust man. "I'm your lawyer. I'll be representing you in this case. From what the sheriff has told me, I recommend that we plead guilty to a charge of second-degree murder. We can claim it was a crime of passion instead of premeditated murder. I think I can convince the jury that you just got in over your head and committed the crime while you were confused by the intense passion you felt when your wife accused you of having an affair."

"Whoa! Wait a minute!" Ted objected. "What are you talking about? I didn't kill anyone. Don't you even want to hear what I have to say about what happened before you decide how you are going to defend me? I would think you would want to know what I have to say! What kind of lawyer are you anyway?"

"A very good one," Mr. Stout defended himself. "I'm one of the best in the state. Don't lose many cases. You can ask anyone in Highpoint. They'll tell you Eric Stout is the best lawyer in this county."

"I'm sorry, Mr. Stout," Ted apologized. "I don't mean to question your legal ability. It's just seems like I can't get anyone around here to listen to me. I didn't kill anyone, and I want someone to believe what I have to say."

"Okay, Mr. Black, let me hear your story," the lawyer said in a rather bored-sounding tone. "Only don't go into too much detail. I'm kind of busy today. I need to get home and have some supper so I can get out the door to an important meeting tonight."

Ted was sure glad that he had organized his thoughts earlier in the day. As quickly as he could, he told the lawyer everything he could remember.

When Ted finished his report, Mr. Stout said, "Well, things don't sound too good, Mr. Black. You really don't have much of an alibi. I'll think about what you just told me and get back to you in a few days. In the meantime I would suggest that you give some serious thought to what I recommended. Old Judge Cox is pretty tough on criminals who waste his time."

With that declaration Eric Stout excused himself and almost ran through the door, while Ted fell back across his bed and began to plead with God for answers. "What in the world is happening, God?" he asked. "Why do I have to go through this? Have I not been trying my best to live for You? Have I failed You in some way? Why aren't You helping me get out of this mess?"

Following a rather bland supper Ted settled in for what he was sure would be another restless night. His lack of sleep the night before had left him exhausted. Before he even had time to think much about everything that was happening to him, however, Ted fell into a deep sleep.

He dreamed about Carla and the enjoyable time they had on their vacation to Hawaii for their twenty-fifth wedding anniversary. It had been a wonderful time for them to be together. They had taken in every tourist attraction they could from visiting the Arizona Memorial to attending a luau. The only bad time came when they tried to go snorkeling. Carla, who did not swim, had fallen off the hard plastic raft she was floating on. The water wasn't too deep for her to stand up, but the waves caused the raft to slam into her legs injuring one of them. Minor treatment to her scrapes left her as good as new after a couple of hours however.

It had been a long time since Ted had seen Carla that relaxed. She was beautiful when she wasn't pressured by her role as a pastor's wife. Unfortunately, Ted was not able to relax as much as Carla did. He was constantly aware of the deadlines he faced as soon as the vacation was over. His stress had even gotten worse after they came home. That was part of the reason why he needed this time away. He just couldn't seem to get everything done. He was constantly carrying work home with him and was finding it more and more difficult to relax.

Ted's pleasant dreams were interrupted a short time later when he heard people whispering. He shook his head to make sure he wasn't still dreaming. As soon as he got his eyes open, he noticed was how dark it was in his cell. It wasn't nearly as bright as it had been the previous night. Ted strained his eyes as much as he could to try to see what was going on around him.

Suddenly two figures dressed in black, with ski masks covering their faces, came toward his cell. It was obvious they did not want anyone knowing who they were. When the figures got close enough, one of them whispered in a raspy voice, "Mr. Black, don't make a sound. When we open the cell door, walk between us without saying a word. We're here to move you to a safer location. Do you understand what I just said?"

Ted didn't have a clue what he meant, so he dared to ask, "What do you mean by 'a safer location'?" Ted wasn't totally sure if he was asleep or awake. In his wildest thoughts he could not even imagine what kind of bizarre twist his life was taking.

When his first question was not answered, Ted dared to ask a second one, "Am I in some kind of danger?" Although Ted asked the question, he was not sure he wanted to know the answer. The way everything else had been going, there was no way of knowing what kind of danger might be lurking ahead.

"Just come with us," the other shadowy figure whispered as he opened the cell door. "And, remember, don't make a sound. One word out of you will mess up our plan and put all of us in great danger."

The other man grabbed Ted's arm and pushed him across the floor. Ted wondered where the deputies were while all this was going on. He stumbled as he walked through the back door of the jail and made his way toward a waiting car that was parked behind the building. One of the men in black grabbed his arm and helped him regain his balance before shoving him toward the car. The other man opened the car door. Ted ducked his head so he could get in. He made a mental note that the car was a silver one. He wasn't sure what kind it was, but it sure was luxurious with wood trim and leather seats. As soon as he got in the car, he raised his head and sat back in the seat.

Just before a blindfold was tied over Ted's eyes, he looked around. He was surprised when he spotted an old man across the side street. In spite of the limited light of the dark night Ted could tell it was the old man that had shared his cell for a couple of days. His eyes met the old man's eyes for a split second before everything went black from the blindfold.

"Why is that old man up at this time of night," Ted asked himself beneath his breath. He was careful not to utter a sound aloud however. He sure didn't want to put himself in any kind of danger. Nor did he want to upset his escorts. He wasn't sure what they might be capable of doing.

"Why would anyone, especially a man his age, be across the street from the jail in the middle of the night?" Ted continued to ask himself in his thoughts. He was not sure what time of night it was, but he knew it had to be late enough for most people to be asleep.

One of the two men in black slid into the driver's seat while the other got into the back seat beside Ted. As the car started, Ted felt something pushing into his side. He started to look down because he was sure it was the barrel of a gun, but the blindfold kept him from seeing anything.

"Don't you make a sound or try to call attention to us in any way, or I will use this thing," instructed the man in black beside him. Trying something heroic was the last thing on Ted's mind at this moment. He had too much for which to live.

Ted decided to memorize which way each turn took them as they drove away from the jail. He wasn't sure how that might help, but it was the only thing he could think of. Maybe it would help in some way. It wasn't long before Ted lost count of the turns, however.

There were far too many twists for him to remember. He sat back in the seat and resigned himself to the trip.

After traveling for what seemed like a long time, Ted began to hear the sound of rocks hitting the underside of the car. He told himself that the car had turned off the paved road. "That must mean that they are taking me somewhere in the woods outside of town," Ted silently guessed.

A short time later the car stopped, but the driver didn't turn off the engine. Not another sound could be heard. The man in black beside him released the pressure of the gun in Ted's ribs as he whispered, "Get out of the car. Stand still and wait for me to tell you what to do next."

Ted did what he was told. While he was standing there, the car pulled forward a few feet and stopped again. Ted knew that there could be no more than one man guarding him now, but he also knew that man had a gun and Ted didn't have any idea where the man was. He stood frozen in his tracks waiting to be told what to do.

A minute later the driver joined his partner. They grabbed Ted by his arms and pushed him along. When they had walked about twenty-five feet, one of men spoke aloud for the first time since they had first appeared. "Mr. Black, you are standing in front of your new home away from home. Please step up one step and then up again on the porch," he told Ted as he pulled on his arm.

Ted did what he was told. After taking a few more steps, he could tell he was walking through a doorway. Ted heard the door click behind him. Seconds later light flooded his eyes, blinding him with its brightness. Ted squinted as he waited for his eyes adjust to the light before he said anything.

"Where am I?" he asked.

"You don't need an address," said one of the men. "You won't be getting any mail anytime soon." The second man must have considered this a joke. He laughed loudly at his partner's comment.

Before Ted could ask anything else, the men removed their masks. Ted didn't know either of them. "Who are you?" he asked.

"I'm your new host," laughed the taller of the two men. Ted guessed him to be about six feet four inches tall. An ugly scar stretched across his cheek under his left eye. It disappeared into his slightly graying hair.

"And I'm your new cook, Teddy Boy," said the other man as he
let out another loud burst of laughter. This man was probably five
feet ten inches tall, balding, and slightly overweight. It was obvious
that he was easily amused.

Ted's "host" led him through a dark hall toward a room near
the back of the house. "This will be your room," he said. "You are
to stay in this room until one of us comes to get you. If you dare
to leave the room without us knowing it, your life won't be worth
much."

Ted looked around the room. It was a small bedroom with
nothing but a twin bed in it. The small window near the foot of the
bed had been covered with boards that had been painted black. It
was obvious they wanted to make sure Ted was unable to see anything
through the window.

"One of us will be awake at all times," said the host as he
continued giving instructions. "If you attempt to leave the room,
you will be severely punished. Who knows, we might even have the
joy of taking a little target practice at your expense," Ted's captor said
in a way that revealed an obvious desire to inflict harm on someone.

"What if I need to go to the bathroom?" Ted asked innocently.

"I'd suggest you learn how to hold it if you don't have enough
sense to ask if you can go," the man snarled. "You better ask first,
though. If you come through that door without getting permission,
you are responsible for anything that happens to you." The way he
said these words convinced Ted that he didn't want to find out what
might happen.

"Oh, by the way, Mr. Black," the man said. "There will be two
guards stationed outside the cabin at all times. That makes four
against one...and we know where we are and how to get around, and
you don't. So, don't try anything stupid."

Ted agreed that it would be stupid for him to try anything, so he
lay down on his bed and, once again, asked God to help him get out
of the mess he was in. In spite of his attempts to relax, he was unable
to settle down enough to go to sleep. As he lay there, he began to
reflect on the events of the last few days.

CHAPTER FOUR

"I'm sorry, Mrs. Black, but we have no record of a Ted Black being seen at this hospital. I've checked the records two or three times. He hasn't been, nor is he currently a patient here. I've also checked the emergency room records. They have no record of seeing anyone by that name over the last few days. The only patient we've seen from Pigeon Point recently was a drowning victim…but that was a woman," the very friendly nurse at Cleburne County Hospital told Carla after she had regained her composure enough to go in and inquire about her husband. The nurse's smile was enough to make Carla feel like there was at least one person in Highpoint who cared about her situation.

"Thank you for being so helpful," Carla said as she turned to leave. The drab, gray color on the hospital walls matched Carl's spirit as she walked through the sliding doors and into the parking lot. She was greatly relieved to learn that Ted had not been treated at the hospital, but she still wondered what had happened to him.

"If the sheriff doesn't know anything about him and he wasn't brought to the hospital, where in the world could he be?" she asked herself as she made her way across the parking lot. "He couldn't just disappear."

Carla's mind began to swirl with fearful thoughts about what might have happened to Ted. Her vision kept blurring from the unreleased tears that filled her eyes. She wondered if she should try to find the coroner's office, but thinking about going to see him made it harder than ever to hold back the tears that again threatened to burst forth. Her body shuddered at the thought of what she might find out. Deep inside she knew she was not ready to face anything so horrible.

Carla tried to console herself with the idea that the sheriff's office would have known if Ted had died. She wanted to believe that they would have shared such tragic news with her, but she wasn't fully convinced that the awful deputy she talked to would have told her anything even if he knew it.

When Carla started her car, she intended to go back to the lake house to see if Ted had returned. If he had not, she would search for clues she could have easily missed during her first visit. If Ted had gone somewhere, it would be like him to leave a note or something. She admitted to herself that she was too upset by the yellow ribbon to know if Ted had left any clues or not.

By the time she got back to Log Mountain Road, however, a new plan was beginning to form in her mind. Instead of turning right to head toward the cabin, she kept going straight and headed toward home.

The trip back to Little Rock took much longer than her trip to the mountains earlier that day. She kept letting her speed decrease as she got lost in thoughts about her beloved Ted. Occasionally, she would realize that she was traveling far below the speed limit and would speed up. Her increase in speed didn't last long, however, before a new memory would cause her to slow down again.

Carla remembered how happy she was when she first met Ted. "Look at that guy on the library steps," a young Carla Sims had told her best friend, Diana Hopper. "Isn't he the best looking man you've ever seen?" She still thought Ted to be one of the most handsome men in the world...or at least he was.

Thinking of Ted in the past tense shocked Carla so badly that she nearly jerked the car off the road. She had no reason to think Ted was no longer handsome. There had to be a good explanation for his disappearance. Again she struggled to choke back the tears that threatened to spill over.

Memories of how Ted stepped in front of her as she walked as close to him as she dared on her way up the library steps caused Carla to smile as she continued her drive home. She had not even needed to go to the library, but she couldn't let an opportunity like this pass without at least trying to be noticed. It had worked, too. Ted blocked her entrance to the library door.

"Hi! I'm Ted Black," he had spoken to her in the most romantic voice she had ever heard. "And who might this lovely young lady be?"

That's the way Ted was…sweet, but direct. He didn't try to use a pick-up line. He just introduced himself to her and asked her name. Excitedly, she introduced herself to him. They exchanged phone numbers as Ted stepped out of her way so she could enter the library.

Carla couldn't even remember anything she did in the library that day. In fact she couldn't remember much of what happened for several days. Every waking hour was consumed with thoughts of that handsome college student she had met on the library steps. He had really swept her off her feet.

After three agonizing days of waiting for a phone call from her knight-in-shining-armor, Carla's phone finally rang. "Hi Carla," the voice on the phone said. "This is Ted Black. I met you on the library steps a few days ago. I would be most honored if you would join me for lunch tomorrow. Will you be able to?"

Carla remembered how hard she had tried to act like she had to take time to consider the invitation she was dying to accept. "Well, I think I can make it," she had finally responded as calmly as she could. Deep inside, however, she was thrilled beyond measure by the invitation.

They quickly made arrangements to meet near the student center before Ted hung up. Carla floated around the dormitory that day telling anyone and everyone who would listen to her about her date. She had never been this excited in her entire life.

As Carla continued her trip toward home, her memories darted from one dating experience to another and finally landed on the night Ted had asked her to marry him. They had been dating for two and a half years by then and had discussed marriage several times, but she had no idea this would be the night. She just thought they were enjoying a day together near the water.

They had driven to the canyon near Ted's home town. Ted had told Carla so much about it she was anxious to see what it looked like. After climbing around on the rocks for a couple of hours, they stopped near a gentle waterfall and stood there looking into each other's eyes as the last rays of sunlight disappeared behind the trees.

Ted had pulled her close to himself and kissed her. Then he spoke in the most serious tone she had ever heard from him. "Carla, I have something I need to discuss with you," he said in a way that sent chills down her back. She was afraid he was going to tell her that he wanted to go another direction in his life.

Instead he said, "Carla, I love you more than I've ever loved another person in my life. In fact, I have wanted to ask you to be my wife for some time now. Before you could ever agree, however, you would have to think about what you would be doing. As you know, God has called me into the ministry. I must fulfill that calling no matter what it costs me in life. I may not always serve in large churches. Sometimes I may not know how things will work out financially. In many ways my future will always be uncertain, and I won't have much to offer a person. But Carla, I would be totally committed to you. You would never have to worry about my love. I realize it is a lot to ask, but I would really love it if you would face that future with me."

As he spoke, Ted got down on one knee, pulled a ring from somewhere and said, "Carla, will you marry me?"

"Yes, yes I will! I want to spend my life with you!" Carla nearly screamed the words. She wrapped her arms around his neck and said, "I've thought about this many times. I want to be your wife no matter what the future holds. As long as we have each other, we can make it." Then their lips met in the most passionate kiss they had ever shared.

Again Carla's happy memories were dashed by the sudden realization that she didn't really have Ted at this instant. He was gone...missing...somewhere alone. She was alone, too. "Why, oh why, have you allowed us to be separated, God?" she asked aloud as she fought back the tears.

Soon the day of their wedding filled Carla's thoughts. Ted looked unbelievably handsome in his white tux as he stood at the altar in the front of the church. When she walked through the door into the sanctuary that day, her heart was bursting with excitement and pure joy.

Just thinking about the beauty of the church in which they exchanged their vows lifted Carla's spirits. Everything was perfect. Well, almost everything. The cake wasn't decorated like it was supposed to be at the reception, but no one seemed to notice except Carla and her mother. It was the happiest day of her life.

Suddenly, the happiness of her wedding day caused Carla to think about the sadness of the events of this day. Her heart ached to know what had happened to Ted. Where was he? Visions of that yellow ribbon kept flashing through her mind in spite of her efforts to block them out. She was afraid something awful had happened to Ted, but no one seemed to know anything about it. She was so confused. People don't just disappear...or do they? A tear slipped down Carla's cheek as she entered the city limit of Little Rock. This had to be one of the saddest days she had ever encountered.

As the first rays of sunlight broke through the early morning darkness the next morning, Carla was stepping out of the shower. She had important business to take care of today. She quickly put on her make-up, got dressed and forced down a piece of toast. She certainly didn't feel like eating, but she knew she had to keep her strength up. The last thing Ted needed right now was for her to get sick.

Perhaps a little earlier than she should have, Carla dialed the phone number she had written down the night before. It was the number of Ben Albright, a former city policeman from their church. Ben had recently retired from the police force and opened his own private investigation business. She had no idea what the name of his business was, but she was able to find his home phone number in the church directory.

"Hello. This is Ben Albright," the familiar strong voice of her friend said after the phone had rung three times.

"Hello, Ben. This is Carla Black. I've got something very important I need to talk to you about," Carla said with a note of urgency in her voice.

"Oh. Hi, Mrs. Black," Ben responded. "How is Pastor Black enjoying his retreat? Is he getting any rest?" Ben asked, sincerely wanting to know about his pastor's well-being.

"That's what I want to talk to you about," Carla said. "Ben, something has happened to Ted. He has disappeared. I went up there yesterday. His car was there, and so were his books. But I couldn't find Ted anywhere. I went to the sheriff's office and to the hospital, but no one had seen him. There was a yellow ribbon near the lake by the house, but the deputy said he didn't know anything about it. The lady at the hospital said he had never been there. He couldn't go anywhere without his car. Ben, something has happened to him. I know it has. Would you help me find him?" Carla knew that everything was coming out in a jumbled-up mess, but she didn't care. She had to help Ben know how serious things were.

"Whoa, slow down a minute, Carla," Ben said. "I'm not sure I understand all of what you are telling me, but I will certainly be glad to help you any way I can. It sounds like we need to meet so you can explain it to me again. I may need to ask you a few questions as well. Could you come to my office at nine o'clock?"

"Yes, I'll be there, Ben." Carla answered. "Where is your office? Oh, Ben, I'm so scared. You are the only one I could think of who would know what to do. Thank you so much, Ben. I don't know what I would do without Ted. We just have to find him."

"My office is at 951 Cedar St. I'll do my best to help you get to the bottom of this, Carla," Ben reassured her as best he could. He made sure Carla had written the address correctly and then hung up the phone so he could get ready to go to work.

Carla couldn't wait for nine o'clock to come. She was in the parking lot at 8:30 just to make sure she wasn't late. As she sat there waiting, the minutes dragged by. Carla's mind swirled, jumping from one thought to another. She would pray for a while and then relive every experience she encountered the day before. None of it seemed to make any sense. Someone had to know something. Repeatedly she wished she could have spoken to that old man at the jail. He might have given her some valuable information. For some reason she was sure he knew something.

At 8:55 Carla slammed her car door shut and walked resolutely toward the door with the carefully lettered name, *Ben Albright, Private Investigator*. As she pulled the door open, she was greeted by Sherry Meyers, Ben's secretary. Carla quickly told Sherry that she had called Ben that morning and had set up an appointment to meet him at the office at 9:00.

"Ben isn't here yet, Carla," Sherry informed her. "He should be here any minute. Would you like a cup of coffee?"

"No. Thank you, Sherry." Carla answered. "Do you know how long he might be?" Carla asked nervously. Before Sherry could answer, the door opened and in walked Ben Albright, much to Carla's relief.

"Hi Carla," Ben said with obvious concern in his voice. "Sorry I'm late. I got caught in traffic. Please come back to my office so we can get started. I want to know everything you know."

Ben led Carla down a short hall and through a door to their right. His office was tastefully decorated with dark, cherry furniture. The framed credentials hanging on the walls assured his clients that Ben was well-trained and widely recognized for his work. Such things were of little concern to Carla right now however. She knew Ben was good at what he did. She just wanted him to get started. They had to find Ted before something even worse happened to him.

"Now, Carla, let's start at the beginning. Tell me everything you can remember from the day Pastor Ted left home for the mountains," Ben instructed Carla as he reached for a legal pad and pencil. He was in the habit of taking detailed notes on what clients told him. His notes were always helpful as cases unraveled.

Carla told him everything. She talked about his visit with the neighbors before they left for vacation. She mentioned the deer, the white dog, his daily walks, his favorite reading place and how happy he was to be where he was. Ben stopped her occasionally to ask a few questions, but mostly he just let her talk.

When she began to talk about how worried she was when Ted stopped calling her at night like he always did, tears slipped down Carla's cheeks. She started to dig into her purse for a tissue, but Ben grabbed a box of tissues from his credenza and made them available. Carla gladly pulled one from the box, dabbed her eyes and continued her account of what had happened.

As she told Ben about her visit to the lake house, Ben seemed especially interested in the crime scene tape and her visit to the sheriff's office. He even asked her to describe the old man she had seen that day.

Carla had to stop frequently to wipe away the tears and regain her composure, but Ben seemed to understand. He never showed any sign of irritation nor did he seem to be in a hurry. When she had told him every detail she could remember, Carla asked, "What do you think, Ben? Do you think something horrible has happened to him? Do we have enough to get started? Where do we go next?"

"Carla, at this moment I don't know what might have happened to Pastor Ted, but we certainly have enough to get started. I'll study my notes and decide what to do first. In the meantime, why don't you go home and try to get some rest," Ben told her. He could not help but notice the signs of stress and worry etched into Carla's face.

Resting sounded impossible to Carla. She wanted to do something. She wanted Ben to do something, but she knew Ben was more skilled than she was. Trying to digest the information sounded logical, so she got up to leave.

"Ben, I want to help however I can. If I can go with you to show you where things are, I would be happy to. I certainly can't just sit around and wait. Please keep me informed and call me when you know something. Ben, you've got to let me help. I'll go crazy if all I can do is sit at home. Ted needs me. Please call me as soon as you decide what to do first," Carla requested. She knew Ben would call her. He was that kind of person. She was sure he would even let her help, but she just had to tell him anyway.

"I will, Carla. You've already been a big help, but I may need greater help along the way. May I have your cell number in case I have any questions and can't reach you at home?" Ben asked.

Carla gave Ben her cell number and then turned and left his office. Her shoulders were a little downcast. She had hoped Ben would jump into action immediately. She didn't know if she could stand waiting much longer. Ted was out there somewhere and he needed her. She had to find a way to get to him.

"God, please help Ben know how to find my husband. Please! You know how much I need Ted. Please help us find him!" Following her simple prayer, Carla broke down and sobbed for several minutes before she wiped her eyes, started the car, pulled into a lane of traffic, and headed home.

As soon as Carla left his office, Ben grabbed his calendar and began to study it. Disappointment spread across his face when he discovered that he had two important appointments that afternoon that could not be cancelled. When he realized he could not leave immediately for Highpoint, he studied his schedule for the next day to see how early in the morning he could leave. He breathed a huge sigh of relief when he saw that he could leave right after he finished a small amount of paper work at the office.

With a sense of urgency Ben buzzed his secretary and said, "Sherry, would you please clear my schedule tomorrow? I'm going to go to Highpoint to see if I can find out what has happened to Pastor Ted Black. This sounds like it could be a time consuming trip, so don't promise anyone I will be back during the day. Tell them I'll call them day after tomorrow unless it's an emergency."

"Alright, Mr. Albright, but you are scheduled to speak at the Everett Community Senior Citizen's Club tomorrow night at 7:00. Will you be back for that?" Sherry wanted to know. "They are counting on you to speak to them about safety, and you had to postpone your appointment with them last month."

"Thanks for the reminder, Sherry," Ben replied, trying to hide the hint of irritation in his voice. He enjoyed speaking to the senior adults, but this new assignment was much more urgent. "I'll plan to be back in time. It might be tight, but I should be able to make it as long as I don't run into traffic problems."

Concentrating on his work that day was difficult. Ben kept thinking about Ted. His interest was more than a professional one. Ted had been his pastor from the time Ben first started attending Hillside Community Church. Ted had offered Ben guidance and advice many times. In fact, Ted was the one Ben consulted when he started his business.

Ben needed to know what happened to Ted almost as much as Carla. He was disturbed by Carla's report of seeing yellow crime scene tape near the cabin. He was not particularly fond of the way the sheriff's deputy had treated Carla either. Something was going on, and he was going to get to the bottom of it.

CHAPTER FIVE

B en's alarm rang at 5:30 the next morning, but he was already up. He was anxious to wrap up a couple of things at the office so he could head for Greers Ferry Lake and the nearby town of Highpoint. He had debated with himself about taking Carla with him, but decided he wanted some time to gather facts on his own. He would invite Carla to meet him later in the day so he could discuss his findings with her...if he had found anything by then. He had a feeling this case was not going to be solved quickly.

At 8:00 a.m. Ben called Carla's cell phone. "Carla, this is Ben," he greeted her when she answered the phone.

"Hello, Ben," Carla responded. Her voice sounded tired. Ben knew she had probably not rested very well during the night. Then, as if a page in a book had been turned, Carla's voice was charged with a spark of excitement. "Are you ready to go already?" she asked. "It will take me another 45 minutes to be ready to leave. But I will get ready as quickly as I can, Ben." Carla promised.

"Carla, that's why I called," Ben said. "I want to spend some time by myself while I do some of the initial investigation. Could you meet me at Colby's restaurant near the town square in Highpoint at 1:30 this afternoon?"

"Oh, Ben, I don't know if I can wait that long. I want to feel like I'm doing something useful. Can't I go along now? I promise to stay out of the way," Carla objected.

"Carla, you can really help me, and Ted, too, if you will give me a few hours alone while I get started. I need to see some of the things you've already seen. I'm ready to take off immediately, and want to leave within minutes. You can come on when you want, but just make sure you are at Colby's by 1:30," Ben instructed.

"Okay, Ben, you're the professional. I guess I should let you make the decisions as we look for Ted. I promise to be at Colby's by 1:30. In fact I'll probably be early in case you get finished earlier than you expect, Ben," Carla said hopefully.

"Okay, Carla," Ted chuckled. "I'll see you at 1:30." With that, Ben hung up the phone, packed a few things in an attaché, and walked briskly to his car, a white, *Toyota Avalon*, that had served him well for several years now. With low traffic volume he could be in Highpoint before 10:00 he thought to himself. This was one case he was looking forward to investigating and solving.

The drive into the mountains was uneventful. There was very little traffic so Ben was able to make it to the area around Greers Ferry Lake by mid-morning just like he had hoped. As he drove along, Ben kept reviewing the information in his head. When he neared Highpoint, he decided he would go to the lake house first. He wanted to see if he could spot something Carla had missed.

When Ben arrived at the cabin, he was shocked to find the driveway empty. There was no trace of Ted's car anywhere. He checked the address in his notes to make sure he was at the right place. Ben climbed out of his car slowly and went to the side door of the cabin, where he tried turning the door handle. It was locked just like he expected. He cupped his hands and looked through the window. He wanted to see if Ted's stuff was still in the house. It wasn't, but the cabin looked unusually clean. Nothing at all seemed to be out of place. Ben did notice the corner of something sticking from under the couch. He couldn't tell what it was, but he sure wanted to find out. As Ben turned away from the door, he noticed a silver *Lexus LS* creeping slowly past the driveway. He couldn't help but wonder who would have such a fancy car out here in these woods.

Confusion invaded Ben's thinking as he made his way down the hill toward the lake. He couldn't find the chair that was supposed to be there, nor did he find any yellow crime scene tape anywhere.

He did notice that the bushes and weeds along the edge of the water had been trampled by something. It was obvious that something had taken place at this very site. Footprints along the bank told him that several people had walked there recently. He used his cell phone to snap several photos of both the bushes and the footprints.

Ben walked back and forth along the bank, carefully inspecting every foot of ground as he went. As he slowly made his way up the hillside, he found four small holes in the dirt. They looked like they would line up perfectly with a chair. He stepped off the spot from the lake and from a nearby tree and recorded the location in his notepad. Then he took out his cell phone and took pictures of the holes. It was obvious that a chair had been on this spot at one time. As Ben continued to examine the area, he checked for a signal on his phone. He had a strong signal so he dialed his office.

"Sherry," he said when his secretary answered. "I'm going to send you some pictures. I want you to enlarge them and print them off for me. Have them on my desk so I can get them when I get back tonight. And, please find out who owns the cabin on lot 53 on Log Mountain Road in an area called Pigeon Point near the town of Highpoint. When you get a name, call them to see if you can rent the cabin next week."

"But, Mr. Albright," Sherry objected. "Didn't you tell me that Mr. Black had the house rented for the entire month? Wouldn't he still have it through next week?"

"Yes, Sherry." Ben answered. "You know that and I know that, but the owner won't know that we know that. Just ask the question and see what kind of answer you get. Oh yes, Sherry. Please record the information you get very carefully. I have a feeling I may need to verify it sometime."

Sherry assured Ben she would get right on it. She often wondered why Ben asked her to do some of the things he asked her to do, but she was confident he had a good reason. More than once, his unusual requests had proven to be the key to solving some unusual case.

After Ben ended his call, he inspected the trees nearby to see if he could find any evidence of crime scene tape. He didn't find any remnants of the tape, but he could tell that something had applied pressure to the bark of the younger trees about four feet above the ground. He was confident that this was where crime scene tape had been tied, so he carefully recorded the location of the trees in his notebook.

Ben returned to the cabin and carefully inspected it from all sides. He tried his best to look in all the windows, but some of the shades were closed. Finally, he was satisfied that he had gathered all the information he could at this time. Before he left, he looked through the window in the door again. He could still see the edge of an object under the edge of the couch. More than ever he wanted to know what was under that couch.

When Ben turned away from the cabin and started to walk around his car toward the driver's door, he was surprised to see the silver *Lexus* drive by the driveway again. He had a strong feeling that someone was keeping tabs on him, but he acted like he didn't even notice the car. As soon as it passed, he looked at it carefully trying to find some way to identify it if he needed to in the future.

Since his initial investigation of the site was complete, Ben started his car and backed out of the driveway. He headed in the direction of Highpoint. As he took off, he looked in his rearview mirror. The first thing he saw was the *Lexus*. The driver of the car turned around and started following him from a safe distance. Ben knew what was happening. He had done it many times himself.

Ben had only driven a few miles when he realized that the silver *Lexus* was right on his bumper. He decreased his speed hoping the *Lexus* would pass him. That would allow him to get a good look at this mysterious driver. When his strategy didn't work, Ben increased his speed. Unfortunately, the driver of the *Lexus* matched his speed and stayed just a few feet from the back of his car. For four or five miles the driver of the *Lexus* stayed right on Ben's bumper, but would not pass.

When they approached a fairly straight section of highway, the driver of the *Lexus* speeded up and started around Ben's *Avalon*. As it came alongside of his car, Ben realized that the driver of the *Lexus* was trying his best to crowd him off the road. Ben inched his car toward the edge of the highway. He knew he couldn't let the wheels drop off the pavement however. As soon as they hit the loose gravel, he would be in danger of skidding out of control. The driving skills he had learned during his years in a squad car kept Ben from losing control on the narrow road. Ben tried to sneak a glance at the driver who was attempting to force him off the road, but he had to concentrate on the road too much to see anything.

Just before he heard the scraping sound of metal against metal, the *Lexus* catapulted ahead of him like a car in a drag race. Ben tried to get the license plate number, but he had to give all of his attention to his driving. He was fully convinced that this episode was no accident. Someone didn't like him snooping around this part of the country, and they wanted him to know it.

Without even thinking about it, Ben noted the time on his watch so he could enter it into his notepad later. It was 11:55 a.m. He still had time to drop by the sheriff's office before his appointment with Carla. On his way to the sheriff's office, Ben drove around town for a few minutes and looked at every vehicle he saw. Unfortunately, he did not spot the silver *Lexus* anywhere.

By the time Ted pulled up in front of the sheriff's office, he had decided not to tell the sheriff about his encounter with the wild driver…at least, not yet. He wanted the focus of this visit to be on Ted Black.

"Good morning, Sir. How can I help you?" a smiling deputy asked as Ben pushed the door open and entered the small sheriff's office. Ben figured this must be a different deputy than the one Carla had encountered in this office a few days ago. This guy sounded much more pleasant than the one Carla had told him about.

"Good morning, Sergeant. My name is Ben Albright," Ben said as he gave the deputy one of his business cards.

"You're a private eye from Little Rock, huh?" the deputy said as he studied the card. "What brings you to this part of the country?"

"I'm here to check out an incident that happened on Log Mountain Road a few days ago," Ted answered. He was purposefully vague, hoping the deputy would give him some information he didn't already know.

"Would that be the drowning of Marla Harris?" the deputy asked.

"Yes, what a tragedy," Ben said, not quite sure who Marla Harris might be or how she might be connected to Ted Black, if at all.

He realized that getting a drowning victim out of the water would account for the broken bushes and footprints he had seen at the edge of the lake. "What can you tell me about it?" Ben asked.

"What do you want to know?" the deputy asked. Apparently he was going to play his own version of a strange *I've-got-information-you-want-but-you're-going-to-have-to-drag-it-out-of-me* game.

"Oh, just the typical stuff," Ben replied trying hard to make everything sound routine. "How long had she been dead? What was the condition of the body? What were the coroner's findings? Do you suspect foul play? Where is the body now? Was she from around here? Does anyone know anything about it?"

"Well, Mr....what did you say your name was?"

"Albright. Ben Albright."

"Well, Mr. Albright, all that is a matter of public record. Why don't you just take a look at the records?" the deputy said in a tone that told Ben he wasn't going to volunteer any additional information.

"I plan to," Ben replied. "Say, Sergeant, could I look at your jail census for the day of the discovery?" Ben asked, fully expecting his request to be denied.

"Why do you want to see that?" the deputy asked.

"Oh, I'm always looking for clues. I thought I might find a good one." Ben said as he chuckled.

"Probably won't find one in our records. If I remember correctly, we only had two men in custody that day," the sergeant replied.

"Is that right? What were their names?" Ben asked.

"One was old man Smith...J. C. Smith. He's a regular... in his seventies at least. Has a tendency to indulge in a little too much alcohol from time to time. He comes here to sober up. The other was a first timer...a Mr. Lindsey, I think. You should have seen him hightail it out of town when we released him. Haven't seen him since," the deputy suddenly spilled forth some of the information Ben really wanted in the first place. Ben stored the names in his memory until he could get somewhere to write them down.

"Sure doesn't sound like any clues there," Ben said as he laughed again. "Sure you don't want to give me a copy of Ms. Harris' investigation record, Deputy? It would save me a lot of time."

"Nope, I can't do that, Mr. Albright. You can look it up same as anyone else," the deputy snarled. Now he was beginning to sound more like the deputy Carla told him about.

"Oh, Sergeant, I have one more question. Do you know anyone around these parts who drives a silver *Lexus?*" Ben asked. He could tell by the reaction of the deputy that he had hit a nerve. The deputy's face bleached white, but he tried hard to cover it up.

"Why you want to know that?" the deputy said as he fumbled with a stack of papers trying to look too busy to continue talking.

"No real reason. I was just out at the site of the drowning before I came here. Some character in a silver *Lexus* followed me part way to town. Passed me like a wild man. Nearly ran me off the road. I thought you might want to watch for him. If he drives like that all the time, he could end up getting someone hurt," Ben said, hoping he made his report sound like he was just concerned about a stupid driver. For a reason Ben couldn't explain he didn't want the sheriff's department to know that he suspected there had been an attempt made on his life.

"Well, that's a pretty fancy car. I'm sure I would know it if someone from around here had an automobile like that. We do get lots of visitors around here, you know. Could have been anyone," the deputy replied.

"Yes, Sergeant, I'm sure you do," Ben said as he glanced at his watch. "I'm going to have to be going, Sergeant. I have an appointment in a little while. If you think of something you think might help me with my investigation, you have my number on that card. You can reach me directly on my cell phone or you can call my secretary in Little Rock. Thanks for your help."

"You're welcome, Mr. Albright," the deputy was suddenly nice again. "You be careful out there on the highways. We wouldn't want something to happen to you," he said with a laugh that made Ben wonder if he was giving him a warning or just trying to sound concerned.

As soon as Ben got in his car and closed the door, he wrote the names of Marla Harris, J. C. Smith and Mr. Lindsey in his notebook. Then he left for Colby's Restaurant. While he was on his way to meet Carla, he called his secretary.

"Sherry, have you found out anything about the lake house yet?" Ben asked his secretary when she answered the phone. "I really need to know who owns that place."

"Yes, Mr. Albright. It's owned by a Mr. Joe Starnes," Sherry replied. "Just like we suspected, he told me that a Mr. Ted Black had arranged to be in the cabin for several more days. Mr. Starnes told me he was in college with Pastor Ted. He said he agreed to let the pastor use the cabin for the entire month. That's about all I could find out...except that it is available for several weeks beginning September 13."

"Great work, Sherry. Did you tell him you were calling for me, or did you make the inquiry for yourself like I told you?" Ben wanted to know.

"I told him I wanted to rent it," Sherry replied, hoping she had understood her boss's instructions correctly.

"Good," Ben said, "Now, Sherry, I want you to call Mr. Starnes back and rent the cabin for four days beginning September 13. Tell him he doesn't need to clean it if he says he won't have time to get it cleaned. Tell him you only have a few days and want to use every minute you can, even if it means you have to do a little cleaning." Ben caught Sherry off-guard with his next statement. "If Jim can get the time off, I want to give you and Jim a few days in the mountains. There's just one catch...I'll be there part of the time during your stay. I'll let you know when I'm coming, and...Oh, yes, I'll expect you to do some of your work from there. Are you interested?" Ben asked.

"That would be wonderful, Mr. Albright!" Sherry said excitedly. "I'm sure Jim can get the days off. His boss has been telling him he needed to get away for a few days of rest. This would be perfect. I'll make the reservation as soon as I hang up. Thanks, Mr. Albright. You are one of the kindest men I know. Jim and I appreciate you so much."

Ben hoped her visit would be as pleasant as she was anticipating. He sure didn't want to disappoint Sherry. "Okay, Sherry," Ben chuckled. "By the way, did you get the pictures I sent? Were you able to enlarge them?"

"They are on your desk, Mr. Albright," Sherry answered. "But they don't look like anything but pictures of some holes and a couple of trees, though. I hope there wasn't supposed to be something else in the pictures."

"No, that is exactly what they are...but those holes could be some very important holes," Ben said before his mind snapped back to his immediate surroundings. He could see the restaurant. Just like he expected, Carla's car was out front.

"I've got to go, Sherry. Make the reservations, and we'll discuss the details later," he instructed.

Carla had driven by Colby's Restaurant at 12:30 p.m. She had given herself plenty of time to get to Highpoint and had arrived a full hour early. She knew she couldn't go in and sit there for an hour before her appointment with Ben. That would certainly draw too much attention to them when he arrived. She had driven past the building and decided to do a little window shopping downtown. She drove around for a minutes and then found a parking place. When she got out of the car, she started wandering aimlessly from store to store, hardly noticing what was in the display windows.

Shock was written on Carla's face by what she saw in the window of the hardware store. For a brief moment the image of the old man she had seen in the sheriff's office earlier in the week appeared in the window. She looked right at him and then turned quickly to see where the old man was...but he was gone. She couldn't spot him anywhere. She looked back at the hardware store window. He wasn't there either. Carla couldn't decide if she had actually seen someone, or if her mind was playing tricks on her. She certainly planned to tell Ben what she thought she had seen.

By 1:15 Carla couldn't stand waiting any longer. She certainly didn't want to risk being late. She was afraid Ben might leave if he showed up and she wasn't there. Without hesitating a minute longer she made her way back to the restaurant and went inside.

Carla had only been sitting at the table for a few minutes when she saw Ben approaching the restaurant. He looked worried...like he had discovered something he didn't like. She hoped it wasn't some kind of awful news she didn't want to hear. When Ben entered the restaurant, he looked around, but looked right past her like he didn't even know her. Carla caught on and took this as a warning. She pretended like she didn't recognize him either, but her heart was about to explode. She couldn't stand to wait much longer. She had to know what was happening.

As Ben walked past her table toward a table in the back corner of the restaurant, he dropped a small piece of paper on her table. She quickly covered it with her hand and slid it toward the edge of the table. After waiting for a couple of minutes to make sure no one was looking, she sneaked a peek at the paper. "Meet me ten miles south of town on Route 63 in the Zion Community Church parking lot at 2:30," the note read.

Carla crumbled the note and dropped it in her purse, ordered a hamburger and forced herself to eat it. A quick glance toward Ben let her know that he had ordered something as well. Both ate quickly and quietly. Carla was about to die from curiosity, but at the same time she wasn't sure she wanted to know why Ben was acting so strangely.

Ben was the first to leave. He paid his bill and walked to his car. After looking around, he climbed in and started in the opposite direction he had told her to go. Carla was convinced that he didn't want to give anyone any reason to think they were going to meet. After waiting for about five minutes, she paid for her lunch, got into her car and started in the general direction of the church parking lot. She took her time getting there since the hour was not up yet.

Carla was surprised to see Ben's car already in the parking lot when she arrived. He had not passed her on the way, but he was there when she arrived. She pulled up beside him and started asking questions, "What's going on, Ben? Have you found out something about Ted? Why were you so secretive back at the restaurant? Has something bad happened? Is Ted alright?"

"I haven't found out anything about Ted yet. At least I haven't found out anything definite," Ben continued, "but I have found out that no one wants me to find out anything." With that he shared with Carla the details about what had happened to him that morning.

Tears began to form in Carla's eyes as she listened to what Ben was saying. "How could there be no trace of him, Ben?" Carla asked between sobs. "I saw his car…his books…the yellow ribbon…his chair. I saw it all with my own eyes. It was there, Ben. I know it was. I know I wasn't dreaming. It was all too real for that!"

Ben assured Carla that he believed her. He told her that someone had apparently moved Pastor Ted's car and cleaned the cabin. When he told her about the silver *Lexus* trying to run him off the road, she got very quiet and turned a little pale.

"I saw that car," Carla said quietly, as if she was remembering something for the first time. "It passed by the lake house when I was up there two days ago. In fact, I can't say for sure, but it may have even passed a second time while I was there. Oh, Ben, what could be going on? Why have they tried to remove any trace of Ted? Who could be doing this?"

"I don't know, but I'm going to try to find out," Ben answered. "Listen, Carla, I want you to go back home. I have one more thing I need to do today before I head toward Little Rock myself. As soon as I take care of that one item, I'll be heading back home as quickly as I can. I have to speak to the Everett Community Senior Citizens' Club about personal safety tonight."

After he told Carla good-bye, Ben dismissed himself and turned his car in the direction of Highpoint. Carla wiped her eyes and slowly pulled out of the parking lot. As she started toward Little Rock, her heart was heavy. Doubts threatened to crush her spirit as she drove along. She wondered if they would ever find Ted before it was too late. Tears started streaming down Carla's face and forced her to pull off the road until she could regain her composure enough to drive again. In spite of her attempts to remain positive, she was beginning to imagine what they might discover over the next few days. Fear engulfed her and tried to snatch every tidbit of hope from her.

Unaware of Carla's emotional struggles, Ben drove into Highpoint and found the coroner's office. He went in and told the aged man who was working there that he needed to get some information for an insurance company. He then asked to see any records he had about Marla Harris' death. The coroner, who had introduced himself as Travis Moore, went to a file cabinet and came back with a file. "Here it is, Mr. Albright," he said. "I think this has everything your insurance company will need to see. I have a copy machine on the wall across the room from my desk if you would like to use it to make copies of the records."

Ben could hardly believe he was finally getting some cooperation. "Thank you, Mr. Moore," Ben said politely as he took the file. "Yes, I would like to have copies of the entire file if I could."

"Sure, go right ahead. Take your time. I'll be here for the rest of the afternoon," Mr. Moore replied as he walked toward his desk.

Ben cringed as he copied the gruesome pictures of the body. He studied the limited information carefully. Marla Harris was a 26-year old female from Highpoint. She had drowned in Greers Ferry Lake, an apparent murder victim. She had been dead for at least a week, but the body was not discovered until a few days ago. It was picked up on Lot 53 in Pigeon Point.

"Mr. Moore, it's kind of unusual to have access to this much information when there is a murder investigation going on. Could you tell me why you are releasing the file?" Ben's curiosity had gotten the best of him and he asked the question in spite of his own fear that his access to the file would suddenly be taken from him.

"Sheriff has already solved the crime," Mr. Moore reported. "He arrested some man at the scene. Said something about a love triangle, I think," Mr. Moore continued.

"Do you know what that man's name was?" Ben asked, hopeful for the first time since he had arrived in Highpoint.

"No, I don't, but I'm sure Sheriff Bixley could tell you. He put the man in his own car and headed to town with him. I saw them leave before I left the scene with the body," Mr. Moore said.

"Could you describe the man to me?" Ben asked.

"No, I'm afraid I can't," said Mr. Moore. "I was too busy with the body. The sheriff and his deputies were all around the man anyway. I never even got a glimpse of him. All I saw was the sheriff leave with someone in the back seat of his car."

"Thanks, Mr. Moore. You've been a great help," Ben said as he finished copying the last sheet from the file. He handed it back to Mr. Moore, gave him some money to cover the cost of the copies, and hurried to his car. He glanced at his watch and saw that he had just enough time to make it to the meeting at the Everett Community Center.

CHAPTER SIX

By the third day Ted was going stir-crazy in such confined quarters. His only reprieve from his tiny bedroom was an occasional trip to the bathroom. He couldn't tell anything about his surroundings from these trips however. He was taken into a small, plain hallway that looked like it had not been painted in years. The paint had faded so much you could hardly what color it had been except for the faint green color in the corners. There were no windows in the hallway, but there was a window over the tub in the restroom. It had been covered with the same boards and painted with the same dull, black paint as the boards over the window in his room.

At least these trips offered him a change in scenery for a few minutes. He made his daily shower last as long as he dared. It was good to be out of the extremely small, little bedroom he was forced to occupy. Ben used to cherish his time alone, but he had so much of it now that he looked forward to seeing anyone…even his unpleasant guards.

At first Ted spent a lot of time reflecting on his life. God had given him a great life in so many ways. He sure couldn't count this as one of those great times however. This was awful. It was the first time Ted had experienced any major challenge to his calm, peaceful lifestyle. The occasional relationship problems that came with being the pastor of a church seemed harmless compared to what he was experiencing now.

Ted was especially disturbed by the battles he had with doubt from time to time. For the first time in his life he wondered if God was really aware of his need. He had spent a lot of time begging God to help him regain his freedom, but things kept getting worse instead of better. Where was God? Why didn't He answer? Why had this happened to him? What was going to be the outcome? The questions came and battered his troubled mind repeatedly during the long hours of each day.

For years Ted had preached messages telling people that God would be with them when they were going through difficult times. Now he was finding out that it is difficult to sense God's presence when things are worse than you ever thought they could be. He wondered if he would ever be able to preach the same messages again.

Suddenly an alarming and troublesome thought struck him. He might never be able to preach again. Ted had no guarantee that he would ever get out of this. He might be convicted of the charges against him, unless one of these guards got tired of him and put a bullet in him first. It would be easy enough to claim that he had attempted to escape. The way things were around this town, no one would even question his death.

Ted wondered if anyone would even tell Carla he had died if, in fact, one of the guards did eliminate him. More disturbing questions invaded his mind. Did Carla have any idea what was going on? Had they told her he was having an affair with that young woman who had drowned? Had they even bothered to tell her anything? He knew she didn't know where he was or she would have already been at his side. Who was offering her comfort and help? How was she standing up under all the uncertainty?

When the questions were too numerous to count and the strain too heavy for him to endure any longer, Ted would try to sing a song, quote a Bible verse, or start declaring his faith to the walls. He would try to remember stories about saints who had been required to endure hardships far greater than his. More than once he had asked his guards for a Bible, a magazine, or anything to help the time pass more quickly. All he got in return were snide remarks and ridicule.

Today was particularly difficult for Ted. Tears flowed down his cheeks as he talked to God about his situation. "God, please give me a reason to keep going. Give me some kind of sign that things will turn out okay," Ted prayed. "I want to believe, but I feel so weak right now. Will you at least show me something that will give me a little bit of hope? I'm not sure I can take much more." Ted was honest with God during his prayer just like he had always been.

After Ted finished his prayer, he stood and walked about the small room like he had done hundreds of times since he was brought to this unknown location. That's when he noticed something he had not seen before. One of the boards covering the window had a strange looking knot along the top edge of it. Ted went over to look more closely. As he did, he realized that the knot was loose. He tried to jiggle it a little...and it moved. It moved! He wasn't sure why this was so exciting, but it was.

Ted stepped across the room and locked his bedroom door. He didn't need an unexpected visit from his guards right now. He knew the men could get in if they really wanted to, but he also knew they would probably knock first if the door was locked. He hoped they would think he was asleep and leave him alone.

When Ted got back to the window, he started wiggling the knot and gently pulled on it. It slipped out rather easily. Ted leaned over and pressed one eye against the knothole. He could see outside for the first time in days. Just a few feet beyond the clearing where the house was, he could see a dense grove of trees. That told Ted they were out in the woods just like he had suspected.

Ted strained to see what was toward the front of the house. As he looked, he caught a glimpse of something shiny...something familiar. It looked like...like...like the front of a car...his car! They had moved his car from the lake house to this place, wherever this place was. He wondered when they had done that. Then he remembered that they had taken all his possessions, including the keys to the car, when he was booked at the sheriff's office. Moving the car would not have been much of a challenge, but why would they have moved it? What else had they brought out here? Had they removed every trace of him? Would anyone ever hear from him again? His mind was full of questions, but, like all of his other questions, these had no answers and no one bothered to tell him anything.

Just then Ted saw something that caused his pulse to quicken. It was a white blur in the trees about twenty feet beyond the clearing. He stained to get a better look, but, just as quickly as it had appeared, it was gone. Was he imagining things? What could it have been? Was he losing his mind? More questions without answers.

Suddenly Ted heard a noise from the other part of the house. He quickly placed the knot back in the hole and unlocked the door. He had barely sat down on the bed when the taller man pushed the door open without bothering to knock. "Today is your lucky day, Teddy Boy," he said in a mocking voice. "We're going to let you get some fresh air."

"Could I go to the bathroom first?" Ted asked, hoping to sound like being allowed to go outside was no big deal to him.

"Sure, take all the time you want," his captor said. "We've got all the time in the world. Unless you try something stupid, we're going to be here for a long time."

While he was in the restroom, Ted tried to imagine what it would be like to finally become familiar with his surroundings. His hopes were dashed when he came out however. A black blindfold was tied tightly around his eyes and handcuffs were placed on his wrists while his arms were stretched behind his back.

In spite of not being able to see anything, Ted was enjoying his few minutes outside the cabin. The breeze felt cool on his face. He listened for familiar noises, but heard nothing but the chirping of a few birds. His companion took his arm and pushed him along on his walk. At first, he could hear gravel crunch beneath their feet. Then he could feel tall grass swipe across his pants. He knew immediately that he had crossed a road and was now walking in a yard or field. He had never appreciated such a mundane thing before.

Much too soon, his few minutes of freedom, if it could be called that, were over, and he was taken back into the house. He dreaded being led to his private quarters. That is what his guards called his room, but to Ted it was more like a prison cell. Sure enough he was taken straight to his bedroom.

Ted settled down on his bed and tried to think. He kept wondering what that white blur had been. Had it been real or was it something he imagined? He wondered why these men, who had not offered him anything before today, had chosen this day to let him go outside. Was something about to happen? Ted longed to take another look through his peep hole, but decided not to risk it. As he sat there thinking, he slowly drifted into a much-needed, dream-filled nap.

As the days dragged by, Ted had to fight harder and harder against depression. Every day seemed routine and monotonous. After his first two or three days, Ted started making an impression in the soft wood of the doorframe with his finger nail. That let him keep track of how many days he had been in this tiny room. It really didn't matter much since no one seemed to know where he was.

At first Ted tried to imagine what Carla and the leaders of his church were doing to try to find him. He wondered if they had talked to the sheriff. Then he realized that the sheriff was probably responsible for his being in this room. Ted was sure that, in spite of his "rescue" by the men dressed in black, the sheriff knew what was going on. They tried to make it look like a kidnapping or jailbreak, but Ted was sure it was all an acting job. He was convinced the men were just a diversion in case anyone saw anything.

By the eighth day Ted was growing impatient and irritable. His "hosts" seldom came into his room. They seemed happy to sit at the table and play cards while Ted spent hour after hour by himself in his small room with nothing to do or anything to read. He didn't have a book, a Bible or even a magazine to help pass the time. Even his looking through the knothole brought him little relief after the second or third day. He could tell if it was cloudy or sunny, but that was about all.

Ted prayed a lot, but usually ended up questioning God more than trusting Him. He couldn't understand why God had allowed this to happen to him. Nor could he come up with any good reason why God had not done anything to bring about his release.

On one especially difficult day, Ted complained bitterly to the Lord. He tried to pray for Carla and the church, but he couldn't focus on anyone but himself. He sobbed as he told God how awful he thought God was being. Never had he imagined he would ever do such a thing. He could remember standing in the pulpit warning people not to question God's love for them. Now he was guilty of doing the very thing he had preached against.

After praying for what seemed like an extremely long time, Ted was suddenly shocked by some searching questions he was sure came from God. "How long are you going to face this alone?" God seemed to ask. "When are you going to let Me take over like you tell others to do? Don't you think I am big enough to handle things like this?"

As Ted pondered the questions, he fell across his bed and confessed, "God, I'm sorry I have been such a hard-headed jerk. I don't mean to question You, but it is just hard to keep trusting when I don't see any results. I really want to surrender my situation to You, but I'm struggling to actually make such a complete surrender. I say I surrender, but I can't seem to let go of things."

Ted continued to alternate between crying and praying for an hour or more. Then he lay quietly and tried to remember some of the promises he had learned from the Bible. As he lay there, Ted felt an unbelievable sense of peace envelop him. He soon drifted into the most restful sleep he had experienced since he came to the cabin.

A couple of hours later Ted woke up with a burning desire to look outside. He got up and took the knot from the board covering the window. As soon as he bent over and looked through his peephole, Ted saw a familiar flash of white. It was Buddy! Ted resisted the urge to call the dog's name. He knew his "hosts" would hear him and come to see what he was yelling about.

Just seeing Buddy brought Ted new hope. Then something wonderful dawned on him. If Buddy was there, Ted could not be very far from the cabin he had rented. If he wasn't far from that cabin, someone would surely find him. He just hoped it would be soon. He wasn't sure how much more of this he could take. The forced isolation was getting to him.

Ted was totally focused on Buddy as the dog sniffed along the clearing between the house and the wooded area surrounding it. He wasn't very far away. Ted tried to will the dog to come closer, but he never did. Instead, he began to go back into the woods. Ted wanted to yell, "No, don't go! I need you here." He forced his words back into his thoughts as he watched the dog wander further and further from the house.

Suddenly Ted heard the sound of one of the men walking across the floor. He glanced quickly across his shoulder and realized that he had failed to shut the door before he removed the knot. He grabbed for the plug so he could quickly stuff it back into the board, but knocked it onto the floor. He held his breath as it bounced away from him. Like a cat pouncing on a ball of yarn, Ted fell to the floor and swiped the knot into his hand before it could make any more noise.

The sounds of walking got louder as he stood to his full height and tried to get the knot to fit into the hole. He turned it around and around trying to find the exact way it fit. Drops of sweat appeared on his upper lip as he kept working. Just before his "host" appeared in the doorway, Ted was able to shove the knot into the hole and take a step away from the window.

In what he hoped was a calm voice, Ted asked, "What's up?"

"Time for your daily exercise," the man snapped back at him. "What was that noise I heard as I came down the hall?" he asked.

Ted was glad the man couldn't hear how loudly his heart was beating as he said, "I don't know. I kicked the bedpost as I walked by it. Maybe that was what you heard."

The man surveyed the room as if he were looking for something amiss. Satisfied that everything was in place, he asked, "You need to go to the bathroom before we walk?"

"Yeah, that would be good." Ted said. He was thankful for the change in subject.

As soon as he emerged from the bathroom, Ted's eyes were covered by the blindfold. He had become all too familiar with this routine. The handcuffs were secured as well. Ted had learned to trust his guide by now and walked confidently across the living space toward the door.

They had barely walked twenty or thirty feet across the gravel drive when his escort suddenly yelled, "Get out of here, Dog! You don't belong around here." He let go of Ted's arm and left him standing there imagining what was taking place.

"Stupid dog! Next time he comes around here, I'll give him a taste of lead for dinner," the man snarled as he grabbed Ted's arm and pushed him along the gravel driveway.

"What kind of dog was it?" Ted asked, hoping to find out if it was Buddy or some other dog.

"Four-legged kind," his guide said, and then laughed as if he had said something funny. Then he said, "Just an old stray. Get all kinds of them through here," he reported. "Guess people dump them on the highway to get rid of them."

"What color was it?" Ted asked.

"What's it to you?" the man responded. "Just shut up and walk. I didn't bring you out here to talk. Let's get you exercised and back in the house." With that comment, he picked up the pace causing Ted to stumble along.

As Ted shuffled along, it suddenly dawned on him that there were not four men guarding him like he had been told. No one was outside or the men would be talking among themselves. It really didn't matter that much however. He had no chance of escaping from the two captors that kept the way to the door securely guarded. He didn't know why it encouraged him to know there were only two, but it did.

CHAPTER SEVEN

Jim and Sherry Meyers arrived at the cabin on Log Mountain Road about 3:00 p.m. on September 13. They unlocked the door and looked inside, but did not enter. Ben had told them not to go inside until he arrived. They were surprised by the cleanliness of the place. Sherry was sure she detected a slight odor of cleaning supplies lingering in the air. Jim was anxious to get moved in and get this vacation underway, but they both wanted to please Ben since he was paying for their time here. So, they closed the door and walked back to the car and then down the hill.

They tried their best to make it look like they were fascinated by the lake as they walked down the hill and went straight to the water. They stood there for a few minutes talking about how beautiful the lake was. Jim even took off his shoes and rolled up his pants legs. As soon as he put one foot in the frigid water, he realized that it was much too cold for wading and did his best to get his leg dry before he put his shoes back on.

During this time they frequently looked up the drive to see if they could catch a glimpse of Ben. He had told them he would arrive on foot and would be hiding when he first arrived. He told them he didn't want anyone to see them together. That made Sherry a little nervous, but she had learned to expect unusual requests from her boss. She reluctantly agreed to follow his instructions.

When they had spent as much time as they dared beside the lake, they walked back up the hill and found the outside stairs to the deck. Before they went up the stairs, they grabbed two magazines from the car. They sat on the deck and looked through their magazines while a couple of hummingbirds flew back and forth to the feeder hanging from the overhang. About an hour later Sherry nearly jumped out of her chair when her cell phone rang.

"Hello," she said timidly. She didn't understand why she felt fearful, but she did.

"It's me, Sherry," Ben said in a calm voice. "Listen carefully. I'm sorry I scared you. Please calm down. I've been watching you and Jim for the last thirty minutes. You guys are great actors. No one has come down the road since you arrived. I don't think anyone suspected you of anything. Sherry, I want you and Jim to go inside and unlock the side door. Don't touch anything. I'll be there in about five minutes. Do you have any questions?"

"No," Sherry answered. She started to tell Ben that this didn't seem like much of a vacation so far, but decided against it. After all, Ben had told them she would have to work part of the time.

Ben waited for five minutes and then started making his way toward the cabin. Just before he stepped into the clearing, he saw a car driving slowly up Log Mountain Road. He ducked behind a tree and waited to see what happened. When he peeked around the tree, he couldn't believe what he saw. There it was, as big as day…the silver *Lexus* that almost crowded him off the road. Unfortunately, he was not close enough to see the driver.

Just before the car turned into the driveway, Ben moved to a better hiding place and waited. He wanted to warn Jim and Sherry, but he didn't dare try to call them now. It would be too risky. He could only hope they would be able to handle whatever happened.

The driver stopped behind their car and cut off his motor. Out stepped a big man Ben had not seen before. He couldn't be sure if this was the same man who had tried to run him off the road, but suspected that it was. He watched as the man went up to the door of the cabin and knocked.

Jim answered the door and looked surprised. The big man did most of the talking. Ben wished he could hear what they were saying, but he was too far away. He would have to wait until later to get a report from Jim and Sherry.

After what seemed like a long time but was really only a few minutes, the big man went back to the *Lexus*, looked around and got in. He backed out of the driveway and headed in the direction of Highpoint. Unfortunately, the man had parked at an angle that made it impossible for Ben to see the license plate.

Ben didn't waste any time. He rushed across the clear space between him and the cabin and opened the door. Jim and Sherry gasped in fear as he barged in. "It's just me. I'm sorry I didn't knock, but I couldn't risk being seen if your visitor decided to return," Ben explained.

Sherry looked relieved to see that it was Ben. She wasn't sure she was cut out for this side of the job. Typing and making phone calls was one thing. Being on site when mysterious things were happening was something else. She tried to voice her fears, but she couldn't get anything to come from her throat before Ben spoke again.

"What did that man want?" Ben asked.

"He said he was hired by the owner to look after the house and just wanted to welcome us to the area," Jim said. "Then he told us there had been some kind of bad incident take place at the cabin a few weeks ago and cautioned us to be careful. When I asked him what kind of bad incident, he said, 'Oh, nothing real serious.' Then he told us again to be careful. We assured him we would and he left. It was really funny, Ben. While he was talking, he kept trying to look around me. It looked like he was trying to see inside the cabin...like he wanted to make sure everything was in place. What do you think that was about, Ben?" Jim asked.

"I'm not sure, but I have a feeling you hit the nail square on the head. He wanted to make sure there were no traces of Pastor Black left in the cabin." Ben answered. Then he opened the bag he was carrying and said, "That's exactly what I want to know as well. We'll just see if we can find something to help us locate Pastor Black."

Then Ben directed his comments to Sherry, "I've got to work quickly to find out what I can. I won't be able to talk much, but I do need you to take notes, Sherry. Here's a legal pad. Would you please keep a record of whatever we find here?"

Sherry took that pad, grabbed a pen and prepared herself to write whatever Ben told her to write. She was much more comfortable with this part of her assignment.

Ben went straight for the couch and bent over to see what was sticking from under it. Before he touched it, however, he took a picture on the camera he had in his bag. He pulled on latex gloves and pulled a book from under the couch. He had Sherry record the name and author of the book and the location where he found it. Then he put the book in a plastic bag and put it in his bag.

Then Ben began checking for fingerprints. He checked the back side of the refrigerator handle, the inside of the phone receiver as well as the buttons of the phone, and even checked the door pulls on the closet doors. He found a couple of pretty good prints and lifted them for possible future identification.

Sherry recorded the location and findings of everything. She even wrote down where Ben found nothing. She had learned to be thorough during the time she had worked for Ben.

Ben gave Jim a pair of latex gloves and a few plastic bags and asked him to look around outside to see if he could find any cigarette butts or anything that looked out of place. He asked Jim to make sure he could tell Sherry where he found every item. Jim went outside and started looking, but he didn't find a thing.

While Jim was looking outside, Ben looked around the house for a vacuum cleaner. When he found it, he poured out the collection bag and began to sift through the contents. Several times he looked something over really good. He asked Sherry to make two or three entries on the legal pad and put those items in plastic bags.

After checking the house meticulously, Ben asked Jim to get the garbage can and bring it in. They found an old plastic painting tarp and placed each item from the garbage can on it. Ben looked at each item in it with great care. He only kept one thing…a box and tray from a T.V. dinner. Sherry wondered what good that would do, but dutifully wrote it down on the legal pad and made sure she noted the fact that it came from the bottom of the garbage can.

"I think I've covered everything. Now you guys can move your stuff in and enjoy the rest of the evening. I promise not to bother you before tomorrow," Ben said as he moved from window to window looking out the window from each side making sure that he could not be seen when he left.

As Ben peeked out the widow toward the road, he pressed himself closer to the wall and said, "Apparently your friend wants to make sure you are still okay. That silver *Lexus* that came by here earlier just went by again."

"Oh, Ben," Sherry moaned. "Is this the way it is going to be the whole time we are here? I'm not sure I'm up for this kind of assignment."

"Sherry, as soon as they are sure you are not connected with Pastor Black in any way, they will leave you alone. Now here's what I want you to do. I want you and Jim to start unloading the car. Leave the door open as you go in and out. Laugh and giggle a little. Make it look like you have already started your vacation, and are having lots of fun. I'll stay out-of-sight until they leave. Oh, yes, be sure to wave at the driver every time he drives by. I want him to know that you are noticing his frequent trips by the place."

Sherry and Jim reluctantly agreed to do what they were told and were soon actually enjoying moving in. They chattered about how relaxing the trip had already been, how beautiful the lake was and how much fun they were going to have. Sherry even flirted with Jim a little, and he responded just like he would if no one were present. Ben was surprised at how well they did.

The *Lexus* went by two more times, and they waved each time. They might have been tense, but no one would know it. Ben decided they were good actors. By the time they got the car unloaded, it had been several minutes since the *Lexus* went by. Ben looked out the windows while they began to unpack.

After he was convinced that their welcome wagon had closed down for the evening, Ben told Jim and Sherry he was going to leave. Before they could even object, Ben grabbed his bag, slipped out the door and was gone from their sight. He had not been gone for more than five minutes when the silver *Lexus* drove by. Out of habit and training Sherry wrote down the time of the trip right under her record of the previous trips.

She was totally surprised when Jim grabbed her around the waist and said, "Welcome to my humble vacation abode, Mrs. Meyers. It's time for us to really begin our vacation. The rest of the business can wait until later. You have some more important business to take care of right now."

Sherry was in full agreement with his comment, but she chuckled at his attempt to sound romantic. She laid her head back against his shoulder and felt herself relaxing for the first time since she arrived.

Bright and early the next morning Ben drove back to Highpoint. He had made a quick trip back to Little Rock to give the fingerprints he had found to a friend to see if he could match them to anyone in the police system. Ben then drove back to the area of the lake and spent the night in a motel just a few miles away. He wanted to get an early start on some important business he wanted to tackle. Ben knew that staying nearby would let him start much earlier than he could if he stayed in Little Rock. He was tired from all the extra driving he did the night before, but he was up and on his way to Highpoint as soon as he saw the first sign of daybreak.

When he got to town, he found a coffee shop near the center of town. Ben found a seat near the back of the restaurant where he could see the door. Then he ordered bacon and eggs and coffee. He watched as the regulars began to arrive. Before long a group of men gathered around a long wooden table in the back of the restaurant. Ben was sure this was the group with whom he wanted to visit, so he refilled his coffee cup and moved over to their table. He grabbed an empty chair and introduced himself without telling them his line of work. He quietly listened to their conversation for several minutes.

When Ben was sure the group was comfortable with him being with them, he asked, "Do you guys know where I might find J. C. Smith?"

"Why do you want to find J. C.?" one of the men wanted to know.

"I think he may know a friend of mine," Ben said honestly.

"If it was 6:30 at night instead of 6:30 in the morning, I would tell you to go to the tavern over on Fifth Street," one of the men offered. The others chuckled as if they knew exactly what he meant.

Finally, one of the men said, "I'm not sure old man Smith has a place he calls home. You see him at all hours, day and night, roaming the streets. I see him most within a few blocks of the jail.

If you really want to contact him, I'd suggest you talk to some of the businessmen and clerks around there. They can tell you if they have seen him recently. I haven't noticed him for several days myself, but they might have."

Ben thanked them for the information and let the conversation drift to other topics. He didn't want to raise too much suspicion. He enjoyed the conversation and even offered a few comments himself. After one or two men left the group before him, Ben got up to leave. He walked up to the counter, paid for his meal and walked slowly out the door.

As soon as his eyes adjusted to the sunshine outside, he noticed something he had not seen as he walked into the coffee shop earlier. It was right across the street from the coroner's office. He had been here just a few days ago without noticing this particular restaurant.

As soon as Ben left the coffee shop, he went to every grocery store and gas station he could find. He showed them pictures of Ted and asked them if they had ever seen him. Most had not, but one man at the gas station near the edge of town thought he recognized him. "I'm sure he bought some gas in here a time or two. Haven't seen him in a week or two, though" he said.

Ben quickly jotted down the man's name, asked a few more questions and told him that he might need to visit with him again at a later time. Ben had hoped to get more information, but at least he had one man who could verify Ted's presence in this strange little town.

When Ben got to Nick's Grocery Store, he found another person who had not only seen Ted, but could positively identify him. "I believe he told me he was a preacher from Little Rock," Nick Barnes, the store owner reported. "My dad was a preacher so we had a lot in common. Every time he came in we told each other stories about funny things that happen in churches. He probably came to the store two or three times a week for about three weeks. His visits stopped about a week or so ago, however. I just figured he had gone back to the city. I think he said he was here on something like an extended vacation. He said he was staying over on Pigeon Point. Sure was a nice guy. Is he in some kind of trouble? Has something happened to him?" the man wanted to know.

"Well, he might be in some trouble. I'm not sure. We're having trouble locating him. Did he say anything that would make you think he went anywhere with someone he had met up here?" Ben asked.

"No, never said anything about going anywhere. He had his own car if he needed to get anywhere, though," Nick replied.

"Thanks, Nick," Ben said. "I've written all this down. I may need to talk to you again. Is this the best place to catch you? Would you mind giving me your phone number in case I think of something else I need to ask about?"

Nick gave him the number for the store and told Ben that he was at the store from sunup to past sundown just about every day except Sunday. He took that day off to go to church and be with his family.

As soon as Ben got in his car, he made two phone calls. First, he called Carla to tell her that he was finally finding some people who could confirm the fact that Ted had been in Highpoint. Before he could say anything else, Carla exclaimed, "That's great, Ben! I'll be on my way to Highpoint right away."

"Wait a minute, Carla," Ben cautioned her. "If you come up here right now, I'm afraid it would raise too much suspicion."

"I hate to admit it, but you are probably right, Ben," Carla said reluctantly. "It will be hard, but I will wait for your permission before I start to Highpoint. Please call me if you find out anything else."

Ben agreed to keep her informed and then made his second call. It went to Sherry, his secretary. When she answered, Ben asked, "Have you heard anything about the fingerprints yet?"

"No, but it usually takes a couple of days. Hopefully they will contact me by tomorrow," Sherry replied.

"Sherry, I need Jim to take care of a couple of things for me if he is willing. Could I talk to him? Oh, before you go, Sherry, have you seen the *Lexus* anymore?"

"Not since last night," Sherry answered his last question first. "I'm sure Jim will help you out." She wanted to add the words *as long as it isn't dangerous*, but decided that Ben would not asked them to do anything dangerous if he knew it was dangerous. "He's right here. I'll put him on," she said as she handed the phone to Jim.

"Hello, Ben," Jim greeted him by name as soon as Sherry handed him the phone.

"Hi, Jim," Ben returned the greeting. "Say, would you flag down the mail carrier and ask him if he saw Ted during the time he was up here. You might ask him if he saw anything the day Marla Harris was found. Find out anything you can, Jim. There's one more thing I would like for you to do. Would you drive to the neighbor's house about a mile back toward the highway? See if anyone there remembers having a conversation with Ted before they left on vacation."

"Sure, Jim, I'll be glad to do both of those things. I'm not much of an investigator, but I am kind of snoopy, so it shouldn't be too hard for me," Jim laughed as he spoke.

"Thanks, Jim," Ben said as he hung up. He wanted to head toward the jail to see if he could find Mr. J. C. Smith, but realized that he didn't have enough time to make the trip. He had to return to Little Rock to take care of a couple of other cases that afternoon. He hated to leave since he felt like he was finally making some progress, but he knew that he had to keep the rest of his business going as well.

As soon as he got to Little Rock, he called Carla and shared more details about the information he had gathered. She was like a kid celebrating a birthday. It was good to see her excited again. Ben was sorry to deny her request to accompany him the next day, but he felt like he had to. He could pretty much stay invisible as long as he was alone. He could only hope she would understand and wouldn't do anything against his wishes.

By the time the alarm went off the next morning, Ben was already up and headed in the direction of Highpoint. He had to find J. C. Smith. He was certain the old man could give him some of the information he needed.

Just before he got to the jail, Ben saw an old man cross the street a block ahead of him. He quickly parked his car and practically ran up the street to see if he could find the man he had seen. After looking in every store for two blocks, Ben finally gave up. If it was Mr. Smith, he was certainly an elusive old codger.

Ben talked to every merchant in a two block square. All of them knew Mr. Smith, of course, but none of them had seen him today… or at least that is what they told Ben. He couldn't be sure if they were telling him the truth or if they were just saying what they had been told to say.

About noon Ben was startled by the ringing of his cell phone. It was Sherry. "Mr. Albright, I'm sorry to tell you this, but neither of those finger prints belonged to Pastor Black," Sherry said, expecting Ben to be disappointed.

Instead of expressing disappointment, Ben exclaimed, "Good! Whose fingerprints are they?"

"They belong to a Mr. Saul Mitchell. He is the owner of a cleaning service in Morris Bluff," Sherry answered.

"Great work, Sherry!" Ben responded. "I'm on my way to Morris Bluff to pay Mr. Mitchell a visit. What is the name of his business? Did you get an address? By the way, I'm going to stop by for a couple of hours after I get back if that would be alright. I'll call you before I come. Do you mind?"

"That will be fine, Mr. Albright," Sherry said. "Jim and I will be glad to see you, and besides, you're paying the bill, you can come when you want. Mr. Mitchell's cleaning service is A-1 Cleaning and Restoration. It's located at 920 Centenary Street."

As soon as he hung up the phone Ben jumped into his car and headed toward Morris Bluff. He had barely driven five miles before he realized that someone was following him. Not wanting a repeat performance of his first day in these mountains, Ben decided to take quick action and watched for an opportunity to switch places with his tag-a-long.

The opportunity came when Ben passed a semi in the right lane of a long stretch of highway that had a passing lane. As soon as he rounded a curve that would keep him from being seen from behind, he pulled in front of the truck and forced the truck to stay right on his back bumper by matching his speed to that of the truck. He could only hope the truck would keep him from being seen by the driver following him.

It worked! The driver flew by the truck and looked startled when he looked over and saw Ben's car in front of the truck. Ben couldn't believe his eyes. The driver looked like the deputy from the sheriff's office, but he was not in uniform. Ben couldn't be absolutely sure of the identity of the driver, so he quickly pulled in behind the car and followed him closely. As he did, he pulled out his cell phone and called Sherry.

"Sherry, I need you to call my friend, Joe, and have him get me information on Arkansas Plate, DSZT-506. Once you get a name, find out everything you can about the owner...where he works, where he lives, and so forth. Call me back when you get the information. I've got to go right now. I'm following this guy closely, and he's trying to ditch me. Get me whatever information you can."

Sherry barely had time to respond before the line went dead. She breathed a prayer for her boss, and started making phone calls.

In spite of repeated attempts by the driver to get him off his tail, Ben was able to stay right with the alarmed driver. It was obvious that he didn't want any part of a confrontation. He quickly turned right onto a county road at the very last second. He was going so fast that he nearly overturned. Ben went on by without attempting to follow. He had the information he needed, and the driver knew he had been exposed.

A couple of miles up the road Ben pulled behind a gas station to see if his pursuer had resumed the chase. After waiting and watching traffic for about ten minutes, Ben pulled back on the road and continued his trip to Morris Bluff.

Locating the address for the A-1 Cleaning and Restoration business was difficult. Ben's GPS unit didn't recognize the address so he stopped by City Hall and looked at a city map. He couldn't find it there either. When he asked the clerk, she told him about a new shopping center on the street Ben was trying to find and gave him directions to it.

As Ben pulled in a parking place a couple doors down from the cleaning service, he noticed a familiar-looking man come out of the front door of the business. It was the man who had been following him. Ben slumped down in the seat and watched from his vantage point. The visitor got in his car, and squealed his tires as he left in the opposite direction from where Ben sat.

Immediately, Ben jumped out of his car and ran into the cleaning service. The man he had seen at the door with his tag-a-long entered an office near the back wall as Ben stepped through the door. The receptionist greeted him and asked how she could be of service.

"I need to see Saul Mitchell," Ben said as he kept his eyes on the office in the back.

"I'm sorry, Sir," the receptionist replied. "Mr. Mitchell is not in today."

"Yes, he is, Ma'am," Ben replied, hoping he had guessed correctly about the identity of the man who had entered the office. "I just saw him go in that office right back there."

"Oh, that was Paul Mitchell, his twin brother," the receptionist laughed. "People get them mixed up all the time. Would you like to talk to him? He's one of the owners as well."

"Yes, I would," Ben replied without taking his eyes off the office door.

The receptionist buzzed the office and told Mr. Mitchell someone wanted to see him. Without even asking who it was, the man came from the office and approached Ben.

"Hi, I'm Paul Mitchell," he introduced himself. "How can I help you?"

"I'm pleased to meet you, Mr. Mitchell. I'm Ben Albright, a private investigator from Little Rock," Ben said as he handed the man his business card. "I'd like to visit with you about a cleaning job you did near Highpoint recently. Could we visit in your office?"

Mr. Mitchell agreed to Ben's request and led him back to his office. He denied that they had ever done a job in the Pigeon Point area near Highpoint until Ben told him that he had found two of his twin brother's fingerprints in the house. Mr. Mitchell's shocked expression revealed the fact that he had just been exposed, but he reacted calmly and said, "Well, let me check our records. It's always possible that Saul did a job I don't recall."

As he pulled up the information on his computer screen, Mr. Mitchell asked, "Why are you so interested in a cleaning job there?"

"Well, my client disappeared from that location right after a body was discovered in the lake nearby," Ben replied purposing keeping his reply very general. He didn't want to go into a long explanation if it wasn't necessary.

Mr. Mitchell looked a little shocked and the color drained from his face when he heard the information about the body and the disappearance. "Well, that's too bad," he said. "Let's see," he seemed to be considering more than the list that must have appeared on the computer screen as he ran his finger down the list. "Oh, yes, here it is. We cleaned that house on August 30."

"Who hired you to clean the house, Mr. Mitchell?" Ben asked.

"Let's see... You know, I don't know, Mr. Albright. That information isn't on the screen. Since I didn't do the job, I don't know who asked Saul to do it. Saul's out of town right now, so I can't ask him."

It was obvious that Mr. Mitchell was lying, but Ben decided not to make an issue of it yet. Instead he asked, "Mr. Mitchell, did your brother remove anything from that house when he cleaned it?"

"Oh, nothing except a little trash and some dirt, I'm sure," Mr. Mitchell said with a chuckle. "You know, a person can get in a lot of trouble if he removes personal items from a residence," Paul Mitchell replied with an air of arrogance about him.

"Yes, I'm sure he could, and would if I were to find out he did," Ben dropped a veiled threat into the conversation. There was no reaction, so Ben continued. "Mr. Mitchell, would you know if anyone else was present when Saul cleaned the house?" Ben dared to ask even though he was fairly certain what the reply would be.

"No, Mr. Albright, I would have no way of knowing that. Saul might have had a helper along, or he might have done the job himself. I just don't know."

"I see," Ben said pensively. "Mr. Mitchell, it sounds like I'll need to talk to your brother when he returns. When did you say he would be back in town?" Ben asked.

"I didn't say, but he should be back in a couple of weeks," Paul Mitchell replied. "He took his family on a little outing before the weather turns cold."

"Good for him," Ben said sincerely. He knew how important it was for families to spend time together when they got a chance. "By the way, Mr. Mitchell, what were you and Sheriff Bixley's deputy talking about just before I came in the door?"

Another shocked expression spread across his face Mr. Mitchell's face before he responded, "Now, I think that's a little personal, Mr. Albright, don't you?"

"Yes, perhaps it is, Mr. Mitchell... unless he told you not to share anything with me. In that case it could make you an accessory to kidnapping. If the sheriff had anything to do with the disappearance of my client, you could be charged as well. As you said earlier, a person could get into a lot of trouble if he were to help cover-up a kidnapping or a murder."

"Now, wait a minute, Mr. Albright. I'm sure Saul didn't have anything to do with any kidnapping or any murder," Mr. Mitchell defended his brother. Ben noticed that he was beginning to perspire and his hands were trembling a little.

"I'm not saying he did, Mr. Mitchell, but withholding information that could be useful in the apprehension of someone who did commit a felony is pretty serious. It could even carry some prison time," Ben stated as he watched Mr. Mitchell turn red and begin to tremble even more. "When did you say your brother would be back?" Ben asked.

"He'll be back one week from today," Mr. Mitchell said. Ben noted the fact that the length of his vacation had just been cut in half. He even suspected that it might be much shorter once he heard about this conversation.

"Well, Mr. Mitchell, I would suggest that you give him my phone number and have him call me when he gets back in town. In fact, I would suggest that you contact him and have him call me in the next day or two. We sure wouldn't want anyone to get in trouble just because he cleaned up a house, would we?"

"No, we wouldn't, Mr. Albright," Mr. Mitchell answered trying to sound calm. "I'll see if I can get hold of Saul and have him give you a call. I'm sure he can give you more information than I can."

"Oh, yes, Mr. Mitchell...if Saul did take any personal belongings from the house, I would suggest he let me have access to them. Destroying evidence is another crime that has gotten a lot of people in trouble."

"I doubt if Saul would have done that," Mr. Mitchell answered defensively. "But I'll be sure to ask him. If he did, we'll be sure to let you know."

With that assurance Ben dismissed himself and left the office. He wanted to believe Mr. Mitchell, but something told him he would not get anymore information unless he contacted Saul himself. It was very unlikely that Saul Mitchell would volunteer anything that would help Ben find Pastor Ted.

Ben glanced around as he walked back to his car and almost hesitated as he caught a glimpse of a silver *Lexus* sitting at the Sonic Drive-In across the street. He wasn't sure if it was the same one he had seen at least twice before, but it sure looked familiar. Ben jumped in his car, pulled away from his parking place and drove toward the drive-in as quickly as he could. Apparently the driver of the *Lexus* didn't want to be seen up close, because he slammed his car into gear and pulled out before Ben could drive through the traffic and get close enough to see who it was.

Ben knew he would have to make sure he wasn't being followed as he made his way back to Highpoint. He certainly didn't want another challenge by the driver of the *Lexus*. He breathed a sigh of relief when he entered the city limits without seeing anyone behind him.

CHAPTER EIGHT

Sheriff Bixley's deputy was annoyed by the ringing of the telephone as he sat in his crowded office the afternoon of Ben's visit to A-1 Cleaning and Restoration. Stacks of papers and journals cluttered his desk leaving him only a few inches of work space in the middle of his desk. "Hello," he growled without even knowing who was calling.

"Deputy Pitts, this is Paul Mitchell," the caller identified himself. "Is Sheriff Bixley in? I just had a visitor…a Ben Albright. He said he was a private investigator from Little Rock."

"No, the sherriff isn't here now. He left me in charge. I heard that private eye has been snooping around these parts," Deputy Pitts said as he laid aside what he had in his hands to give the caller his full attention. "He even came by here a few days ago. He's trying to stir up trouble. He said he was representing an insurance company or something. What did he want, Paul?"

"He was asking questions about Saul cleaning the house on Pigeon Point," Paul answered. "He wanted to know if we had found anything in the house."

"You didn't tell him anything, did you?" the deputy demanded in an urgent tone. It was more of a command than a question.

"No. Well, not much anyway. I did have to admit that we cleaned the house. He said he had found Saul's fingerprints inside the house. I don't know what is going on, Deputy, but I don't want any part of covering up any murder...or kidnapping...or anything else for that matter."

"Is that what he told you, Paul? You already know that Marla Harris was murdered at that location, but we have the perpetrator in custody. We found him at the scene. There isn't any cover-up. There is nothing to cover-up. Don't you worry about a thing! I'll take care of this," Deputy Pitts said, trying to sound reassuring to Mr. Mitchell.

"What about Saul?" Mr. Mitchell asked. "He won't get in any kind of trouble, will he? He doesn't need that. He's been trying his best to stay clean since he was released last fall. His parole officer has warned him many times not to get tangled up in any kind of legal problems. I even helped him get this business up and running. He is trying to go straight, Deputy, and I don't want anything unraveling what he's been able to do so far."

"He's not in trouble, Paul. That private eye was just trying to shake you up. He may not even have the fingerprints he claimed to have. Besides, what's wrong with a cleaning service leaving a couple of fingerprints?" the deputy asked. "It just sounds like Saul just got a little careless. Where is he? I may need to have a talk with him."

"He's at home, but I told the private eye that he was on vacation with his family," Paul answered.

"Good work, Paul. It sounds like you handled it very well," the deputy said in a matter-of-fact way hoping to calm the man down.

"Deputy, what about all those books and clothes, and all that other stuff we have in the warehouse? The man said we could be charged with being an accessory to a kidnapping or something. Are we going to get into trouble for keeping that stuff here?"

"Calm down, Paul," the deputy said. "I told you there was no crime committed. The man he is asking about hasn't disappeared. I know right where he is. This guy has some weird idea that he is missing. You don't have a thing to worry about, but don't let our Dick Tracy know you have the stuff. He has no reason to know about it. Besides you are merely providing a storage place at my request. You have nothing to do with anything. Don't let him scare you, Paul. Now, you get in touch with Saul and tell him to give me a call. I have a few things I need to discuss with him."

"I will," Paul said and hung up the phone.

Paul Mitchell sat in his office for a long time after his conversation with the sheriff's deputy and reflected on what had happened over the last few hours. He didn't like what was going on, but he didn't know what to do about it. Finally, he picked up the phone and called his brother. "Saul, you and I need to have to have a long conversation," he said as soon as his brother answered the phone.

"What's the matter, Paul?" his brother asked. "You sound worried. Has something happened to the business? Did someone cancel their contract? Are we in some kind of financial trouble? What's going on, brother?"

"Saul, I just had a visit from a private investigator from Little Rock. He wanted to know if we had cleaned the house on Pigeon Point. I told him, 'No,' but he said he had found your fingerprints in the house. I pretended like you had cleaned it without my knowledge, but he kept asking questions. Saul, he told me that a man had disappeared from there on the day Marla Harris' body was discovered, and said we could be charged with accessory to a crime if we had anything from that house. I told him we didn't have anything, but I'm not sure he believed me. Saul, do you know anything about this?"

"Of course not, Paul," Saul assured his brother. "One of Sheriff Bixley's deputies called me up one day and told me he had to get that house cleaned up right away. He said he was managing the property and had someone wanting to rent it. He told me the man had left without taking his stuff and asked me to store it for him until he could track the guy down. Sure I cleaned the house, but I don't know anything about anyone disappearing. Did you call the sheriff's office to see what was going on?"

"I just got off the phone with them. Deputy Pitts told me not to worry about anything. He said they knew where the man was. Pitts told me not to worry about anything, but I think there is more to this than meets the eye, Saul. And it could get you into trouble if your parole officer finds out about it," Paul stated letting his concern show in his tone of voice.

"Well, it sounds to me like we don't have anything to worry about," Saul said. "All we did was provide a legitimate service for a paying customer. That's what businesses do."

"But they don't get involved in hiding somebody's belongings," Paul objected. "I don't like it. Something sounds fishy to me. By the way, both the deputy and the private eye want to talk to you." Paul gave Ben's number to his brother and urged him again to give him a call as quickly as he could.

As soon as Ben got back to Highpoint, he drove toward the area around the jail. His mind was swirling. He knew he needed to find old man Smith, and he sure wanted to talk to Sheriff Bixley, but he didn't feel good about doing either. Ben had learned that feelings of uncertainty can often be one of the tools God uses to give His children direction. Instead of heading for the jail, Ben drove around until he found a secluded spot behind a warehouse. He was glad he couldn't be seen from either direction while he was sitting there. It was there that Ben asked God what his next step should be.

Once Ben felt like he had an answer, he pulled out of his hiding place and headed toward Pigeon Point. He knew he couldn't take his car to the cabin in case the *Lexus* showed up again, and he certainly didn't want to draw suspicion to Sherry and Jim. He decided to make a visit to the neighbor's house a mile down the road from the lake house.

As Ben pulled into the drive, he could see a curtain close. Immediately he wondered if these people had been warned not to talk to him. He decided it was worth a try so he knocked on the door of the aging farm house and waited for someone to answer.

A thin, frail-looking lady with graying hair opened the wooden door. Ben introduced himself and told her about his search for Pastor Ted Black.

"There was a man here just recently asking about him," the lady said politely. "I told him we met Reverend Black before we went on our trip, but we really didn't know much about him." She told Ben about their conversation, but he already knew most of what she said.

Ben told her about what had happened while they were on their trip. Her reaction told Ben that she had not heard anything about it. "I can't believe that anything so horrible could happen in this peaceful neighborhood," she kept saying.

After visiting for a while, Ben dropped a bombshell on the lady. "Ma'am, I was wondering if I might pull my car behind your shed and leave it there for a couple of hours. I want to take a walk up the road toward the cabin to see if I can spot anything I might have missed from the car."

"Well, I don't know about that," the frightened little lady objected. "I'm not sure what my husband would think about me letting our property become a parking lot."

"I can certainly understand your concern. That's why it would be best to put my car behind the shed. It would be out of your way, and wouldn't give others the idea they could start parking here on a regular basis. I would park at the cabin, but I don't want to alarm whoever is staying there now." Ben tried his best to sound reassuring.

"Oh, that would be Mr. Jim Meyers. That's the man who was here earlier. He was such a nice man. I sure wouldn't want to cause him any concern," the lady said. "I guess you can leave it there for a while if you promise to move it before dark. I don't want you coming around here after dark."

"I promise, Ma'am, and thank you so much. You'll never know how much I appreciate how kind you have been," Ben said as he turned to make his way to his car. He quickly pulled it behind the shed where it would be completely hidden from the road.

As soon as he got out of the car, Ben started walking up the road. He quickly made his way into the woods, though, as soon as he was out-of-sight of the house. He couldn't risk being recognized if some of the sheriff's men decided to take one of their rides down Log Mountain Road.

He had barely gotten off the road when he saw a flash of light ahead of him. Ben figured a vehicle was coming so he crouched behind a tree and waited to see if it was one of his recent followers. As the car approached, Ben recognized it was Jim and Sherry's car. He stepped out of his hiding place just enough for them to see him. He was sure they spotted him, but they didn't slow down. That's when he noticed another car coming behind them. Quickly he jumped back behind the tree and made sure he couldn't be seen from the road. As soon as he was out of sight, his cell phone rang.

"Hello," Ben said quietly.

"Ben. It's Sherry. We're being followed. We saw you, but we knew we would put you and us in danger if we stopped." Sherry didn't wait for an answer. She kept giving information Ben needed to hear. As the car roared past Ben, Sherry said, "The *Lexus* has been driving up and down the road every half hour for the last four hours or so. Ben, it's like he is looking for something or someone. We knew you said you would be here this afternoon, so we decided to take a ride. Hopefully, we can get him to follow us to see where we are going. We left the back door unlocked. You can get in if you need to, but be careful. I don't know how long we can keep this guy on our tail. What do you want us to do next?"

Ben told Sherry how proud of her he was. "You're becoming a real detective, Sherry," he said. "Keep him with you as long as you can, but let me know if he gives up and disappears. You might try stopping at some places that look like the kind of places where people might meet. Maybe he will give you a few minutes to see if anyone comes. Sherry, have Jim keep looking at his watch as if he is waiting for an exact time. If you can keep our *Lexus* driver entertained for an hour or so, that will be a big help."

A nervous Sherry said, "Ben, be careful. You may be used to this stuff, but I'm scared to death. I'll let you know if anything changes." With that she was gone.

Ben stayed among the trees, but practically ran to the cabin. He carefully made his way toward the back door. Just before he pushed the door open with his foot, he heard a noise from inside the cabin. He ducked behind an LP gas tank and listened carefully. Everything was quiet so he went around the house and tried to look in the windows to make sure the house was empty.

It wasn't. Ben could see the toe of a boot in the doorway to the bedroom. He wasn't sure if these hoodlums had tried to harm Jim and Sherry or if one of them had been waiting for them to leave and had entered the house as soon as they left the driveway. Because of Sherry's call, he figured it was the latter. Either way Ben decided he didn't want to go in the cabin. He made his way back into the woods and started hiking in the opposite direction from his car.

He had only gone about a quarter of a mile when he saw something that made him stop in his tracks. Ahead of him was a familiar-looking big white dog. "Buddy," Ben said beneath his breath.

The dog gave a couple of barks and looked in his direction. Ben knew any continual barking could put him in danger, so he shrank back and remained quiet. The dog stopped barking, but kept coming toward Ben with his tail wagging as if he was glad to see Ben. When he got close enough, Ben kneeled down on the ground and spoke to him. The dog trotted over to Ben and waited to be petted.

"Buddy, what do you know about all this?" Ben asked as if the dog could give him an answer. Buddy just wiggled and squirmed. He was enjoying being petted, but Ben knew he had another problem. Buddy could expose his hiding place. After thinking about things for a minute or two, Ben decided to keep moving away from the cabin and deeper into the woods. Buddy followed along, just like Pastor Ted had told Carla he did on Ted's walks.

Ben was deep in thought trying to figure out what to do next when he suddenly realized that Buddy had trotted back across the road and had disappeared. Ben wanted to know what happened to Buddy, but he knew he could not cross the road. He would be easily spotted from a car if one were to appear from around the curve behind him.

After thinking about things for a while, Ben made his way back through the woods. He looked carefully at the cabin as he passed by, but did not dare let himself be seen. About a half-hour later he was back to his car. After checking in both directions for any cars, he quickly ran across the road. He waved at the little white-haired lady just before he disappeared behind her shed and jumped into his car.

Before Ben could even put his key in the ignition, he heard a car coming up the road. He found a position from which he could watch the road and waited. A minute later Jim and Sherry drove by. Subconsciously, Ben counted the seconds until the second car, the silver *Lexus*, appeared as well.

Ben was worried about Jim and Sherry now. What if the man with the boots were still in the house? Would he harm them in any way? Ben decided to risk a phone call and hit the speed dial for Sherry's cell phone.

"Hello," Sherry whispered.

"Sherry, this is Ben. Don't talk. Just listen. Someone was in your house when I got there. Fortunately he made a noise before I walked in on him, so I left. I don't think he saw me. You and Jim need to be careful in case he is still in the house. I'm hoping he got a call from his buddy and has already left the house. He's probably waiting somewhere to be picked up. When you get to the cabin, stay outside for a while. If you have to, walk down to the lake. Better still…open your trunk and act like you are looking for something. That way you can see when the *Lexus* drives by. If you can get a good enough look, try to see how many people are in the car. The driver was alone when he passed me. Be careful, Sherry, and call me if you sense any trouble. I'm close by and can be there in a minute or two. Give me a call when you know something. Bye."

By the time Ben said good-bye, a couple of tears trickled down Sherry's face. She was really scared. She wanted all this to end. This sure wasn't the vacation she had in mind. Sherry dabbed her eyes and told Jim what Ben said just before he pulled into the driveway.

"Ben knows what he is doing," Jim said, trying to reassure his wife. "He is pretty sure the guy is out of the house, or he would have told us to keep going." With that comment, Jim stopped the car and got out. He and Sherry tried to act like it was just an ordinary day. They opened the trunk and started moving stuff around.

In a few seconds the *Lexus* drove by. Sherry looked at the car. No one was in it but the driver. It kept going up the road and soon disappeared.

"Jim, we can't stay here behind the car any longer without drawing suspicion. We've got to come up with another plan," she told her husband.

Jim had a plan in mind already. "Here are your tennis shoes, Sherry," Jim said as he pulled them out of the trunk of the car. "Put them on. I'll put mine on and we can go for a walk down the road. There's no reason why we can't go for a walk before we go in, is there?"

"Jim, I'm so scared. What if the man in the *Lexus* stops us? What will we tell him?"

"We'll just tell him we are out for a walk to get a little exercise."

"What if he wants to know why we stopped at all those places, Jim? What will we say then?" Sherry kept asking questions hoping to feel prepared in case something happened.

"He won't ask us about that," Jim replied with confidence. "Remember, he doesn't know that we know he was following us. He won't want to give that fact away. He probably won't stop us, but if he does, let me do the talking. I think I can handle it without making him suspicious."

Sherry was glad to turn things over to Jim. He was such a strong man. She couldn't help but admire the way he took care of her. Being with him helped her feel safer than she would have felt otherwise.

Jim and Sherry had barely changed their shoes and started up the drive when the silver *Lexus* flew back down the road. The car was right in front of them so they had a clear view of the *two* men inside. Sherry waited for a few minutes and then called Ben.

"Hello," Ben said as he started his car.

"Ben! It's Sherry. When the *Lexus* passed us the first time, there was only one man in it. When it came back by, there were two men," Sherry reported.

"Good!" Ben exclaimed. "That means there is no one in your house. You two can go inside now. Judging from the speed of the car as it went by here, the men gave up and headed back to town. I'm going to drive cautiously just to be sure. You and Jim go on in and check on things. When I'm sure things are okay, I'm leaving for Little Rock."

"We're going in right now," Sherry said as she and Jim pushed the door open and walked into the cabin. Everything looked like it had when they left. Nothing looked like it had been moved. Everything seemed to be in place.

"Sherry," Ben said with a chuckle. "Your Uncle Harry is going to visit you very early in the morning. He'll be coming in his old truck. Try to get some sleep, but be up and ready to entertain by 7:00 o'clock in the morning."

"We'll be ready," Sherry said. She knew that Uncle Harry was one of the disguises Ben used when he didn't want to be recognized.

CHAPTER NINE

Ted kept trying to shake the nagging feeling he had every time he let himself think about the men in the other room. He had been around them for many days now, and he had not once attempted to talk with them about spiritual things. He wondered how many times he had urged his congregation to draw people into conversations about God. He had not even thought to do so until now. Quietly he asked God to show him how to speak to the two men who were his "hosts." He wanted to tell them about God's love if he ever had an opportunity. Ted shuddered as he thought about the fact that they might be the last people he would have an opportunity to talk to about God.

Ted had barely finished asking God for an open door when the taller of the men hollered from the other room, "Hey, Preacher! Where are you?"

"I'm right here," Ted yelled back as if they didn't know where he was.

"How in the world did you get yourself accused of murder?" the man asked as he shuffled down the hallway toward Ted's room.

Ted felt a tremor go through his body, and it didn't come from the question. He was wondering if God was already giving him the opportunity he had asked for. That would have to be some kind of record for an answer to one of his prayers.

"It's a long story," Ted said. "Why don't you get your chair and I'll fill in the details." Ted was surprised when the man walked back up the hallway and got one of the kitchen chairs. Apparently he was interested in finding out what had happened to Ted.

"Way I see it, we got lots of time, so give me all the details you want to give," the man said as he came back with the chair. Ted noticed that he closed the door as he entered the room. He also placed his chair directly in front of the door, so no one could open the door until he moved.

Ted started at the beginning and told him about his need for a break, his first two weeks at the cabin and then about the day he found the body. He was glad to have an opportunity to talk to someone. He shared all the details he could remember. He didn't want to miss this opportunity to actually use his voice for more than asking to go to the restroom.

"Well, did you do it, Preacher?" the man asked when Ted finished giving the last details of his story.

"Of course not," Ted said. "I'm fully aware that the Bible tells us not to murder. I wouldn't do anything like that anyway, but I sure wouldn't want to do anything God tells me not to. I try my best to live my life in a way that pleases God."

"That's something I've never been able to understand," the man said. "For years I've heard people talk about God telling them things, but I've never had God tell me anything. What does God's voice sound like anyway?"

"God doesn't speak in an audible voice," Ted replied. His courage began to grow as he looked into the man's eyes. He could tell the man was really interested and not just playing a game with him. "I've never actually heard God's voice...and I doubt if anyone else has either. Mostly God speaks through the Bible. That's why I've wanted one ever since I've been here. I need to find out what God wants to tell me about my situation."

"I ain't read the Bible much," the man admitted. "Got two or three of them around the house, but I never could make much sense out of them...never could tell who they were talking about with all them *thees* and *thous* and the *camest and runneth* stuff in it. If the Bible is supposed to help us know what to do, why didn't they write like we speak?"

"They really did. They wrote it in the language the people spoke in that day," Ted informed his visitor. He was excited to be able to give a positive answer to his question. "You have been trying to read a really old translation. It was written the way they talked in the days when it was translated. Some of the later translations speak more like we do. You need to try to read one of them."

Suddenly the man shocked Ted by asking, "Preacher, if I get you a Bible, will you answer some of the questions I have about it?"

"You better believe I will," Ted said. This was the most excited he had been since he was first moved to this place…wherever it was. This whole conversation was going a lot better than Ted thought it might.

"I got one more question before I leave you alone," the man said. "What do you Christians mean by *getting saved*? I've heard that all my life. What do you have to be saved from? Are you in some kind of danger or something?" Then the man chuckled. "I guess you really do need to get saved, don't you, Preacher? You really are in danger. I sure wouldn't want to be in your shoes. I don't mind making sure you stay here and keep your mouth shut, but I sure don't want to be tried for murder, like you're going to be. Maybe you ought to ask God to save *you*," the man said with a cynical laugh. "Maybe he would send someone in a helicopter to swoop in here and lift you out of the mess you're in. Then you could tell your congregation that you were saved." The man burst into loud laughter at his own remarks, but Ted didn't find them to be very funny.

"I do ask him to save me from this situation I'm in, but that's not the kind of being saved Christians are talking about," Ted said as he prayed for the words to explain how God can transform a person's life. "Christians are asking God to save them from sin. You do know what sin is, don't you?" Ted asked.

"Well, I always thought it was doing stuff you know is wrong… you know, stuff like murder, stealing, gettin' drunk and stuff like that," the man answered.

"That's a good definition for it," Ted complimented the man. "But it doesn't have to be such bad things. It includes anything that would displease God. A person would still be guilty of sin by telling lies or cheating on something. The good news is…"

"Hank, you in there?" a loud voice echoed through the room in spite of the closed door. It came from the other room, interrupting Ted in the middle of his sentence.

"Sounds like Bo woke up," Hank whispered. This was the first time Ted had ever heard their names, so he stored them in his memory. "Don't you breathe a word of what we were talking about to Bo. He don't take kindly to talking with the prisoner, if you know what I mean." Then Hank lowered his voice to a whisper and continued, "I'll get you a Bible...and I'll try to get me one of them that reads like we speak. I got lots of questions for you, Preacher, but I'll have to ask them later."

"Yeah, I'm in here," Hank shouted back to the man in the other room. "I've been grilling this guy to see if I can find out more about what he's done." Hank quietly opened the door, grabbed his chair and headed down the hall toward the living room.

From the animated exchange that followed, they must have been disagreeing with each other about Hank spending time in the room with Ted. He couldn't hear their words, but Ted could tell by the tone of their voices that it wasn't a pleasant conversation.

As soon as Hank left his room, Ted began to ask God some questions. "Why did Bo have to wake up now, Father?" he asked. "I was getting ready to tell Hank about Jesus. Please give me another chance," he prayed.

About ten minutes later Ted got up slowly and shut the door. He went to the window and pulled the knot from its hole and looked outside. When he did, he was surprised to see Buddy sniffing at the wheels of his car. Deep down inside Ted knew that Buddy knew he was in the house. His hopes began to soar as he thought about how Buddy might let someone know where he was.

Ted's hopes were quickly dashed when he heard one of the men in the other room yell, "There's that stupid dog again. I told him last time he came snooping around here I'd give him some lead to eat if he ever came back. He must be hungry so I'm going to feed him! You watch the prisoner, Hank. I'm going to get me a dog!"

Ted heard the front door of the cabin open. He watched helplessly as Buddy took off like a streak. The sound from the gun seemed to echo through Ted's head over and over. His heart sank as he heard a yelp just before Buddy disappeared.

Ted quickly replaced the knot and opened the door so he could hear. "I'm not sure if I got him or not," the man said as he closed the front door behind him. "The way he yelped, I was mighty close if I didn't hit him. I don't think he'll give us any more trouble, though," the man said with obvious delight.

Ted wondered about Buddy. Until his opportunity to visit with Hank just now, Buddy had been Ted's only encouragement for days. Deep inside he wondered if it was okay to pray for the safety of a dog. Finally, he quit debating with himself and asked God to let Buddy live. Ted felt like he needed Buddy more while he was locked in this room than he ever had while he was taking his walks.

CHAPTER TEN

B en was up a long time before daybreak the next morning. With experienced hands he glued a salt and pepper colored beard on his face and touched up his eyebrows. Then he pulled on a grayish hairpiece that had plenty of unruly hair. He was always amused at the way his appearance was transformed by a little hair and make-up. He quickly pulled on his beat-up pants, a threadbare shirt and an old beat-up hat. He stood in front of the hallway mirror and inspected himself to make sure he had not forgotten anything. In just a matter of minutes he had made himself look twenty to thirty years older. He silently prayed that he would not have to convince anyone he really was Uncle Harry, but he was prepared if it became necessary. He had even secured a fake driver's license if he had to use it to *prove* who he was.

Ben walked briskly down the drive and climbed into his twelve-year-old pickup truck. He had owned the truck for about five years, and had planned to get the dents removed so he could get it painted. There never seemed to be enough time or money, however, so he drove it like it was. The engine seemed to be in perfect condition. In fact, the truck ran as good as any new truck on the road, so he felt no fear about making the trip from Little Rock to Pigeon Point.

As Ben made his way through the city streets, he thought about the day ahead and the many things he hoped to accomplish. He was so glad he had not gotten the truck painted and repaired. In its present condition, it seemed to be exactly the kind of truck he thought Uncle Harry would drive. His disguise would allow him to be at the lake house with Jim and Sherry without putting them in danger. It would also allow him to see if he could make contact again with the white dog. Ben didn't understand why, but he had a hunch that the dog would prove valuable in some way.

The sun was coming up as Ben turned onto Log Mountain Road. When he entered the driveway at the cabin, Ben was struck with the beauty of the sunrise. The fog over the lake had been forced to let go of its grip on the water and was now dissolving as it lifted into the trees. A bright orange, early morning sun was reflecting in the water of the lake and dispelling the dark shadows from the trees. Everything looked so serene and peaceful. No wonder people enjoyed living in the mountains. Ben could not believe he was here to investigate the disappearance of his pastor who was accused of being connected in some way to a murder. This just did not seem to be the kind of place where anything like that could take place.

He breathed a sigh of relief when he saw a light in the living area of the cabin. He was afraid that he might have arrived too early for Jim and Sherry, but the light indicated they had gotten out of bed at least. He quickly turned the truck around and backed it into the driveway as close to Jim and Sherry's car as possible. He sure didn't want anyone seeing his tag. A registration check right now would reveal his true identity.

The cool, morning air bathed Ben's face as he got out of the truck and made his way to the door of the cabin. He knocked gently in case someone inside was still asleep. Jim answered his knock and whispered as he pushed his way out of the door, "Sherry just got up. She's in the shower. You probably ought to wait out here for a few minutes."

"Sure thing," Ben replied. "I really need to look around a little bit. I'll walk up the road for a ways and then come back."

"That will be great," Jim said. "I'll try to hurry Sherry along. I hope you'll sit down and eat a bite with us. I was just getting ready to cook some bacon and eggs. Will you join us, Ben? We would love to have you eat breakfast with us. By the way, you look great. No one will ever know who you are in that get-up."

Ben agreed to the breakfast. He had not even thought about eating until Jim said something about food. Suddenly he felt ravenously hungry. "I would be happy to eat breakfast with you and Sherry, Jim. Thanks for the vote of confidence. I hope I look old enough to your Uncle Harry. I'll be back in about twenty or thirty minutes. Will that give Sherry enough time?"

"Plenty of time. See you in a few minutes," Jim replied as he opened the door and went back into the house.

Ben walked slowly up the drive and down the road in the direction he had walked the day before. He muttered to himself as he walked along and stopped frequently to look out over the woods. He didn't think anyone was watching him, but he wanted to get used to acting like an eccentric old man. After he meandered along for about ten or twelve minutes, he turned around and returned to the house, once again taking his time as he shuffled along the road. Jim met him at the door and invited him to come in.

Jim had prepared a breakfast fit for a king. Even the coffee tasted especially good this morning. Ben didn't say anything to Jim and Sherry, but he saw a car drive slowly past the cabin in both directions. He figured the occupant of the car was curious to know whose old truck was in the driveway. As they ate, Ben gave Jim and Sherry instructions so their stories would agree in case anyone came snooping around.

Following breakfast Ben made his way back up the driveway. This time he was on a mission, but he was careful to walk along the road as if he were an old man getting some exercise. About three-fourths of a mile from the house Ben saw the old white dog coming his way. His pulse quickened with excitement as he saw the dog. Deep inside he hoped he would not be disappointed.

"Hello, Buddy," Ben said as he knelt down and extended his hand toward the dog. There was blood matted in the fur of the dog's left hip. "Where did that come from?" Ben asked as he examined the dog.

"You're a might lucky dog," Ben told Buddy. "It looks like a bullet might have grazed you, but it didn't do much damage. It just broke the skin enough to make you bleed a little. Who was shooting at you anyway? Were you in some kind of trouble?"

Of course the dog couldn't answer Ben's questions, but he did look at Ben in a way that seemed to communicate both fear and the need to say something important. Ben scratched the dog's ears for a moment or two and then started meandering down the road. Buddy followed him closely.

About a quarter of a mile down the road, Buddy suddenly passed Ben and started down a small path that led away from the road. Then he turned and came back to Ben before starting down the path again. He repeated his actions at least three more times. Finally he turned and looked at Ben as if to ask if he understood.

The actions of the dog convinced Ben that the dog wanted him to follow him, so he carefully checked the road to make sure no cars were in sight. Then he stepped into the path and followed Buddy through the tall grass. He didn't know where they were going, but he was convinced Buddy had something to show him.

As he followed Buddy across the trail, Ben realized how hard it was to see where the trail was going. He couldn't see more than five feet ahead. Unless someone knew the trail was there, he could easily walk right over it without even seeing it. Ben breathed a little easier when they went over a knoll that prevented anyone from seeing him from the road. He was even more grateful when they made it to the trees beyond the tall grass.

About a half-mile later Buddy suddenly crouched low to the ground. A muffled growl not much louder than a whisper crept from the dog's throat. Ben knew danger was nearby. Almost unconsciously he touched his gun to make sure it was in place. He also pulled his binoculars from his pocket. He was glad Jim had suggested he take them along.

"What is it, Buddy?" Ben whispered as he got down beside the dog. When the dog looked at him and then at the path that led over the crest of the small hill they were climbing, Ben realized that whatever danger was present was just over the hill. He crawled along beside the dog until he could see what lay ahead. In a clearing at the bottom of the hill was a small cabin. Ben grabbed his binoculars to take a look.

"What have we here?" he asked himself as he surveyed the scene ahead. A light in one of the windows led Ben to believe that the cabin was occupied. He couldn't see through any of the windows, but he was sure someone was inside.

When his binoculars fell on the car that was parked beside the cabin, Ben nearly stood up from the adrenalin rush he felt. It was the same make and model as Pastor Ted's car. Ben focused his binoculars and strained to try to get a clear view of the license plate. He had to move a few feet to his left, but was finally able to read the letters and numbers on the plate. "N...S...P...0...3...4...9," he whispered to himself.

Without giving it much thought, Ben pulled his cell phone from his belt and dialed Carla Black's number. His heart sank when he realized that he was in a dead spot and could not complete his call. He didn't have any paper with him so he memorized the number from the license plate. Repeatedly he quizzed himself to make sure he had the number correctly memorized.

Ben started to crawl toward the house, but Buddy grabbed the leg of his pants and pulled against him. "What's wrong, Buddy?" Ben whispered. "You don't think I ought to risk being seen from the cabin, do you? Well, all right. I'm going to trust you with this one. You got me this far. I can't ignore you now."

With that comment Ben lay flat on the ground where he could see the front door of the cabin. Buddy lay as close to Ben as he could get and never moved a muscle. About a half hour later Ben noticed the door open just a little. Then it closed again. Buddy's ears perked up, but he still didn't move. Ben quietly assured the dog, "It's okay, Buddy. I'm used to this kind of surveillance." Then he put the binoculars back to his eyes and examined the cabin again.

That's when the front door of the cabin suddenly flew open and a short man came out obviously engaged in animated conversation with someone inside the house. Ben strained to hear what the man was saying, but he was too far away to make out the words. The man on the outside walked around for a few minutes looking around to make sure everything was like it should be. Then he stomped back into the house.

Ben wondered if there was some kind of disagreement going on with the occupants of the house. He continued to watch for another half hour. Buddy never moved from his side. Slowly Ben turned away from the cabin. He was convinced that the car belonged to Pastor Ted. He hoped the pastor was safe inside the house, but he had no way of knowing. Whoever was inside could have done something to Pastor Ted and stolen his car for all Ben knew. Right now he needed to get back to the lake house before he put Jim and Sherry in danger. He also wanted to find out for sure if the car belonged to Pastor Ted or not.

Buddy seemed to be glad they were leaving. He ran along the path away from the house acting as if he were relieved that he had finally been able to let someone know about the house in the woods. By the time they got to the edge of the trees and into the tall grass Buddy was nowhere to be found.

Ben had barely reached the road and walked twenty yards down it when he saw a car come around the curve a mile or so away. He pulled his binoculars from his pants and started looking up into the trees while he shuffled along. He kept peeking around the eyepiece of the binoculars to keep track of the car as it came closer and closer. When the car was right beside him, he pulled his binoculars from his eyes and waved at the driver like a friendly old man.

"You wouldn't believe how many different kinds of birds I've seen this morning," Ben said before the driver could say a word. "I just watched a woodpecker drill a few holes in that tree right over there. I sure wish I could see one of those Ivory-billed Woodpeckers everybody talks about. This is a bird-watchers paradise. Oh, by the way, my name is Harry Easton, but most people call me Uncle Harry. What's your name?" Ben asked as he extended his hand toward the man sitting in the car.

"Name's Henry Menokin," the man in the car replied. His words seem to be coated in ice as he spoke. Then he asked, "What are you doing up in these parts? I don't think I've seen you before."

"No, you probably haven't. It's my first time up here. It sure is a pretty place," Ben said, before adding, "Have you ever seen one of those Ivory-billed Woodpeckers, Mr. Menokin?"

"No, and no one else has either," the man answered, obviously irritated by Ben's question. "I don't think they really exist. It's just another scheme to get people excited so they'll spend some money. But that really doesn't matter. You didn't answer my question. What brings you to these parts?"

"Oh, sorry Mr. Menokin. I'm up here visiting my niece. She's one of the sweetest people you'll ever meet. She and her husband are renting the cabin right down there," Ben said as he pointed in the general direction of the lake house. "They're leaving later today. They called me yesterday to invite me to come up before they left. They think this is one of the most beautiful places on earth. I would have to agree with them. I sure wouldn't be surprised if they come back real soon. Do you live in one of these other houses, Mr. Menokin?"

"No I don't. I live in town just past the Shell station and to the right. I'm sure your niece knows where that is." Mr. Menochin's voice was a little softer, but he still looked at Ben with an icy stare that would intimidate most men.

"Sounds like you're a far piece from home," Ben said. He wondered how much information he could get out of the man. "What brings you all the way out here?"

"I'm helping the sheriff out," the man said matter-of-factly. "I'm not really a deputy, but the sheriff asked me to keep track of all the comings and goings out here. For some reason the sheriff is especially interested in what happens around that cabin your niece rented. I don't really know why...but some of the guys in town say there was a woman murdered around there. I don't know if the sheriff is afraid whoever did it will show up again or what. All I know is that he wants me to let him know everything that happens. I'll even be telling him that I met you out here."

"Well, that will sure be nice," Ben said. "I don't think I've ever had a sheriff want to know about me before. Does that mean I'm on some kind of watch list or something? I'm not in some kind of trouble, am I?"

"No, nothing like that, Sir. Sheriff Bixley just likes to keep track of people. There is one guy he really wants me to watch for, though...some private detective from Little Rock. The sheriff said I'm supposed to call him immediately if I see him. Haven't seen him today, though. Don't know what he's done, but the sheriffs don't seem to like him much."

"What's he look like...maybe I could help you keep an eye out for him...if I knew what he looked like, I mean?" Ben did his best to sound like a nosey old man.

"That's okay, Mr. Eason. I appreciate your offer, but this is a job I can handle on my own. I take pride in my ability to stay aware of what is happening. I don't think there are very many people who can get by without me knowing they are here."

"I'll bet you are right about that," Ben replied. "You are probably the best watchdog in the whole area, Mr. Menokin. Where in the world would I find you, if I see anyone that looks suspicious?" Ben was fishing for information so he would know what areas to avoid when he came back to Log Mountain Road.

"I usually park just off the road near where it turns off the highway. There is a nice little place right next to the store you'll see there. From there I can see everyone who turns into this area. They can't see me, though, unless they are looking for me. If you see anything, turn in and come around the south side of the building and you'll see me there." The man gave him more information than Ben expected.

"I'll keep my eye out for anyone acting suspicious, Mr. Menokin. If I see anyone, I'll come down there and tell you what I saw. You can count on me. I've always been a law-abiding citizen. Helping the sheriff get his man would be something I would enjoy doing," Ben said, trying to sound as helpful as an old man could hope to be.

"I'll bet you would. I've got to go now, Mr. Eason. You keep your eyes open and let me know if you see anything. Bye for now. You enjoy our mountains now, you hear? It is one of the most beautiful places in the whole state of Arkansas!"

"I will, and I'll tell my niece and her husband I met you. You have a good day." Ben breathed a sigh of relief when the car drove off. He put his binoculars back to his eyes and looked back up into the trees. He was sure his disguise and actions had convinced the man that he was nothing more than an eccentric old man.

CHAPTER ELEVEN

"If everyone will please take a seat, we'll get started," Mr. Jeffries raised his voice as much as he dared. He didn't want to sound like he was scolding the people gathered into the meeting room of the governing board of Hillside Community Church. The conversations in which the people were engaged slowly stopped as each group noticed that the others were finding their way to a place around the long, mahogany table in the center of the room. Several of the people looked at the empty chair where the pastor usually sat. When they did, sadness spread across their faces.

"Folks, this is going to be as difficult for me as it is for all of you, but I feel like it must be addressed. That's why I asked all of you to come tonight. As you know, Pastor Ted has been missing for quite a while now. No one seems to have any idea where he might be. According to his wife, he just disappeared one day. It is my understanding that Ben Albright has been trying to locate him, but hasn't had much luck. All of us have been praying for his safety, but, as of today, we haven't received any encouraging news at all. We hope he will be located soon, but we have no way of knowing when, if ever, that will happen." Everyone stirred uneasily as they listened to Mr. Jeffries state what all of them already knew.

"I'm sure many of you have joined me in thinking a lot about the future of our church. I've begun to wonder what will happen to it if we continue without any pastoral leadership much longer. Those who have filled in for Pastor Ted have done an admirable job, but I'm not sure how much longer we can expect them to carry such a heavy load. I assure you that I'm not wanting to hurry the process up, but you know as well as I do that finding a new pastor can take several months. I, for one, think it is time for us to get started in the search process." Mr. Jeffries' tone made his last statement sound like it was the only choice the leadership board could possibly make.

"Don't you think you are jumping the gun just a little?" Tiffany Lee spoke up. She was certainly not ready to give up yet. She was convinced something had happened to Pastor Ted, but was just as convinced that he would be found and everything would return to normal. Several others seemed to be in agreement with her...if she read the expressions on their faces correctly.

"Not at all, Ms. Lee," Mr. Jeffries responded coldly. "I know you have been close to the pastor's wife, and would naturally want to wait for as long as possible so it would not look like we are getting impatient. But we have to think about the church. We certainly don't want to do anything that would harm the church in any way. Waiting could be detrimental if Pastor Ted is never located."

"I'm certainly not in favor of hurting the church either, Mr. Jefferies," Tiffany responded with a confident determination. "If we move too quickly, however, we could harm the church more than we will if we wait a little longer. What kind of message would it send to our pastor if he is found, but we have already begun the process of replacing him? He has given many years of his ministry to this church. We sure don't want to abandon him just because he is a couple of weeks later in returning than he planned."

"What makes you think we would harm the church if we go ahead and get started on a lengthy process that could be stopped at any point?" John Ingles asked.

"Think about it, ladies and gentlemen," Tiffany responded. "If we replace the pastor quickly, it would convince people we don't have any compassion or love for our pastor. I know we can't wait forever, but a couple of extra weeks hardly seems like we have given the authorities as much time as they need to find out if Pastor Black has been harmed. Besides, we haven't even talked to Ben or Carla to find out what they have discovered. They might have some news for us. Did you take the time to contact either of them before you called this meeting, Mr. Jeffries?"

"Well, no," Mr. Jeffries responded, a little embarrassed to be backed in a corner by such a young person. He took a great deal of pride in his business knowledge and didn't like to admit he had been careless in his preparation.

From his seat near the end of the table on the opposite side of the table from Tiffany Lee and Jerry Jeffries, Joe Hawkins mentally noted who nodded their heads in agreement with Mr. Jeffries and who seemed to affirm Tiffany Lee's position. It was obvious to him that this would be a stand-off if a vote were taken. The group was divided right down the middle. After listening to a few comments that mostly repeated what had already been said by both sides, Joe spoke up. "In the few months that I have served on this board I have never seen us as divided as we are on this issue," he said. "It seems to me like we need to develop a strategy that will let us proceed with unity. Isn't that what the Bible teaches us? Aren't we supposed to 'dwell together in unity'?"

"Well, yes, of course we are," stated Mr. Jeffries sounding almost conciliatory in his response.

"What did you have in mind?" inquired Tiffany Lee.

"The way I see it; it is simple. We ought to start by spending some time in prayer. If I remember correctly, we sought the Lord's direction when we granted Pastor Ted's extended leave. I think we ought to seek His leadership in our next step as well. Next I think we ought to talk with Carla and Ben before we do anything else. We could call Carla tonight, but contacting Ben will take longer. I understand that both he and his secretary and her husband have been out of town conducting his search for Pastor Ted. Since we might have to wait a day or so before we can locate Ben, we could wait until tomorrow to talk to Carla as well. There's no need to upset her at this hour. If either Carla or Ben has found out anything hopeful, then I think we should wait to do anything until we see if it will produce any results. If they haven't found anything yet, and don't by this time next week, then I think we ought to begin the development of a pastoral profile for this church. Once that is done, we could announce that we are officially beginning the process of searching for a new pastor."

"Well, that sounds like a pretty lengthy delay in my book," Mr. Jeffries growled. "I would much rather start on the profile right now, but I guess waiting for one more week won't hurt us too much as long as our pastoral supply is willing to continue. I sure don't want you all to get the idea that I don't love Pastor Ted. He is the best pastor this church has ever had. I just don't want us to let our feelings for him cause us to be negligent when it comes to doing what is best for the church. I can support your strategy, Mr. Hawkins. What about you, Tiffany?"

Tiffany wasn't totally pleased with the limitation of one more week for finding clues about finding Pastor Ted, but realized that this was a very logical approach given the circumstances. She also knew that developing a pastoral profile would take another week or two. That would mean that any official announcement of a pastoral search would be delayed at least two or three weeks. Her voice was a little weak when she started to speak. "Most of you know that I really admire Pastor Ted and Carla. I have spent a lot of time with Carla over the last few weeks just like I agreed to do when we granted Pastor Ted his leave. She is such a strong, confident person. I sure don't want to do anything to hurt her. It won't be easy for her to face the fact that the church cannot continue waiting indefinitely. She is totally convinced Pastor Ted will be found alive and well. Providing another week to look for Pastor Ted would have the additional benefit of giving us the opportunity to show her the support she needs right now. As the week draws to a close, some of us could begin to try to help her understand our position in the matter. With these things in mind, I guess I can agree with Mr. Hawkins strategy although I would personally like for that week to be a month." Carla's voice cracked a little as she said the last sentence.

"Since both of you are in agreement, I move that we adopt this strategy and express our vote by calling upon God in prayer," Sam Tucker said as he pushed his chair back and fell to his knees beside it.

"I second that," said John Ingles as he joined Sam on his knees.

One by one each member of the board joined them in this humble posture of prayer. Tears flowed down many cheeks as different board members cried out for Pastor Ted's protection, for guidance for Ben Albright, for support for Carla Black and for a clear sense of God's direction for Hillside Community Church. Silently several of them thanked God that a split of the board had been avoided. They realized that they needed unity now more than ever.

After the group had prayed for about thirty minutes, Mr. Jeffries rose to his feet. The other board members soon joined him. "I have two things I want to say before we leave tonight. First, we must continue to make this a matter of prayer. Our prayer effort must not be limited to this prayer time. We must each one pray every day for the things we have prayed about tonight. Secondly, I want to thank Tiffany Lee for speaking up. She is one of the strongest Christian ladies in our church. Tiffany, I admire your walk with God. I also want to thank you, Joe. You kept us from being divided. Thank you for showing us a way to proceed in unity."

Both Tiffany and Joe expressed their appreciation for Mr. Jeffries. There were many hugs and expressions of appreciation among the entire group as they made their way out the door that night. All of them were aware of a greater level of unity than they had ever experienced as a leadership board before. Maybe…just maybe… Pastor Ted's disappearance would be used for their good just like God promised in the Bible.

CHAPTER TWELVE

"Preacher, you awake yet?" The question bounced around Pastor Ted's mind like a pin ball as he struggled to figure out what was happening. Was he asleep? He certainly had been before he was startled by the loudest voice he had heard in weeks. For a minute or two he thought maybe he was dreaming. Then he realized that the question came from one of the men who were guarding him.

"Well, I am now," he yelled back.

"Good," replied the unseen speaker. Ted could tell from the sound of the voice that the man was making his way down the hall. "Bo had to go into town for supplies," the voice said. "He also needs to look up the sheriff and take care of a couple of other things. He's going to be gone for two or three hours, so I thought maybe you and me could continue the conversation we started the other day."

"Sure, that would be fine," Ted said. For a few seconds he thought about looking for a way to get past the man. Then he realized that he had no idea where to go if he got out of the house. As far as he could tell he was deep in the woods. Besides, his guard had a gun strapped under his shoulder and Ted had no doubt that he would not hesitate to use it if he tried to escape. At least he was still alive. That was something for which to give thanks.

As Ted raised his head from the pillow, the figure of the taller of the two guards filled the doorway. "I got you that Bible you asked for, but you will have to keep it hidden. You shouldn't let Bo see you with it. Keep your door shut when you read it. Sit where you could stash it away if Bo ever comes down the hall. It's in my bag in the other room. I'll get it and my chair while you go to the bathroom and do whatever you need to do to get ready. Then we'll have us that conversation we were going to have. I still got lots of questions, Preacher." Hank sounded very eager to engage him in a serious discussion of spiritual matters.

"Yeah, sure," Ted replied. He was still struggling to get fully awake. "Uh, give me a few minutes to take a quick shower and brush my teeth. Then we'll see if we can find some answers to your questions," he said as he began to pray for the wisdom to answer the questions Hank had. He also prayed for the opportunity to invite Hank to pray a prayer for forgiveness.

As soon as Ted finished getting dressed, Hank came into the room carrying a chair and two identical Bibles. He carefully placed his chair where it blocked the doorway. Hank might not know much about the Bible, but it was evident he knew a lot about making sure no one got the upper hand on him.

Hank handed Ted one of the Bibles as he said, "Okay, Preacher, if God loves people so much, why does he allow someone like you – one of His preachers – who probably ain't never hurt nobody – why does he allow you to be accused of something as serious as murder? Why didn't He protect you like He should have?"

Nothing like starting with the hard questions first, Ted thought as he formulated an answer in his mind. "Well, Hank, one thing we soon learn about God is this: He works in ways we don't always understand. Sometimes He uses things that look bad for one person so He can do something good for someone else. For example, He may have allowed me to be in this situation to give you an opportunity to have this conversation with me."

"I doubt that," Hank objected. "Ain't nobody cares much about what happens to me. I ain't been much good most of my life... not good enough for God to let someone as good as a preacher face murder charges just so I can have a chance to talk. That sounds pretty harsh if you ask me. Looks like God would be better off just to get rid of me so He can get you out of this mess."

"Believe me He could do that if he wanted to, Hank, but apparently He doesn't want to. And, here's something else you need to know. God does love you...a whole lot more than you realize. The good thing about God is: you don't have to be worthy of love for Him to love you. He loves you even when you don't deserve it. If fact none of us deserves God's love, but He loves us anyway."

"That would be good to know if it was just true," Hank said with a note of despair in his voice. "If He loves me so much, why am I so bad? Why do I do things I know I shouldn't? And why do I feel so awful after I get drunk and do some really bad stuff?"

"The answer to those questions is pretty clear, Hank. When we do things we know are wrong, we are sinning against God. God makes us feel bad so we will know that we are doing wrong. It's His way of letting us know that there is a better way for us to live. He wants us to turn away from those things and start living the way we should. I have some good news for you, Hank. You don't have to keep doing things you know are wrong. God will help you keep from it. And there is something even better. He will forgive you for the wrong things you have already done."

"I don't know why He would forgive me. I sure don't deserve it," Hank objected.

"You're right, Hank. None of us deserves it...but God offers it anyway."

"Well, I sure don't seem to be able to keep from doing wrong. I may do pretty good for several days, but as soon as I get with the guys, I find myself doing stuff I know I shouldn't. Just the other day I was with Jerry and Ken. I know you don't know them, but they're friends of mine. Anyway, I was with them and I was doing pretty good, behaving myself and all. Next thing I know Jerry pulls out a fifth of whiskey. That's all it took. One bottle led to another. We all got drunk and beat some poor man half to death out by the drive in. That's what I'm talking about. I'm a bad person, preacher," Hank said with a note of sadness in his voice.

Ted was surprised by Hank's openness. The people in his church always tried to cover up their sins. They didn't want Ted or anyone else knowing how bad they had been. Their prayers seemed more like attempts to convince God they really weren't all that bad instead of honest pleas for mercy. In a strange way Hank's honesty was refreshing.

Again Ted tried to assure Hank that God could change him and give him a whole new start in life. He helped Hank turn to verses in his Bible like John 3:16, John 1:12, Romans 6:23 and 1 John 1:9. Those verses reinforced the message Ted was sharing. Ted underlined some of the verses in Hank's Bible so he could read them later.

Time seemed to fly as Hank peppered Pastor Ted with his questions. Ted did his best to answer as many of them as he could. More than once he encouraged Hank to pray for forgiveness. Time after time Hank just asked another question instead of praying. Ted felt like he was in a struggle that was bigger than the one between two men meeting in the bedroom of a shack in the woods.

Pictures of angelic beings, dressed in dazzling white, kept flashing through his mind. They were always fighting against ugly, impish "things" dressed in black. Pastor Ted knew that these were not necessarily accurate pictures of angels and demons, but he recalled the words the Apostle Paul recorded in Ephesians 6: 12 (NIV), *"For our struggle is not against flesh and blood, but against the rulers, against the authorities, against the powers of this dark world and against the spiritual forces of evil in the heavenly realms."* Ted's body tingled with excitement as he realized he was doing much more than answering the questions of a man with limited understanding of the Bible. He was actually engaged in a battle for Hank's soul. Humbled by that thought, Ted prayed more earnestly than ever for Hank.

Right after Hank rejected the opportunity to pray for forgiveness another time, he stood up from his chair. "Preacher, we better stop for now. Bo will be back before long, and I don't want him to catch us reading the Bible. He would be madder than an old, wet hen if he did. I'll think about what all you said. You keep your Bible out of sight. If you get caught with it, Bo will know I brought it to you and I'd get in trouble. Are you listening to me? I'm serious. If you get me in trouble, you will wish you hadn't."

Ted didn't need for anyone to convince him of the truth of that statement. "I'll keep it out of sight. Bo hardly ever comes back here, so it won't be much trouble. Thanks for the Bible, Hank. You're a good man. Let me ask you to do one more thing. Would you start reading the gospel of John? Maybe we can talk about it when we get another chance to discuss the Bible. I'll be praying for you to ask Jesus to forgive you and give you a new start, Hank. Anything else you want me to pray for?

"No," Hank mumbled as he grabbed his chair and left the room. Just before he turned toward the door, Ted noticed moisture forming in the eyes of the hardened man. He was sure God was speaking to Hank so he decided to pray for Hank every day.

Hank had barely left Ted's room before Ted heard the crunch of gravel under the wheels of a vehicle. He was tempted to remove the knot from its hole to see if he could see anything, but decided against it. His mind was so full that he needed to spend some time talking to God.

CHAPTER THIRTEEN

Ben sat by the fireplace stroking his chin as he contemplated his next step. He had arrived home late last night…too late to call Carla Black. He wanted to find out if the car he had seen by the cabin in the woods belonged to Pastor Black, but he didn't want to alarm Carla, nor did he want to get her hopes up too much if the car he had seen didn't belong to the pastor. He certainly didn't know if Pastor Ted was in the rustic old house or not. Somehow or other he needed to figure out a way to find out if his beloved pastor was being held in that place.

Ben's wife, Joan, refilled his coffee cup and sat down beside him. "Why so glum?" she asked softly as she gently stroked his hair.

It took Ben a moment or two to realize she had spoken. "Uh… what, Honey?" he asked, embarrassed by his neglect of his beautiful spouse. She had always been supportive of his work as an investigator. His assignments often took him out of town for periods of time and sometimes caused him to be aloof because of the way they took over his life. Never once had she complained. He considered himself fortunate to have such a wonderful person as his mate.

"I asked why you were looking so glum this morning," Joan said with a touch of frustration in her voice. She was used to him being absorbed by his cases, but this one seemed to have special significance to him. She could understand why. Pastor Ted meant the world to both of them. She couldn't bear to think about what might have happened to him. In her prayer times she had asked God over and over to help her husband locate Pastor Ted before something awful happened to him.

Quickly Ben told her how a white dog had led him to the house in the woods and how he had seen a car parked there that looked like Pastor Black's car. "I'm trying to figure out how to share this information with Carla without getting her hopes up too much in case it isn't the right car. I also need to develop a plan to find out if the pastor is inside," he shared. "I'm not completely sure what to do next. I'm not even sure how to get to the house except through the path in the woods. I can't burst out of the woods and walk up to the house and ask if they are holding a pastor from Little Rock against his will. That would be a sure way to get them to move Pastor Ted to another location if he is there at all. I certainly don't want to cause the pastor more trouble than he has already been through."

"Why don't you call Carla and ask her if she could tell you what her husband's license plate number is without telling her why you want to know? If it is the same number, then you could tell her you may have spotted the car. If the number isn't correct, you could tell her you just needed to know so you could identify it if you do spot it," Joan suggested. "As for the entrance to the cabin, let's look at *Google Maps* on the computer to see if we can spot the cabin. Surely it has some kind of drive leading up to it."

"Joan, you're a genius. Just another reason why I made a very smart move when I asked you to marry me," Ben said as he pulled his wife close and pressed his lips upon hers. She was the ideal detective's wife. She was flexible enough to handle his unpredictable schedule and interested enough to offer good suggestions when his thinking wasn't providing obvious solutions.

Ben resisted the urge to continue showing affection to his lovely wife. He had to find out what he could about that car in the woods. If it did belong to Pastor Ted, he needed to move as quickly as possible. This was the best lead he had regarding the location of the pastor. While Joan logged on the computer, Ben picked up the phone and called Carla's number.

Carla was startled by the ringing of the telephone. Who could be calling her this early in the morning? Quietly she answered, "Hello."

Ben noticed how tired Carla sounded as she answered the phone. "Carla, this is Ben."

Before he could say another word, Carla began to ask questions with an excitement in her voice that had been missing moments before. "Oh, Ben, what have you found out? Have you got good news for me? Do you know where Ted is? I've been waiting to hear from you. Is Ted okay?"

Ben ignored Carla's questions by asking a question of his own, "Carla, I need to know what Ted's license plate number is on his car. Would you happen to know what it is, or could you find it for me?"

"No, I don't know it, but I could probably find it. My husband has a file on our cars. He should have the number recorded in it somewhere." The tired feeling quickly returned to Carla's voice. It made Ben want to disclose his reason for calling. It was obvious that the stress of the last few weeks was taking a toll on Carla.

Ben offered to wait while she looked for the number. While he waited, he jotted down the number he had memorized the day before. Joan let him know that she had the computer ready for him to begin his search as soon as he finished talking to Carla.

"Ben, I think I found the number you're looking for," Carla said as she returned to the phone. The hopelessness in her voice nearly broke Ben's heart. "Does this sound like the number you need... NSP0349?"

"That's it, Carla!" Ben exclaimed. "Carla, I don't want you to get too excited, but I have some good news. I spotted Pastor Ted's car yesterday."

Before he could say anything else, Carla said, "Where is it, Ben. I'll go immediately. If we know where his car is, we know where he is! He will be somewhere near it. Oh, Ben, I'm so excited. We're going to find Ted. I just know we are! When can I go see him? I can be ready in 15 minutes. Can you take me there now?" She was obviously excited again.

"Wait a minute, Carla. I know this has been hard on you, but I don't know where Pastor Ted is yet. I just know where his car is. You can't go there. In fact, I haven't even been close to it yet. I only saw it from a distance. It is parked in a remote place. I've got to find out more information before I dare get close." Ben was glad he had not shared all the details about what was happening near the cabin. "Carla, the best thing you can do at this point is stay in Little Rock. Get some people together and pray for God's direction. This is one case that is only going to be solved if God gives us wisdom and guidance."

"Oh, Ben, you can count on that. Please don't take too long. I don't know how much more I can take." Carla's voice broke as she pleaded with him. "Ben, I have to tell you something." There was a strange sound in her voice now. It was almost like she was suddenly under a black, storm cloud. Ben braced himself for what was coming. "Ben, the leadership board met last night. I'm not sure what they discussed, but rumor has it they were considering calling a new pastor." Before she could continue, Carla broke into heart-wrenching sobs.

"Oh, Carla, I'm so sorry. Let's not assume too much. Maybe they just wanted to gather for prayer, or to update all the members on what has happened in the search for Pastor Ted. Maybe they need to hear some good news. Carla, I'm going to ask Joan to come over in a few minutes to give you more details. Then I want you and Joan to call Tiffany Lee. Invite her to come for coffee. Share with her what Joan tells you. I'm sure Tiffany will know what happened in the meeting last night, and will also know what needs to be done now." Ben tried to sound as reassuring as he could.

"Okay. I hate to be such a bother," Carla said as she tried to choke back the sobs that threatened to erupt again. "Ben, could you ask Joan to hurry? I really need to have someone with me right now. I feel like I'm going to fall apart."

"She'll be there as soon as she can get dressed, Carla," Ben replied. As soon as he hung up the phone, he told Joan what was going on.

"Oh, Ben, that poor lady...how could they do that to her? Don't they know what she is going through?" Joan asked as she started through the den toward their bedroom.

"Don't go jumping to conclusions," Ben cautioned Joan. "You don't know what the meeting was about yet. That's why I suggested you and Carla meet with Tiffany. She is on the board and can tell you exactly what happened last night."

"I know, Ben, but I just don't like the way it sounds," Joan said as she disappeared into the bedroom to get dressed.

Ben turned his attention to *Google Maps* and started narrowing his search for the cabin in the woods. He had to know how to get to that rustic old house. Five minutes later he finally spotted what he was sure was the right place. He was surprised to see that the road leading to the cabin left Log Mountain Road on the opposite side of the road and meandered through the woods before finally ending up at the house. Someone had obviously gone to a lot of trouble to keep this place isolated.

By the time Joan was ready to leave the house Ben had formed a new plan. "I'm going to rent a car and go back to the mountains. I've got to find out if Pastor Ted is in that house," he told Joan, as she grabbed her keys and headed toward the garage door.

Joan changed directions and went to where Ben was staring at the computer screen. "Ben, be careful. If Pastor Ted is in that house, he is being held against his will. This could be dangerous. Please consider getting some help," she begged as she massaged his broad shoulders. "I couldn't stand it if something happened to you."

"I'll be careful," Ben tried to sound confident and calm as he stood to face his wife. "I'll even try to think of someone I might invite to accompany me, but this kind of assignment usually goes better without help," Ben said. With that he pulled his wife close and kissed her. Their lips lingered together as each one of them pushed away the thoughts that tried to invade their minds.

As soon as Joan left the house, Ben took a quick shower and got dressed. He grabbed a quick bowl of cereal before making his way across town to his office. As he drove along the familiar streets, he felt a new excitement that had not been there since he had begun working on this case. He thrived on this excitement. It was what kept him in this line of work. He could easily have taken a job with less stress and uncertainty, but he knew he would have been bored and soon would have abandoned such an arrangement. He liked the excitement that came when he was about to unravel a complex case…and he felt that excitement this morning.

As he made his way to the office, a plan began to form in his mind. By the time he was a block from his parking spot, he knew that Wellington Enterprises, a fictitious company that only existed in his mind, was about to need his services. When Joan's suggestion flashed through his mind, he decided to call Harvey Garnett to see if he would consider working for Wellington Enterprises for a day.

"Hello, Harvey. This is Ben Albright," Ben identified himself and engaged in small talk for a few minutes before he got to the purpose of his call. "Harvey, could you help me out tomorrow or the next day? I'm investigating a missing person case and think I may have located the missing person, but I'm not sure yet. I want to try to verify my suspicions before I proceed. Here's what I want to do..." Ben carefully explained his plan of action to his friend, who was also a private investigator. They agreed to make their visit to the secluded cabin later that morning instead of waiting until the next day.

Ben went into the restroom and prepared himself for the visit. Another one of his disguises would be necessary since he would certainly be seen by the man who kept track of everything that happened on Log Mountain Road. As he applied the last touches of his new look, a car horn sounded. He looked out the window and saw Harvey's car. Harvey had offered to rent the car and drive it so it could not be could not be traced to either of them or to their businesses.

The two men refined the scope of their mission as they made their way from Little Rock to the mountains of North Arkansas. As they turned on to Log Mountain Road, Ben expected to see the car on the south side of the store on the corner, but it was missing. He breathed a huge sigh of relief and hoped this was a good sign.

The two men began to stop at every house on Log Mountain Road. They knocked on each door and asked every resident the same questions. They only found a few residents at home however. It was obvious that many of the houses were vacant since it wasn't a popular vacation time. When they stopped at the house just a mile from the Lake House where Pastor Black had disappeared, the lady who answered the door kept looking at Ben as if something about him seemed familiar. That made Ben uncomfortable. He was afraid his disguise wasn't enough to keep the authorities from recognizing him if he came face to face with any of them.

After spending about an hour and a half stopping at the cabins along the road, Harvey pulled the car to the side of the road and they started on foot toward the secluded cabin at the end of a long and twisting drive. Both men were tense and alert as they walked toward the cabin. They first thing Ben noticed was the vacant spot beside the cabin. Pastor Ted's car had been there before, but nothing was there now. What did that mean? Had the pastor been moved, or were his captors just using his car for transportation? Had someone gotten suspicious? Had his investigation endangered his pastor? Ben quietly shared his thoughts with Harvey as they approached the house.

Ben had never noticed how loudly walking on gravel sounded before today. He had hoped to catch whoever was in the house by surprise, but he was sure the loud, crunching sounds beneath his feet announced their presence. By the time Ben and Harvey got within 10 feet of the house, two angry-looking men stepped onto the porch.

"That's far enough!" the shorter of the two yelled. "I don't know what you two are selling, but we don't want none! Now why don't you turn around and leave the same way you came?"

"We're sorry to disturb you, Mister," Ben said. "My name's Gary and his name is Justin. We're doing a survey for Wellington Enterprises. They are interested in starting a business in this area and want to know how receptive people would be for their services. I'd like to ask you a few questions if I could. We've already stopped at all the other houses on Log Mountain Road today. Would you give us about five minutes of your time?"

"Don't need no businesses in this area!" the man snarled. "And I ain't got time for no survey. Now, why don't you do what I asked you to do and git yourself out of here?"

"We sure will, Mister, but could you at least tell me how many people live here and what the gender of each is?" Ben dared to press the man for the information he wanted.

"Don't know that that is none of your business," the man spit the words at Ben and Harvey as he picked up his rifle which had been leaning against the wall. "Now, are you guys going to get out of here, or am I going have to convince you to go?"

"Whoa, now, calm down, Mister," Ben said as he put away his pen and lowered his clipboard. "We don't mean to cause anybody any trouble. We're just trying to earn a living. Only thing is, we don't get paid for coming here unless we get at least one answer to our questions. Would you help me out by just answering the one question I asked you? Then I could get paid and you could go back inside and enjoy the rest of the day." Ben was surprised by his own reluctance to turn and leave. From the look on Harvey's face, he would be more comfortable if they were already headed back down the shady road that led through the trees back to Log Mountain Road.

"They's three of us," the man muttered. "Now will you get outta here? Don't make me do something you and I will both regret!"

"Okay," Ben answered. "I guess that is the two of you and the lady of the house." Ben was fishing for as much information as he could get, but he also knew he was about to push the man as far as he could. As he looked out of the corner of his eye, he noticed that Harvey's face was colorless. The gun was a whole lot more than he had bargained for when he agreed to help Ben out on this trip.

"Ain't no lady here," the man snorted. "Don't need one. The two of us can take care of everything we need."

"What about the third one? Doesn't he do anything?" Ben dared to ask.

"He ain't much help," the man replied. "Keeps to himself most of the time. In fact he only comes out of his room once or twice a day." Suddenly the man realized that he had given the two men more information than he had intended. "Now, git out of here right now!" he growled. "You got your answer. You'll be able to git your pay. If you keep standing here talking, I'm going to pay you with some lead from the barrel of this here gun. Did you hear me? Git going!"

"We're going. Thanks, Mister," Ben said as he started walking away. He really didn't want to turn his back on these two, but knew he had to make his visit look authentic and innocent, so he did. As he turned Ben noticed a few drops of sweat run down Harvey's face. He felt sorry for his friend. He had not intended to put him in a place of danger.

When he heard the yelling from outside, Pastor Ted had a strong desire to hear what was being said. He closed his bedroom door, went to the window and pulled the plug from the hole. He put his ear down to the opening and strained to hear the exchange of words. He couldn't hear everything, but he could hear enough to recognize one of the voices he heard. It was the voice of Ben Albright.

Ted was tempted to yell at Ben and run out the door of the cabin, but decided he needed to exercise caution. When he heard Bo mention the rifle and threaten to shoot the men, the pastor's heart sank. He didn't want to place his friends in greater danger than they already were in. As the men turned to leave, Pastor Ted replaced the knot, opened the door and fell on his bed. As he lay there, a sense of peace enveloped him. Ben's presence surely meant that he was being hunted for and that they thought he was in this cabin. He tried to think of ways to get a message to them, but no ideas would come to mind. Ted closed his eyes and pretended to be asleep hoping his guards would think he had missed the entire visit.

As soon as Harvey and Ben rounded the curve, Bo told Hank to follow them to make sure they left the area. Bo stormed into the cabin and stomped down the hall toward Ted's room. When he caught a glimpse of Pastor Ted on his bed apparently sound asleep, he turned around and went back up the hall instead of saying anything. Ted breathed a sigh of relief. As he lay there, he tried to control his emotions, but his hopes soared for the first time in weeks. He was not forgotten. Someone was on his trail. He wondered how long it would be before he would be found.

The edge was taken off his emotions, however, when he heard Hank return. "They walked straight out of here and went to an SUV with one of them magnetic signs on the side of it. I stayed out of sight, but read the words, *Wellington Enterprises*, on the side of it as they turned around. I guess they were legit, but we'll let the sheriff decide that."

"You better believe we will," Bo replied. "In fact I'm going to walk up to the road and give him a call right now. You keep an eye on the prisoner. He slept right through the whole thing. I'll be back in a few minutes. If you get some time, you might get some lunch started. I'm hungry after that little encounter."

Before Hank started fixing their lunch, he walked down the hall to look in on Ted. Ted was still pretending to be asleep. Convinced that what Bo told him was true, Hank went back to the kitchen and started getting some lunch ready. For some reason Ted felt more like eating than he had in days.

As soon as they got in the car, Ben apologized to Harvey for what had just happened. Harvey pretended like he wasn't scared, but Ben knew he wasn't prepared for what they had just been through. As they drove along, they discussed what they needed to do now. They were sure their presence was being reported to the sheriff so they decided to make their survey look legitimate by driving to another part of town. Ben could not help but notice that the car was still gone as they passed the store at the entrance of Log Mountain Road. He wondered if they were no longer patrolling the road. Somehow he suspected the car to be back within hours.

Ben kept looking over his shoulder as they surveyed house after house on the east side of town. He wasn't sure he knew what he was looking for, but he had to stay aware of his surroundings. Too many strange things took place in this little town for a man to be caught by surprise. A shiver went down his spine as when he saw a police car approaching. He tried to convince himself to stay calm, but his heart was racing a mile a minute.

The police car went down the street and stopped beside their car. Ben figured that the officer in the car was running a check on the plates. He sure was glad they had rented a car. They would get the name and address of the rental company, but little more. Any attempt to trace Wellington Enterprises would come up empty. Fictitious companies don't have addresses or profiles or anything people can trace.

The police car soon turned and came up beside them as they walked from one house to the next. "What do you boys think you are doing?" the deputy in the car asked. Ben recognized him as the man he had met at the desk in the jail.

"Hi, Officer," Harvey replied. "We're doing a little survey work for a man in Little Rock. He is thinking about starting a business up here and wants to have some information about the need for his services." Ben kept his head turned slightly so the officer could not get a good look at him.

"Is that right?" the man inquired. "Do you boys have a permit to conduct surveys in this community?"

"Oh, no sir," Harvey answered. Ben almost chuckled at the way Harvey was acting nervous and totally rattled. "We didn't know we needed one. No one told us anything about a permit. We were just hired to come up here and get the responses of a certain number of people. We aren't in any kind of trouble, are we, Officer?"

"Well, yes you are, young man. You are in violation of City Code 0849. But I tell you what I'm going to do. If you will close up shop and get in that car down the street and head back to Little Rock, I'll let you go this time. Do you understand me? If you go to one more house, you are going to be taken in and charged with a crime. Now, did I hear you say you were on your way out of town?" the man asked with a malicious grin spreading across his leather-like face.

"Yes sir!" Harvey squealed. "We'll leave right now, won't we, Gary?"

Ben grunted a yes through clenched teeth as they wheeled around and headed toward the car. The patrol car turned around and fell in behind them as they drove away. Ben told Harvey about his experience when he was followed by the *Lexus* and suggested that he be prepared for anything to happen. There was no repeat performance, but the police car did stay on their bumper until they passed Log Mountain Road and headed toward Little Rock.

As soon as Harvey dropped him off, Ben went into his office and removed all traces of his disguise. Suddenly he felt totally exhausted and collapsed in one of the chairs in the waiting area. Sherry had gone home much earlier, so he was alone with his thoughts. For about an hour he wrestled with the challenge he faced.

The facts surrounding the case seemed to rise up like a mind-numbing barricade that kept him from seeing any possible way to locate Pastor Ted. He had seen the pastor's car, but it was now missing again. There were three men living in a secluded cabin in the woods, but he didn't know for sure that Ted was one of them. Someone had tried to run him off the road, but he couldn't identify who the person was. All he had was the make and model of a car... no tag, no VIN number, nothing. The sheriff's deputies were rude and seemed to want him out of the way, but he could bring no legal charges against them. A cleaning company had cleaned up the house where Ted was staying when he was accused of murder, but that's what cleaning companies do. There was no evidence that they had taken anything from the house. His mind swirled as he tried to see through the barricade.

It was getting late and Ben knew he needed to get home. Joan would be getting worried about him, but he needed to take care of one important item of business before he called her to tell her he was on his way home. With a heavy heart he slid from his chair and fell on his knees with his face nearly touching the floor. "God," he said. "You told us in the Bible, *if any of you lacks wisdom, he should ask God.* I'm admitting that I lack the wisdom to solve this case. I can't figure out what to do next. I've been working on it for weeks now and nothing seems to add up. I really need your help on this one." Ben had prayed about many cases over the years, but this one seemed more complex than all the others. He was also more passionately involved in the outcome.

Ben continued his prayer, "You told us in another place, God, that the Spirit of Truth, Your Holy Spirit, would guide us into all truth. I need that guidance, dear Lord. I really need Your direction and help. The only thing I know to do now is to leave this in your hands. I'll be listening for Your answer when You are ready to let me know what to do next. Thank You for Your promises. I'll stand on them as I proceed. I offer my prayer in the name of Your Son and my Savior, Jesus Christ. Amen"

Ben felt a deep sense of relief. The case was no longer his alone. He knew he could trust God to be his partner in this one. With that he walked into his office and picked up his cell phone. He called Joan to let her know he was headed home.

"Oh, Ben, I've been so worried about you. Harvey called and said he dropped you off over an hour ago. Why didn't you answer your phone? I've been trying to reach you for an hour or longer. Is anything wrong?"

"Nothing is wrong, Honey. I'm okay. I'm sorry I had you worried. I left my phone on my desk while I went into the bathroom to remove my disguise. I guess I left it there for the last hour while I tried to sort through the facts about Pastor Ted. I've been in the waiting room spending some time talking to God about what to do next. I couldn't hear the phone ringing. Forgive me, please. I'm leaving to come home right now. What did Harvey want?

"He said he had an idea he wanted to run by you. He said he would give you a call tomorrow. Please, come straight home, Sweetheart. I've been so worried. I won't rest until you get here"

Ben apologized again, assured Joan he would be home in a few minutes, turned off the office lights and made his way to his car. He was exhausted, but had a strange feeling that he was about to see God at work.

CHAPTER FOURTEEN

B en woke up the next morning with one thought drumming its way through his head. "I need to put the cabin under surveillance," he thought. The idea kept pounding its way through his mind over and over. As soon as Ben could, he called Harvey to see what kind of idea he had and to see if he could cover a couple of his other cases over the next few days. He quickly explained to Harvey that he was going back to watch the cabin to see for sure if Ted Black was, in fact, being held in the cabin. Harvey told him to be careful and agreed to help him out. The men exchanged ideas and information before assuring each other of prayer. As soon as he hung up the phone, Ben jumped into his vehicle and started toward Greers Ferry Lake.

Ben had been watching the cabin for about thirty minutes when Buddy, his white, furry friend, came to where he was and laid down right beside him. Buddy stayed close to Ben without moving a muscle for the next couple of hours. Ben was amazed that a dog could lay that still for that long, but he sure was glad to have Buddy there. It gave him a strange sense of security to have the dog by his side.

Hunger pains shot through Ben's stomach causing him to make plans to take a break to get something to eat. Before he could move, however, the front door of the cabin slammed against the front wall of the building. Three men barged through the opening. Ben looked at them carefully, but none of the men was Pastor Ted. One of the men pointed in his direction and said something to the other two. It was obvious they were arguing about something. Ben strained to hear what was being said, but he couldn't hear a word. The men kept arguing and kept pointing in Ben's direction. He knew he could not be seen, but the pointing made him feel tense and extremely uncomfortable.

As the hours passed, Pastor Ted's newly found optimism began to diminish. He had been certain that Ben knew he was in the cabin. He had expected someone to come to his rescue before now. Old questions kept forcing their way back into his mind in spite of his attempts to keep them away. Why was he here? Where was God? Was he going to be set free? Was that really Ben he had heard? Could he have been dreaming? Perhaps his hopes had caused him to imagine that it was Ben. Who was this third man? Ted recognized Hank's voice and Bo's voice but he had no idea who this new visitor was. The men seemed to be arguing. Ted nearly jumped out of his skin when the door slammed against the front wall and the arguing men forced their way outside.

Ted lay quietly for a few seconds and then jumped up and removed the plug from its place in the window. What were the men arguing about? They were saying something about a second way to the cabin. He heard something about being suspicious of a recent visit. That was all he could hear. Ted heard a noise that made him think the men were coming back in. He pushed the plug into place and fell across his bed. He held his breath, but could not hear anything else.

As Ted lay on his bed, he began to pray for protection for both himself and his friend, Ben. He wasn't sure what was going on, but sensed something was about to happen. He wasn't sure he liked what was happening, but what could he do about it? He was locked in the tiny confines of his bedroom.

Buddy stirred slightly, causing Ben to jump. For some reason his nerves were on edge. He looked at Buddy, who had drawn his legs under him and was now in a slight crouch. He could tell by the dog's posture and demeanor that Buddy sensed danger. What was happening? Were they in danger? "Maybe I ought to get out of here," Ben said to himself. He quickly glanced back at the men by the cabin. There were only two of them now. The third man had gotten into a car and was driving away.

Carla, Ted's wife, woke with a start. She had fallen asleep while trying to watch television. It was not uncommon for her to fall asleep when she sat down and got quiet, but she didn't usually wake up feeling a crushing burden. For some reason Carla was certain that Ben and Ted were in trouble. After breathing a quick prayer, she grabbed the phone and called Tiffany.

"Tiffany? Could you come over here? I know it is short notice, but I just woke up feeling an urgent need to pray for Ben and Ted. Could you come over and pray with me?"

She must have sounded urgent, because Tiffany said, "I'll be there in 15 minutes." She didn't ask any questions. She just agreed to come over.

When Tiffany got there, she had two ladies with her. One was Joan, Ben's wife. The other was Betsy, a lady from the church who had the reputation for spending large amounts of time in prayer. As soon as they arrived, Carla told them what she could about the burden she was feeling and the ladies began praying.

Suddenly Ben heard noises behind him. He strained to see what was causing the noise when he caught a glimpse of three shadowy figures coming down the path toward him. Ben realized he was trapped. Behind him was the cabin. He sure couldn't go in that direction. In front of him now were three unknown men making their way toward him.

Before Ben could figure out what to do, Buddy crept away from him staying low to the ground. When he was about 30 feet away, he suddenly started barking and charged the men. One of them let out a string of curse words and raised his gun toward his shoulder. Before he could pull the trigger, however, Buddy left the trail and was soon engulfed in the tall grass. He must have stirred up some rabbits because several trails of waving grass started moving in all directions. It was impossible to tell which one might be Buddy so the man lowered his gun and said, "Dad-blamed, dog. He just about scared me out of my wits." The others with him laughed quietly as they resumed their trek toward Ben's hiding place.

Ben used the time when their attention was on Buddy to slip into a thick stand of pine trees nearby. Buddy was an even greater hero in Ben's mind, now. That dog seemed to have a way of knowing what to do. As he stood among the trees, he hoped he had not been seen as he moved.

Standing quietly behind one of the larger pines, Ben hardly dared to breathe. He wanted to peek around the tree to see where the men were, but decided against it. One glimpse of him and his life could be cut short in a hurry. As Ben stood there for what seemed like a long time, he wondered what was happening. Just as he decided to risk peeking around the tree, he felt a sudden pain in the back of his head, and everything went black.

Ben's eyes were blurry when he tried to open them. He could tell someone was sitting beside the bed he was stretched out on, but he couldn't tell who it was. As Ben stirred slightly, the figure leaned over him and, in a whispered-voice, urged him to be quiet. He knew that voice. He had heard it many times before. He was sure it was the voice of Pastor Ted. Ben started to say something, but Ted put his hand over his mouth and told him to be quiet. That's when reality began to set in. He had found his beloved pastor, but not in the way he had hoped. Instead of locating him so authorities could rescue him, he was now a prisoner with him in this cabin in the woods.

The men only managed a few words of greeting before one of the guards came into the room. He saw Ben was awake and started giving him a rough time. "Way to go, Detective," he said. "I see you found your man." With that came a belly laugh that lasted for what seemed like several minutes. In an instant his countenance changed and he started giving orders. "Both of you...grab your things and come with me. We've got some unfinished business to take care of."

Noticing his own gun in the man's gloved hand caused Ben to shudder. The stranger motioned toward the hall as he ordered Ben and Ted to move in that direction. "Now, Preacher, when we go outside, I want you to start walking slowly across the yard toward the trees on the other side of the road. Do you understand? What did you say, preacher? Do you understand?"

"Yes, I understand," Pastor Ted replied. Ben could sense the resignation in the pastor's voice.

The man giving instructions continued, "And, De...tec...tive, (the man drawled the word out as if he wanted to show his disdain for Ben) I want you to stay with me on this side of the road. You're going to be the witness to something awful, but you can handle it, can't you, De-tec-tive? What did you say, De-tec-tive? I can't hear you. Can you handle it?"

It didn't take long for Ben to catch on to what was happening. The men were going to shoot Pastor Ted with Ben's gun and then put his gun in his hand and force his hand to pull the trigger as he held it to his own temple. They were going to make it look like Ben shot himself after he had accidentally shot his pastor. He had no choice about answering. "Yes, sir, I can handle whatever happens here."

If their lives had not been at stake, Ben would have been impressed by their plan, but now he was trying to figure out a way to get out of what looked like certain death. If he ever needed God's help, he sure needed it now. As he began praying for deliverance, Ben realized that Pastor Ted must have come to the same conclusion because his lips were moving as he walked along. Ben joined the pastor in praying for deliverance from their enemies. Somehow Ben felt comforted by the fact that he was with Pastor Ted.

The ladies gathered in Carla's living room were weeping and praying. They didn't know what was happening at the cabin in the mountains, but they knew they needed to pray for the protection and safety of both Pastor Ted and Ben. Urgently and repeatedly they cried out to God, asking Him to take care of the men at that very instant. Each one of them felt the crushing burden that Carla had described earlier.

As they were praying, Tiffany suddenly stood up and grabbed her cell phone. She quickly dialed Ben's office number and talked to his secretary. "Does Ben have any friends on the police force?" she asked as she shared her fears with Sherry.

After getting a name, Tiffany called the man and began to spill out the whole story...especially the part about the cabin in the woods and Ben's plan to keep the cabin under surveillance. She couldn't tell if the man would be impressed by their burden for the safety of the two men, but she shared that as well. Carla interrupted her with the name of the other private investigator who had accompanied Ben to the cabin on one of his earlier trips. Tiffany quickly gave the policeman Harvey's name and begged him to check things out. She told him how certain the ladies were that the men were in danger.

Sergeant Blight thought this was the strangest call he had ever received in all of his 26 years on the police force. He tried to explain that the area near Greers Ferry Lake was out of his jurisdiction. "I'm not sure what I can do, Ma'am," he said. The ladies were so convincing and so insistent, however, that he agreed to see what he could do.

As soon as Sergeant Blight hung up, he called Captain Hendricks, his supervisor, and asked his advice.

"Is there a missing person's report on Pastor Black?" Captain Hendricks wanted to know.

"I don't think so, Captain. Just a minute. I'll check and see," Sergeant Blight said as he turned to his computer and checked for a listing. "No, it doesn't look like there is anything on file."

"That's where you start then, Sergeant," the captain suggested. Then he continued, "Have his wife come down to the station to file a missing person's report. That will allow us to investigate the matter."

"Captain, sir, these ladies have convinced me that time is really important in this one. If I can get them to agree to come down right now, would you allow me to go on up to Highpoint and start the investigation?" Sergeant Blight asked even though he expected his request to be turned down.

"Will your case load allow you to make that trip?" the captain asked.

"As long as I am not gone more than a day, I should be able to do it," Sergeant Blight answered.

"Permission granted, Sergeant. I'd suggest you get to moving if you are going to get anything done in one day. And, Sergeant, make sure those ladies get down here immediately so I can have the preacher on the list by the time you get to Highpoint."

"I will, sir, and thank you. I'll see you when I get back," replied the sergeant.

As soon as he hung up his phone, Sergeant Blight dialed Tiffany's number. When she answered, he told her that Mrs. Black needed to go to the police station to file a missing person's report. That action would give him official permission to go to Highpoint to look for Pastor Black.

Carla assured him that she would make sure the Mrs. Black filed the report as soon as they hung up.

With that assurance in mind, Sergeant Blight hung up the phone and dialed Harvey's number. Silently he wondered if this private investigator could help him any. When Harvey told him about Ben's suspicion of the local police chief, Sergeant Blight realized this was a more complex case than he thought. Sergeant Blight told Harvey that he had been given permission to investigate the missing person's report. "Would you be able to accompany me to the hidden cabin in the woods," the sergeant asked the investigator.

"I can be ready to go in five minutes," Harvey replied. The men arranged a meeting place and began to prepare themselves for the trip to the mountains.

Ted walked slowly across the porch and started down the two small steps that led into the yard when he heard the loud roar of several motorcycles. They sounded like they were coming toward the cabin. The men quickly pushed Ted and Ben back into the house and told them to get back in the bedroom. All the men in the house began yelling at once. Neither Ben nor Ted could understand what they were saying, but both men knew they were trying to decide what to do now.

Ted quickly removed the knot from the board across the window and peered through it. What did it matter if he got caught now? He was almost a dead man anyway. He could see two men from the group messing around the yard like they were getting ready to make some repairs to the cabin. They tried to look calm and relaxed as if they were simply taking care of things like any other cabin owner in this area.

Ben didn't join Ted at the window. He stood near the door to their room. Cautiously he stuck his head out the door and glanced down the hall. No one was looking his way. Their attention was drawn to the sounds from the motorcycles. It was obvious the bike riders were getting closer. Ben could see one of the men standing against the wall beside one of the windows with his gun drawn. He had no doubt that the others were standing by other windows as well. One wrong move from the motorcycle riders and they would open fire. Reluctantly Ben pulled his head back inside the room and went over to the window where Pastor Ted was still looking through the knot hole. "Can you see anything?" he whispered.

"Just the two men outside trying to act like nothing is wrong. They are trying their best to make it look like they are getting ready to take care of some maintenance or something. I just wish I could figure out a way to alert those guys on the bikes. They could be in trouble."

Before Ben could say a word, Ted told him he could see at least a half dozen riders turning around and pulling alongside the men. The men waved, attempting to be friendly. One of them yelled, "Hello, boys. Are you having a good day?"

"Sure are, old timer. Nice woods you got up here. We're having a blast." With that comment he gunned his bike. The rest hit their accelerators as well and the bikes were gone as quickly as they came. It was obvious that they were just some joy-riders who happened to see a narrow road through the trees and decided to see where it went.

When the men outside the cabin came back into the living room, a loud argument broke out. "I say let's kill them now!" one loud voice exclaimed.

"Too dangerous," Hank's voice rose above the rest. "Those riders saw you guys. If bodies were discovered here, they would put a finger on you two in a minute. We can't get rid of them here. We've got to come up with another plan. Now let's get our heads together and figure out what to do." With that he grabbed a chair and pulled it up to the rickety old table in the middle of the eating area of the kitchen. The others copied his actions.

Pastor Ted and Ben sat down on the bed, more than a little stunned by what had just happened. After sitting there a minute or two, with each man deep in his own thoughts, Pastor Ted invited Ben to join him in prayer. Ben was glad for the opportunity to pray. If he and his beloved pastor ever needed prayer, it was right now. Just a few feet from where they were sitting, men were plotting their death. They needed God to intervene, and they needed it quickly.

Sergeant Tom Blight and Harvey Garnett had agreed to meet in the parking lot of a nearby Wal-Mart store to discuss what to do next. The misty, overcast sky of that fall morning matched Harvey's overcast spirit as he jumped into Sergeant Blight's bright red, sports car as soon as the LRPD officer pulled alongside him. They exchanged a few words of greeting and then headed in the general direction of Highpoint, Arkansas, a charmingly beautiful, little town nestled in the mountains of the northern part of the state. It was the closest town to the lake cabin where all this had begun. Harvey was glad they were taking the sergeant's car. He was not sure he was ready to handle it if anyone suddenly tried to run them off the road. His mind was also full of all kinds of disconnected information that he needed to try to connect.

As they made their way across town, a raging debate regarding their strategy upon arriving in Highpoint began. Sergeant Blight spoke first, "We need to go to the sheriff's office as soon as we get there," he said. "I don't want to bypass the local authorities in this little town. We could create more trouble than we could ever resolve if we give them the idea we think they are incompetent. They would think we are down on them just because they are from a small community. If we strike out on our own without the backing of the local police, we could find ourselves doing battle with the police as well as the criminals, whoever they are. Let's at least talk to them and try to get them to cooperate."

"That sounds good on the surface, Sergeant" Harvey replied a little more forcefully than he intended, "but you are forgetting about one important fact. The police in Highpoint are probably the ones who kidnapped Pastor Ted in the first place. We might as well sign death certificates for both men if say one word to the police. One thing is sure. We won't get any help from anyone in Highpoint, and we might end up placing Pastor Ted and Ben in greater danger than they already are in."

"You don't know that for sure," Sergeant Blight argued. "You said yourself that none of you had actually talked to the sheriff. We might be able to convince him to help us if we at least talk to him. The rest of the police force might sound kind of harsh and might even be corrupt, but I doubt the sheriff is. Let's insist on talking to him in person. If we don't get anywhere with that, then we can come up with another plan."

"I don't like that strategy at all," Harvey countered. "By the time we develop another approach they would move the men to another location or do away with them altogether. I would rather round up some men, go over to the secluded cabin and force our way inside. We could surround the cabin by hiking through the woods, and then speak over a loud speaker demanding all those inside to come out with their hands up." He had to admit his plan sounded more like a scene from an old Dick Tracy movie than any modern strategy, but it was all he could think of.

"Yeah, and you would be placing the pastor and the detective in even greater danger. If they are in there, you might get them killed.

You said the men you talked to when you were doing the survey threatened you with a gun. What makes you think they would just come out with their hands up now? Gunfire could erupt whether they are in the cabin or not. Others could be killed as well. We don't even know for sure Ted and Ben are in the cabin. What would happen to us if people were killed and neither of them was even in the cabin? What if it really is just a couple of men who are trying to protect what belongs to them? When it's all over, we could be charged with criminal trespass, murder and who knows what else. I don't think my captain would be very happy with me if I go to another town and start shooting things up. That's just not how it is done in law enforcement, Harvey. We have to go through the right channels if we are going to make any progress at all!"

"Well, tipping off the sheriff will only mess things up," Harvey objected. "I'll stake my reputation on that, Sergeant. We've got to come up with a way to rescue these men without involving the local police."

Back and forth the men badgered each other until they finally rolled into the city limits of Highpoint. The two men had finally agreed to approach the sheriff before they did anything else. Harvey wasn't totally convinced, but he couldn't think of another plan that sounded any more feasible. He also knew that he would lose Sergeant Blight's help if he bypassed the local police.

Harvey gulped when they turned onto the street where the sheriff's office was located. Parked in front of the building was a silver *Lexus* like the one Ben had described to him. He wondered if this could be the one that nearly ran Ben off the road. He quickly brought Sergeant Blight up-to-date on the car. The sergeant pulled to the curb a few buildings down the street from the police station.

"We can watch the car from here without being seen," the investigator stated. "I want to see who comes out to that car before we talk to the sheriff."

For Harvey the minutes dragged by, but their patience paid off. About thirty minutes later a well-dressed man quickly emerged from the police station. It was obvious he was in a hurry. He appeared to be about six-two or six-three with black hair and a tanned complexion. He was wearing a navy blue, pin-striped suit with a white shirt and a red and blue striped tie. Harvey pulled his phone from its case on his belt and snapped a couple of pictures of the man. As soon as the man closed the door of the *Lexus*, he squealed his tires and roared down the street.

Sergeant Blight and Harvey gave each other a what-was-that glance before the police officer started his car and pulled into the parking place just vacated by the man in the *Lexus*. Each one took a deep breath and exhaled slowly as if he was trying to prepare himself for what lay ahead. Finally they got out of the car and marched straight toward the door of the sheriff's office.

When they entered the office, a gruff voice inquired from across the room, "What can I do for you?"

"We would like to speak to the sheriff," Sergeant Blight said sternly.

"Oh, you would now," the man said sarcastically. "I'm the deputy in charge here today. Whatever you want to see the sheriff about, you can take up with me. Sheriff Bixley has asked me to handle things today. I'll get whatever information he needs. Who did you say you were, Mister?"

"Just tell him Sergeant Tom Blight from Little Rock homicide is here to speak to him about some business," the sergeant said as he offered the deputy his identification. "And, if you don't mind, Deputy, I'll take up my business with the sheriff himself. I'm sure you can handle things, but this one is kind of important. Now will you get the sheriff for me?"

"He ain't here," the man replied. "He just left."

"Was he the man who just got in that silver *Lexus*?" Sergeant Blight inquired.

"No, of course not! Sheriff Bixley can't afford a car like that. And he sure wouldn't wear them fancy duds if he could," the deputy sneered as he walked across the room toward the two men. "That was Mr. Big Shot from across the lake. He really thinks he is something just because he has a lot of money. He tries to run everybody's business in the whole area. He needs to stay on the other side of the lake if he knows what's good for him. Someone's gonna clean his plow someday."

Harvey and Sergeant Blight were caught speechless by the venom spewing forth from this deputy. After a few tense moments, Sergeant Blight recovered and asked, "What has he been trying to do now?"

"Oh, nothing really. I shouldn't be talking about him, but he just gets under my skin sometimes," the deputy said almost apologetically. It was obvious he knew he had been out of order.

Before the sergeant could ask another question, a voice came from behind a partially closed door. "Who's out there, Deputy?"

The deputy pretended not to hear the question. Instead he turned to the men in front of him and started talking, "Like I said, the sheriff has asked me to take care of th…"

Before he could finish his sentence, however, the owner of the voice pulled open the door and reprimanded the deputy, "I just spoke to you, Deputy. Did you hear what I said or do you plan to ignore me again?" The stocky man of average height who came through the door seemed to growl when he spoke. He was obviously irritated with his deputy.

When he saw the two men standing at the counter, he approached them, stuck out his hand and said, "I'm Sheriff Bill Bixley. "How can I help you men today?"

"Hello, Sheriff, I'm Sergeant Tom Blight from the LRPD homicide division, and this is Harvey Garnett, a private investigator from Little Rock." Both men offered their identification to the sheriff.

Harvey noticed the color drain from the sheriff's face. He turned a pasty, white color for a few seconds before he started to regain his color. After looking at their identification for a few seconds, he spoke with a firm voice, "I'm happy to meet you gentlemen. Now, how can I help you?

"Well, Sheriff, our business is of a rather private nature. Could we speak to you in your office?" Sergeant Blight asked.

"That won't be necessary. We don't have secrets around here. But I am late for an appointment right now. If you gentlemen don't mind, could you come back later this afternoon? I could sit down with you and discuss whatever you have on your minds." Before they could even answer his question, the sheriff pushed past them and was out the door, leaving them standing there dazed.

Harvey looked at Sergeant Blight as if to say, "I told you so," and the two men left the building. Once on the sidewalk, Harvey said, "See what I mean. You don't get an ounce of cooperation around here. Come on, let's go for a ride. I want to show you the cabin Pastor Ted rented and let you look around a little. You need to get familiar with the area and I could use a refresher course."

The men jumped into the car and drove quickly to Log Mountain Road. Shortly after making a right turn onto the road, both men were shocked to see blue lights behind them. They could not imagine what they had done wrong, but Sergeant Blight pulled to the curb and prepared to do battle with what he figured was a rookie cop who was anxious to impress his superior with the number of tickets he could write. They were so surprised they couldn't say a word when they looked up into the grim face of Sheriff Bixley. He came alongside their car carrying a ticket book in his hand.

"Good afternoon, gentlemen," the sheriff said with a smirk on his face that made Harvey want to give him a piece of his mind. "I'm sorry to have to meet you men like this, but some strange things have been happening around my office lately. I didn't think we could really have any privacy if we stayed there, so I followed you out here. We can't stand here very long without drawing too much attention. I suggest that you men meet me at Colby's restaurant just south of town in 20 minutes. I'm going to give you this blank ticket to make it look like I stopped you for a reason if anyone is watching, and then I'm going to take a round-about way of getting to the restaurant. You men look around here for a few minutes and then meet me there. Does that sound okay to you?"

"Sure, Sheriff," the men answered in unison. "We'll be there."

Without saying another word the sheriff handed them a ticket that had the address of and directions to the restaurant drawn on it. Then he got into his car and left.

Harvey and Sergeant Blight sat there speechless for a full minute before the sergeant pulled away from the curb. As they drove down Log Mountain Road, Harvey pointed out the cabin where Pastor Ted had stayed and then excitedly pointed to the driveway that led to the secluded cabin where he was sure Pastor Ted was now. He described the house they had found back in the woods when they were taking the survey and briefly described the men they had talked to and the area around the house as best he could remember it.

"My question is," Sergeant Blight began. "If the sheriff knows where the cabin is that Ted was staying in, wouldn't he also know about the cabin down that drive?"

"Sure he would," Harvey acknowledged. "And he may or may not know the pastor is being held there." Sergeant Blight noticed Harvey's change in position. He had earlier insisted that the sheriff knew all about where Pastor Ted was.

Without discussing anything else, the men rode silently toward the restaurant. Both men were a little anxious and kept looking around to make sure they were not being followed. The fear of what had happened to their mutual friend was fresh in their minds. Neither wanted to be forced off the road since they were so close to finding out something they hoped would prove to be helpful.

Harvey noticed that the sheriff's car was not in the parking lot when they arrived at Colby's Restaurant, but the men went inside anyway. They spotted a table all the way in the back. It was off to itself and would offer the perfect place for them to visit with the sheriff. They took a seat and began to wait for the sheriff. Fifteen minutes later the sheriff came through the front door and made his way to the table.

"Sorry about being late, men," He apologized. "I had to take care of one small issue before I could get away without drawing suspicion. Now what kind of private matter do you need to speak to me about?"

"Sheriff, I'm going to be straightforward. We are investigating a missing person's report. Pastor Ted Black, who, as I understand it, was arrested by you a month or so ago seems to be missing according to his wife. What can you tell us about Pastor Black? Do you know anything about where he might be?" Sergeant Blight asked.

"You are right. I did arrest him for the murder of Marla Harris. He was caught red-handed by two game wardens. He said he was tying a rope around her leg as she floated in Greers Ferry Lake, but rope burns on her leg showed that she had already been tied up. He probably tried to tie her to something heavy that would pull her down to the bottom of the lake, but his knot didn't hold and the rope came loose. I figured he had a love affair going with her and was about to get caught. You know how some people can be when they get away from a difficult spouse," Sheriff Bixley reported with obvious pride in what he considered his outstanding police work.

"Sheriff, we are not here to try to determine what he did or didn't do. We are willing to let the courts determine his guilt or innocence. Is it possible for us to talk to him? No one in Little Rock has heard from him since the day before this alleged crime took place," Sergeant Blight cut straight to the point regarding his desire to know where Ted Black was.

"That's the problem," answered the sheriff. "A couple of days after I arrested him, somebody broke into the jail and kidnapped him. I had to let a deputy go because he fell asleep and let it happen. Anyway, I've been looking for him ever since. I went back to the cabin to see if I could find some clues, but someone had cleaned the place up. There was no trace of him. Even his car was gone. Whoever kidnapped him must have stolen his keys and belongings when they broke into the jail. I even set up surveillance on Log Mountain Road for several days. Never got any clues, though."

"Why did your deputies refuse to tell his wife and a private investigator named Ben Albright anything about this? Don't you think his wife had a right to know he was arrested and that he had disappeared?" Harvey jumped into the discussion and asked a question he had been dying to ask for days.

These questions made the sheriff squirm a little, but he soon recovered his composure. "I don't know anything about that," he said. "Who refused to let them know what happened to him? Probably was that deputy of mine…the one I had to let go. Like I said, there have been some strange things happening around my office lately. I wondered why no one ever came looking for him. I thought maybe his wife learned about the affair and decided she didn't want anything to do with him anymore."

Harvey was convinced at least part of what he was hearing was a lie, but he didn't want to antagonize the sheriff, so he kept his evaluation to himself. Sergeant Blight's body language convinced Harvey that he suspected the same thing.

Sergeant Blight spoke up again. "We think we know where Ted Black is, Sheriff. And we think Ben Albright, another private detective from Little Rock...a friend of Harvey's here...is also being held with him. We believe the two men are being held against their will by some armed men. We're asking you to help us set these men free from their captors, Sheriff?"

"Wait a minute, Sergeant," the sheriff objected. "I need more to go on than your ideas about things and what you think might have happened. What makes you think you know where these men are being held? I've been trying to find that out for days now. Just where do you think they are?"

"We know where they are by the detective work of Ben Albright before he fell into the hands of the same people who kidnapped the pastor." Harvey was amazed at the way Sergeant Blight stated their suspicions as fact, but he didn't say a word. The veteran officer continued, "Albright actually found the pastor's car. He didn't actually see the pastor, but he and Harvey, here, verified the presence of an individual in a building near the car. He had the cabin under surveillance when he was captured."

"How do you know that?" the sheriff asked.

"Ben had planned to check in with his secretary every two hours, but she hasn't heard from him since he first placed the cabin under surveillance," stated Sergeant Blight. Harvey was surprised to learn that Ben had planned to check in, but decided to keep quiet. The sergeant seemed to have a reason for stretching the facts. "Will you help us, Sheriff?" he asked.

"Tell me where you think they are, men, and I'll send some men out there to set them free," offered the sheriff.

"We can't do that, Sheriff. You said yourself that some strange things had been happening around your office. How do we know your deputies wouldn't cause some more of those strange things to happen if we tip our hand?" Sergeant Blight objected.

"Well, it sounds to me like you men have a problem. You want my help, but you don't want to give me the information I need to help you. What makes you think I would agree to something as ridiculous as that?" inquired the sheriff.

"Okay, Sheriff, you're right. I guess we are just going to have to trust you" the sergeant seemed to cave in. Harvey was about to scream his objection when the sergeant spoke again, "Since we don't know much about this place, why don't you meet us at that store where Log Mountain Road turns off the main road in one hour and we will tell you where we think the pastor and the investigator are being held. Bring anyone you know you can trust and be prepared to help us."

Harvey wondered what in the world Sergeant Blight was up to and fully expected the sheriff to object. When he didn't, Harvey recognized that he was in the presence of a skilled investigator. Instinctively he knew that anything he said at this point would create problems so he decided to let Sergeant Blight handle things.

"That sounds reasonable enough," replied Sheriff Bixley without asking anymore questions. He stood up, shook hands with both men and headed out the front door.

Harvey was about to compliment the sergeant, when Sergeant Blight said, "I don't trust that man, but he is all we got at this point. Come on, Harvey. Let's get out to Log Mountain Road before they can move the pastor and Ben." Harvey paid for their drinks and followed him to the car. His mind was swirling with questions, but they could wait until they were on the road.

CHAPTER FIFTEEN

As soon as Tiffany and Carla returned from the police station, the four ladies resumed their prayer vigil for Pastor Ted and Ben. Now they added Harvey and Sergeant Blight to the prayer list. As they prayed, Carla broke down and began to sob uncontrollably.

"Oh, Tiffany, I am so worried," Carla managed to say through the sobs that racked her body. She fell into Tiffany's arms and almost screamed, "I know I'm not supposed to worry, but I'm scared to death. I know something bad is happening, and I can't do anything about it. What am I going to do?"

Tiffany held her pastor's wife tightly as she choked back her own tears. She wanted to join her in sobbing, but felt like she needed to try to console Carla instead. "Sergeant Blight and Harvey are there by now, Carla. I'm sure they know what to do. They may have even found the men by now. We just need to keep praying. God is going to be with them. He promised He would be. You know we can trust Him," Carla tried to sound more reassuring than she felt at the moment.

"I know, Tiffany, but I'm so scared. I don't know what I am going to do if something has happened to Ted," Carla sobbed.

Tears were streaming down Joan's face as well, but she managed to say, "Carla, you know Pastor Ted and Ben are both men of faith. God will not abandon them. Their faithfulness to Him will pay off more now than it ever has. Besides, Ben is skilled in this kind of work. He won't let anything happen to Pastor Ted. He will do everything he can to make sure nothing happens to the man he looks up to so much."

Carla suddenly stood up, straightened her dress and dabbed her eyes with an already saturated tissue. "Ladies, I am so sorry. I'm being selfish," Carla said. "I realize you can't stay here all afternoon. Thank you for coming. You don't know how much it means to have you pray with me. I'm sure you have other things you need to be doing right now. Feel free to go. I'll be okay now."

All three of the other ladies glanced at each other. They were amazed by Carla's sudden change of behavior. They wanted to believe that her faith had taken hold and that she no longer needed their comfort, but deep inside they knew Carla was just trying to put their needs ahead of her own. They were sure she didn't want to be a bother to them. They were just as sure they needed to stay with her.

For a moment or two no one spoke. Then Betsy said, "Well, I don't know about the rest of you, but I don't feel like the burden for prayer has lifted. I still sense the urgency to pray for Pastor Ted, Ben, Harvey and that policeman, whatever his name was. If Tiffany and Joan need to go, that's okay, but I would like to stay and pray with you for a while, Carla, ...if that is alright with you, I mean. I don't want to intrude, but I do think we must still pray for the protection of the men. Is it okay if I stay?"

"Of course you can stay, Betsy," Carla answered. "I would enjoy you being here very much if you are sure it won't interfere with anything else."

"It won't," Betsy said.

"I would like to stay, too," Joan said. "I've never felt a burden like I feel today. I couldn't do anything else if I did leave. Would it be okay if I stayed, Carla?"

"I would be happy for you to stay, Joan."

"Well, count me in as well," Tiffany stated as a tear rolled down her cheek. "I told my boss I might not be back for the rest of the day, so he isn't expecting me. And, besides, this is much more important right now."

Following their brief conversation, the ladies started praying immediately. They prayed for the protection of Ben and Pastor Ted.

They asked God to give Harvey and Sergeant Blight the wisdom to know how to handle whatever was going on. At times they couldn't put their prayers into words, but they continued to pray for most of the afternoon.

As Ted and Ben sat on the bed in the small, undecorated bedroom where Pastor Ted had been for a little more than a month, they were surprised by a visit by Hank, one of the guards that had kept watch over the pastor the entire time he was in this house. He was carrying a chair and looked very nervous as he carried it into the room.

"Listen to me, but don't say a word," he ordered as he closed the door quietly. "Something is about to happen that could put you men into more danger than you are already in. As soon as you hear someone outside speak over a megaphone, lock this door and place this chair under the door knob so the door cannot be opened. Get down on the floor behind the bed in case there are shots fired. I can't explain more, but do what I tell you unless I tell you otherwise. The rest of them don't know I brought you a chair so keep it behind the door until you need it."

Hank opened the door and started up the hall. When he neared the living room, he said in a booming voice. "I just checked on the two prisoners. Can you believe it? They were in there praying. Sure hope they have a direct line to God; because they are going to need His help getting out of the mess they've created for themselves." With that he began to laugh causing the others to laugh and make disparaging remarks about Ted and Ben. Soon everyone was talking again about what they should do to the two men.

After listening to them a few minutes, Ben snarled, "I don't like that man. He is probably setting us up again so they can shoot us for trying to block their way. I don't think we ought to use that chair under any circumstances!"

"Wait a minute, Ben," Ted objected. "I've been around Hank for weeks now. He has been the only one who has shown me any consideration at all while I've been locked in here. He even brought me a Bible, and we've had some wonderful conversations about God.

I thought he was close to opening his heart to Him at one point, but Bo came home and he had to leave my room before we could pray. I think he is trying to help us and was covering it up with his last comment."

The men decided to spend time in prayer asking God to show them what to do if things began to happen like Hank indicated they were going to. They knew they couldn't do anything before then, so they sat down to wait. As they sat there, each one imagined what he would do when danger broke out. They played every scenario they could think of over and over in their minds.

Finally, Ben spoke, "Ted, I think you are right. If something begins to happen, you jump behind the bed immediately. Lie on your stomach and cover your head with your hands. Try to slip under the edge of the bed if you can. I'll lock and block the door and jump behind the bed with you. Try to leave me some space if you can," he chuckled.

"Okay," Ted responded weakly. Deep inside he was wondering again how a sincere, loving pastor could be in such a predicament. Where was God and why was He allowing this to happen? Quickly he pushed away the nagging questions about God's faithfulness and started trying to pray. Ben joined him in prayer and the two men asked for protection during whatever lay ahead. Pastor Ted also prayed that they would be found and set free before their captors could harm them in any way.

As soon as Harvey and Sergeant Blight turned onto Log Mountain Road, they decided to drive up the road past the cabin where Pastor Ted had stayed. They decided not to go down the drive that led to the hidden cabin, but agreed they would drive as far as they could before turning around.

Both men spotted a silver *Lexus* in the drive of the cabin at the same time. By the time they saw it they were passing the end of the drive however. Immediately they both felt tense. Sergeant Blight was the first to speak. "Are we driving into a trap?" he asked, knowing that Harvey would have no better idea than he did. "Stay alert," he continued. "There is no telling what might happen next."

As they drove along, they discussed the possibility of following the path through the woods if they could find it, but decided that was too risky. When he spoke, Harvey had a newly found authority in his voice, "We can't go down the road to the cabin, either," he said. "We would be too vulnerable. Whoever is in the cabin down there could hear us from the time we left the pavement. They would be ready for us, and probably wouldn't hesitate to eliminate us if they had half a chance."

Sergeant Blight turned around slowly and started back down the road toward the lake house. Both men were tense. Harvey put his hand on his gun without even realizing what he was doing. He voiced his thoughts aloud, "Wonder where that white dog is that Ben talked about. He just might be able to show us another secret or two about this place."

Before Sergeant Blight could answer, both men spotted Buddy walking down the drive toward the silver *Lexus*. "Well, there's your dog," the police officer said. As they watched, the big, white dog walked down the drive and past the silver car. Before either man could say another word, the dog was out of sight. Harvey couldn't help but wonder if his actions could mean anything.

Before he could put his thoughts into words, however, a man came through the door of the cabin and walked up the drive. Sergeant Blight stopped the car and both men watched the man as he walked up the hill to the road. When he got to the where the drive intersected the road, he turned and walked directly toward them. Now they felt trapped for sure. Behind them was a cabin that contained several armed men. Before them was the man who apparently had tried to force their friend off the road and had irritated the sheriff's deputy earlier in the day.

"There's only one of him," said Sergeant Blight, "so we will head his way if we have to make a run for it. Be ready, Harvey. I may have to floor this thing, but let's at least see what he has to say first." Both men slipped their guns from their holsters and held them tightly in their hands as the stranger approached.

As the man got close, he raised his hands and held out his arms showing them that he wasn't carrying a weapon and had no intent to harm them. Both men breathed a sigh of relief, but kept their guns in their hands just in case they needed to defend themselves.

When the man finally got to the front of the car, Sergeant Blight cautiously rolled down his window a couple of inches. "Good afternoon, Gentlemen. My name is Jim Crane," the man said as he slowly reached into his coat pocket. Both men in the car gripped their guns just a little tighter in case the man pulled out a weapon. Instead he held out an identification badge. Sergeant Blight took it as the man said, "I'm a special agent with the United States Federal Bureau of Investigation."

Sergeant Blight looked at his badge carefully and then handed it to Harvey who stared at it in disbelief. Instinctively both men knew more was happening that day than they realized, and they seemed to be right in the middle of it.

Before either man could say a word, Mr. Crane spoke again, "We have been investigating the activities of the sheriff's department in Highpoint. You men were in contact with the sheriff a few minutes ago. Would you please tell me what you talked about?"

Sergeant Blight wondered how he knew they had just come from a meeting with the sheriff. He was the first to speak. "We are glad to meet you, Mr. Crane. My name is Sergeant Tom Blight. I'm with the homicide division of the Little Rock Police Department. This is Harvey Garnett. He is a private investigator back in Little Rock." Harvey nodded toward the FBI agent who returned his gesture.

Sergeant Blight continued, "A pastor from Little Rock, Pastor Ted Black, disappeared in these parts about a month ago and a private investigator named Ben Albright was trying to find him. I've been sent here to investigate a missing person's report on Pastor Black and Harvey has agreed to help me. We have reason to believe that Mr. Albright has been captured by the same people who kidnapped Pastor Black. We are relatively certain we know where the men are being held, so we met with the sheriff to ask him to help us set the men free."

"Did he agree to do that?" Mr. Crane wanted to know.

"Well, yes, but we became a little suspicious of the sheriff so we told him we would meet him at the store down at the end of this road at 2:20 this afternoon. We didn't tell him where we thought the men were being held. We didn't want to give him, or anyone else for that matter, an opportunity to move the men to a new location."

"Good work, Sergeant," Mr. Crane interrupted him before he could go on. "And just where do you think the men are being held?"

"In the cabin at the end of the gravel road that leaves this road about 50 yards behind us," Harvey answered. He was thankful for an opportunity to add something to the conversation. He had never worked with the FBI before. He relished the idea of having such an experience and was eager to cooperate

"You men have done very good work," Mr. Crane acknowledged. "The men you are looking for are, indeed, in that cabin. My men have that cabin surrounded right now. So I need you to stop your attempts to gain access to the cabin. You could make matters worse for my men and for the men you are trying to help. If you men want to be of help, however I could sure use your help."

"Sure, anything you want," Harvey volunteered.

Sergeant Blight was a little less eager to commit himself before he knew what was being asked of him. He didn't want to put himself into a situation where he could be reprimanded for taking police action outside his jurisdiction so he asked Mr. Crane, "What did you have in mind?"

"I need you to divert the sheriff when you meet with him," Mr. Crane answered. "Tell him you are certain your friends are at an address across town. While you go with him to investigate, my men will carry on with our proposed action. May I count on you to do that for us?"

"We can do that much," Sergeant Blight answered. "Unfortunately, we are not familiar with these parts so we don't know of any possible places on the other side of town. The sheriff would know in a second that we were bluffing."

"I understand," said Mr. Crane. "If you'll get a piece of paper, I'll give you the address of a vacant house that is in a rather remote location. It would be the kind of place where a person could be held for a period of time without raising suspicion. You can take the sheriff there."

Harvey grabbed a notepad from his pocket and scribbled the address Mr. Crane gave him. Then Sergeant Blight asked, "Can we have your phone number, Mr. Crane? The way things have been happening around here, we might need it. Here is my card. It has my cell phone number on it if you need to contact us."

Mr. Crane took the card and recited his phone number to the men. Harvey wrote it down on another piece of paper from his pad. As he did so, Mr. Crane stepped back from the car and said, "You men should go on down to the store. It's almost time for you to meet the sheriff. You sure don't want to be late for such an important meeting."

Both men nodded in agreement and started to say good-bye, but Mr. Crane was already headed back toward the lake house. Sergeant Blight put the car into gear and they headed to the meeting place with the sheriff. When they arrived, they looked for the sheriff, but no cars were visible. Sergeant Blight pulled the car into a position where they would be able to see anyone who approached from any direction. Neither man wanted any surprises at this particular moment.

Sheriff Bixley arrived about five minutes later followed by four deputies in two squad cars. All the men got out of their cars and met at the front of Sergeant Blight's vehicle.

"Okay boys, tell me where we can find these friends of yours so we can get started on 'setting them free' as you put it to me earlier," the sheriff commanded.

"Well, not so fast, Sheriff," Sergeant Blight objected eyeing the deputy with whom he had had the encounter in the sheriff's office earlier that day. "Who are these men? Can they be trusted? We sure don't want anyone working against us while we are on this mission. As you said earlier, there have been a lot of strange things happening in your office lately and we sure don't need for any strange things to happen right now."

"You don't have to worry about these men," laughed the sheriff. "All these men have been with me for a long time. Every one of them will do what he is told to do. Now, are you going to give me the location where you think your friends are, or am I going to get in my car and drive back to town? I don't have time to mess around playing cat and mouse games with you."

Harvey decided to speak up before the sheriff became even more irritated. "I've written the location down on this slip of paper, Sheriff," he said as he gave the sheriff the piece of paper from his note pad.

The sheriff looked at the address thoughtfully for a minute and then said to his deputies, "It's the old Pearson place," he said. "Have any of you guys been out there in the last few weeks?" They all denied being there, so the sheriff continued. "Here's what we are going to do men. We'll drive over there and stop a quarter mile this side of the house. There's a feed store on the left side of the road right there. Let's meet in their parking lot. I'll lead the way. Sergeant you come next and my deputies will follow you. I'll put together a plan for approaching the house while we are on our way."

Before they got in their cars to leave, one of the deputies told the sheriff, "Carlos and I have one little thing to take care of on this side of town before we head that way. If we don't catch up with you before you get there, we'll only be a few minutes behind you. Will you allow us to do that to save the department some time and money, Sheriff?" The sheriff looked irritated, but agreed to their request.

Everyone got into their cars and the sheriff took off like a streak. Sergeant Blight did his best to keep up with him. He was followed by two of the deputies in their car. As he drove, he gave Harvey instructions. "Call Mr. Crane, the FBI agent. Tell him that two of the deputies didn't follow us. Tell him that they headed on up the road toward the cabin. We don't want his project messed up by some unexpected policemen on the scene."

Harvey quickly dialed the number he had written down earlier and relayed the information. Mr. Crane thanked him for the letting him know and hung up. Mr. Crane made a couple of phone calls and then jumped into his *Lexus*. Instead of backing out of the drive, however, he pulled it around behind the cabin so it could not be seen from the road. He had no more than taken his foot off the brake when the police car roared past the drive.

Another phone call from Mr. Crane brought a group of about ten men to the drive. Instructions were quickly given. Just as quickly as they appeared the men disappeared into hiding places on both sides of the road.

Pastor Ted thought he heard something that sounded like a car coming down the drive toward the cabin. He stood to his feet and went to the window. Removing the knot from its place he put his ear down to the hole. He could clearly hear gravel crunching beneath the wheels of a vehicle.

"It sounds like something is about to happen," he told Ben and then bent over to look through the knot hole. When he did, he was shocked by what he saw. "Ben, there's a sheriff's car out there with two uniformed men in it," he reported. No one inside the cabin seemed alarmed, however. It was as if they knew the men were coming.

Suddenly, Ted heard footsteps in the hall. He quickly replaced the knot and turned to face whoever was coming. He breathed a sigh of relief when he saw that it was Hank.

"Plans have changed," Hank whispered. "I want both of you to go with these deputies. They don't know it yet, but they are your road to freedom."

Before he could say anything else, someone yelled from the other room, "Bring them on out here, Hank. We've got to get going. The sheriff is expecting us to join him in a few minutes. We'll take these guys out in the police car. We can tell anyone who sees us that we have apprehended some criminals. You men wait about ten minutes and then you can leave. I'll drop these guys off at Shorty's house. You can pick them up there and take them to their final resting place. It's time we got rid of some bad rubbish."

Hank pulled his gun from his belt and nudged Ben and Ted toward the door. "They're on their way," he yelled.

As soon as they entered the living room, Ben noticed the deputy who had been at the desk when he was at the sheriff's office. He didn't recognize the other deputy. He didn't know any of the other men in the room, but thought one of them looked like the man in the restoration business he had visited. He wondered if this was the twin brother of the man he had interviewed.

One of the deputies started giving Ben and Ted instructions as soon as they got in the room. "When we get to my car out there, I want you two to get in the back seat and stay quiet. One word from you while we are driving down the road will cause your end to come sooner than it's going to anyway. Did you hear what I said?"

"Yes, sir, we heard you. We'll stay quiet. You can count on that," Pastor Ted answered. He didn't want to cross anyone who was threatening his life.

Ted and Ben followed one of the men to the police vehicle and got in the back seat. The two deputies were talking to the rest of the men in the group. After a couple of minutes, they jumped into the car and started back up the long, curving drive. The men had not blindfolded them so Pastor Ted could see his surroundings for the first time since coming to this remote place.

As soon as they reached the pavement, Pastor Ted choked back a gasp. He suddenly recognized where he was. He had walked down this road daily for the two enjoyable weeks he had spent in the lake house. He strained to see past the two deputies in the front seat. Sure enough, there was the lake house just down the road. He had been less than a mile from the lake house all this time. New questions flooded his mind. Why hadn't anyone come around asking questions? Did they not know there was a cabin down that secluded drive? Was the sheriff in on his disappearance? What was going to happen to Ben and him now? Where was he headed? He looked at Ben, who looked at him with a kind of reassurance on his face, or was it submission? Did Ben think they would get out of this, or was he resigned to the fact that he was going to die? Ted longed to speak to his friend, but didn't dare to say a word.

Ben was trying to communicate with Ted without speaking. He wanted him to look down the road again. There were two vehicles blocking the road down by the lake house. Before he could move enough to get Ted to notice what was happening, one of the deputies spoke, "I want you two to lie down in the seat. Do your best to stay out of sight. If the men up ahead try to ask you any questions, act like you are drunk. Do you hear me? Remember one false move on your part and you are the first to die. Now get down right now."

Without bothering to answer both men lay down on the seat. Ben's mouth was close to Ted's ear as they lay there. Ben whispered, "It looks like we may have some help on the way."

Ted wondered what his friend could mean, but he didn't dare ask him. The car was slowing down and he wasn't sure what was happening. In any case it wouldn't take much right now to set the deputies off. They were even more anxious now than they had been earlier.

As the car coasted to a stop, the deputy lowered his window and spoke first, "What's going on? Why are you blocking the road? Don't you know that is against the law? Now, get those vehicles out of the way! I'm on official business or I would give you all a ticket for interfering with the law. Did you hear what I said? Jump in that car and get it out of the way. I've got to get these men back to the jail and then go on another important call. Now, get started...NOW!"

The man on the outside of the window didn't look the least bit frightened. "I see you got a couple of men in the back seat," he said. "Who are they and why are they lying down?"

"Just a couple of drunks," the deputy lied. "We're taking them to jail right now. Now, will you please get your vehicles out of the way before I lose my temper and arrest you as well?"

"I can't do that, Deputy," the man said. "Let me introduce myself. I'm Don Teague. I'm a special agent with Federal Bureau of Investigation. I have every reason to believe that the men in the back seat are Ted Black and Ben Albright. I also believe that you men have something to do with their disappearance." The agent pulled his gun from his coat and pointed it toward the two deputies as he spoke again, "Now if you will just get out of the car slowly, place your guns on the ground and lay across the hood of the car, I would appreciate it."

"Sorry, Don whatever-your-name-is, we can't do that," the deputy who had been driving the car said as he reached for his gun.

"I wouldn't do that if I were you," the agent said as five men on each side of the car suddenly appeared from their hiding places. Each man had a rifle aimed at the deputies. "Now, like I said, if you will get out of the car, place your guns on the ground and lay across the hood of the vehicle, I would appreciate it."

The deputies did what they were told. They grumbled a little about false arrest and the trouble they would cause these men, but neither dared to test the aim of the men with the rifles. Finally one of them dared to make a threatening remark, "You men are going to be in a heap of trouble. We've got some friends that are going to be coming down this road in a few minutes. When they see what you are doing, they will take out each one of you before you will even know what hit you."

"That sounds good, deputy," the agent said with only a slight smile sneaking its way across his face. "The only problem with that is: the men you are referring to are in the same predicament you are. As soon as they left the cabin back there in the woods and got in their cars, they were immediately surrounded by a group of my friends just like you are. They are all being placed under arrest as we speak." With that he turned the men over to another man who had walked up to where he was standing beside the deputies. Once the guns of the police officers were collected, the men who had been standing along the road moved in to assist as well.

Ted and Ben had lain quietly during the entire episode. Ted was afraid to move and Ben knew that they would be less likely to offer the men in the car someone to hide behind if they were not readily available. Both men felt like rejoicing when the deputies got out of the car, but they were somewhat unsure what might happen next, so they remained quiet.

Agent Teague opened the back door on one side of the car as another agent opened the door on the other side. "Gentlemen, you may now get out of the car. Please identify yourselves. If you are who I think, I want you to go in the cabin here and let me know what you know about what has been happening around here over the last few weeks."

A tear slid down Ted's face as he spoke, "I'm Ted Black. I am the pastor of Hillside Community Church in Little Rock. I came up here for some rest and relaxation a few weeks ago. I've got a lot to tell you, but I sure would like to let my wife know I'm alive before I tell you my story. Would you let me do that, Sir?"

"You can call your wife as soon as we get in the cabin, Pastor Black. Then we have some unfinished business," the agent replied. "Please remember that you are still under arrest for murder. You will have to be taken to the jail. I'll do what I can to arrange for you to be released on bond."

"I'm Ben Albright," Ben identified himself. "I was investigating the disappearance of Pastor Black when I was captured as well. I need to let my wife know I'm okay, too."

"That sounds reasonable," Mr. Teague said. "I want you men to go into the cabin with Agent Spooner while I close up some loose ends here. He will let you make your phone calls and then I'll be in to take your stories. Now, if you will excuse me, I have a phone call to make to a Harvey Garnett and a LRPD officer, Sergeant Tom Blight. Do either of you men know either of them?"

"I know both of them," Ben answered. "Are they okay?"

"I'm sure they are," Mr. Teague answered. "They have just been helping me on a little project and I need to give them some further instructions." After saying that, Mr. Teague turned away and started entering numbers into his cell phone.

When the person on the other end answered the phone, Mr. Teague said, "Sergeant Blight, my name is Don Teague. I am an associate of Jim Crane. We have your friends in custody now. Thank you for your help. You do not need to proceed with the plan to go to the vacant house at the address Mr. Crane gave you. I need for you to bring the sheriff and his deputies back to the jail now. You may tell them that the men you were seeking were found in a different part of town. Apologize for having the wrong information. The sheriff will be angry, but will head to the jail. Get there as quickly as you can as well. Thanks again men. By the way, your friends are safe."

Sergeant Blight thanked Mr. Teague for the message and hung up. Harvey was elated when he heard what the man had said. The sheriff didn't seem happy at all. All he could talk about was being misled. When he left, there was no way to stay close to him or his deputy. Sergeant Blight slowed to a reasonable speed and visited with Harvey as they made their way to the jail.

As soon as Mr. Teague hung up his phone, he called for Agent Spooner and told him to take Ted and Ben into the cabin. As the three men entered the cabin, Ted and Ben thought it looked familiar, but it also looked strange to both men. Everywhere they looked was surveillance equipment. Ted couldn't help but wonder what had happened to all his stuff. It was obvious that it had been removed by someone before this operation center was set up.

CHAPTER SIXTEEN

Carla was somewhat annoyed by the ringing of the telephone. She wondered who could be calling now. Reluctantly she excused herself from the ladies who were enjoying a brief break in their prayer vigil. "I ought to see who is calling. It could be someone with a question about something at the church," she said as she made her way to the phone that was just across the room from where the ladies had gathered.

All three ladies in the room with her began to cry when she exclaimed, "It's Ted! They've found him! He's alive!" She turned back to the phone and spoke again, "Ted... Ted... Ted, are you alright?"

Carla was trying to get Ted to respond and he was trying his best to regain his composure, but all he could do was make a few noises as tears streamed down his face. The sound of his wife's voice caused his bottled-up emotions to suddenly erupt. He had wondered so often if he would ever hear her voice again. For several awkward minutes he stood there sobbing. Neither Ben nor the agent in charge seemed to mind.

Finally he was able to speak again. "Carla, it's so good to hear your voice. I'm so sorry I put you through this. I had no idea anything like this would happen. I love you, Carla. I've missed you more than you can imagine."

"Oh, Ted, I love you, too," Carla said as she slumped into a nearby chair. The three ladies came around her as if they could gain information by just being close. "Where are you, Ted? When can I see you? Are you okay? Have they taken care of you? You aren't injured or hurt, are you? Where have you been all this time? What happened to the people who kidnapped you?" Carla knew she was asking too many questions, but she couldn't stop. Her mind was filled with so much emotion right now that she couldn't explain her feelings to anyone if she tried.

"I can't answer all your questions, yet," Ted said. I can tell you this. I am in the custody of the FBI. They rescued me and Ben."

When he mentioned Ben's name, Carla interrupted, "Joan is here with me right now, Ted. Let me tell her Ben is okay."

"Sure," Ted replied. "Tell her he will talk to her as soon as we are finished."

"Okay," Carla said as she covered the phone and relayed the information to Joan. Joan breathed a huge sigh of relief and began to cry softly. Betsy put her arm around Joan in an attempt to comfort her friend.

"Listen carefully, Carla," Ted instructed as he resumed his conversation with her. "I am here in Highpoint. I can't come straight home. I am under arrest for the murder of a lady that I found in the lake. I'll have to tell you about that later. The FBI agent told me he would do his best to arrange for me to be released on bond. I need you to have someone drive you up here to arrange for my release. I don't want you driving. You've been through too much lately, and I don't imagine you are in any condition to get behind the wheel. I don't know how long it might take for me to be released so you might want to bring some clothes with you, and bring me some clean clothes as well. I've been wearing the same thing for days now."

"I will, Ted," Carla assured him. "I'm just so glad you are free and that you are okay. You don't have anything wrong with you, do you Ted?"

"I'm okay, Carla. Please believe me. No one has hurt me in any way." Ted did his best to convince his wife that he was in good health. Then he got a little more personal, "Carla, it is so good to hear your voice. I thought about you so much. I want to hold you in my arms and never let you go. Please get here as quickly as you can."

"I will," she promised. "I'll pack my clothes as soon as I hang up and will be on my way as soon as I can. I should be there in a couple of hours. I missed you, too, Ted. It will be so good to feel your arms around me again. I've been so lonely without you." In spite of her efforts to resist, Carla began to cry uncontrollably.

When it looked like she wasn't going to be able to speak again, she handed the phone to Tiffany who spoke, "Pastor Ted, this is Tiffany. Carla can't say anything right now. She is so grateful you are okay that she is overcome with emotion. We are here with her and won't leave her. I don't know what you told her, but I am willing to bring her up there this afternoon if necessary. I can also make arrangements to stay with her a couple of days if that will help. Pastor, we are so glad you are okay. Our leadership board has been praying for your safety. Everyone in the church has been for that matter. By the way, are Harvey and Sergeant Blight okay as well?"

"As far as I know, they are okay…at least that's what the FBI agent tells me. Tiffany, it would be wonderful if you could bring Carla. I'm afraid for her to make the trip alone," Ted did his best to answer her questions. "If Carla is able, I would like to tell her bye before I let Ben speak with Joan. Do you think she is up to that, Tiffany?"

"I'm sure she is," Tiffany said as she handed the phone back to Carla. "Pastor Ted wants to tell you bye," she told Carla.

"I'm sorry I'm such a baby, Ted," Carla said. "I'm just so thankful you are alive. I was afraid I might never see you again. It was horrible, Ted."

"I know it was, Honey," Ted said. "It was rough on me, too. Carla, I have to give the FBI my story and I need to let Ben speak to Joan. I'm looking forward to seeing you in a couple of hours. I love you, Sweetheart."

"I love you, too, Honey. I'll be on my way as soon as I can get everything together," Carla said as much for her benefit as his.

"Carla, let me lead us in a brief prayer of thanksgiving before we say good-bye," Ted said as he began to tell God thanks for keeping both of them safe and for meeting their needs while they were apart. It was a brief prayer, but it left both of them sensing a special kind of peace.

"Good-bye, Sweetheart," Carla whispered.

"Good-bye, Carla," Ted said and then added, "Please put Joan on the phone. I'm handing the phone to Ben now."

Ben and Joan had a similar conversation. Ben tried his best to convince Joan to stay in Little Rock and wait for him. "I can start for there before you can get here," he said. "I just need to give the FBI my statement and then I can head home."

"But, Ben, I can't just sit at home and wait anymore today. At least by coming with Carla, I'll feel like I am doing something. I want to see you as soon as I can. Besides we can ride home together and you can catch me up on everything that has happened to you while you have been gone," Joan pleaded.

Ben finally agreed to the plan. They exchanged assurances of love and reluctantly hung up the phone. Both men were eager to give their statements to Agent Teague who had just entered the cabin.

Carla, Joan, Betsy, and Tiffany hugged and laughed and danced around the living room for several minutes before Betsy suggested that they thank God for answering their prayers. All the ladies agreed that they should. They held hands as Betsy voiced their prayer of thanksgiving.

After they finished praying, Betsy excused herself to go home. Both Joan and Tiffany excused themselves to go home to prepare for the trip to Highpoint. As soon as everyone was out the door, Carla rushed into the bedroom and began to pack clothes for her and Ted. It felt so good to know where Ted was and that he was safe.

On her way toward her house, Tiffany called Mr. Jeffries, John Ingles, Joe Hawkins and everyone on the leadership team she could reach. To each of them she said, "They have found him. They have found Pastor Ted. He's alive and okay. He still needs our prayers because they think he has done something awful, but he is alive. I'm going to Highpoint with Carla to see him. I'll let you know more as soon as I can. For now let's spread the word that Pastor Black is okay."

Everyone she spoke with was elated. Mr. Jeffries even acknowledged that Tiffany was right when she asked the board to wait to start to pastoral search. He thanked her for speaking up.

"We can talk about that later," Tiffany responded. She had some things she wanted to say, but it could all wait. "All that matters now is that Pastor Ted is okay."

When Tiffany got back to Carla's house, Carla had already placed her suitcase in the trunk of her car. "I was just wiping off the counters," Carla said as she greeted her friend. "I even found myself humming as I worked," she laughed. "It's been days since I have hummed while I worked. Tiffany, I don't think I have ever felt so good."

Tiffany looked at her pastor's wife and was happy to see how good she looked. The last few weeks had taken a toll on this usually vibrant lady. She knew Carla had every reason to rejoice, but in the back of her mind, she was haunted by Pastor Ted's words, *I'm under arrest for the murder of a young lady.* She wondered what that was all about. Surely her pastor could not have done something as horrible as that.

Within five minutes after Tiffany arrived, Joan drove up to the Black's house. The ladies exchanged greetings before Tiffany put her suitcase in Carla's car. Then she climbed behind the wheel of the vehicle and the trio was on their way to see the man who had been the object of so many prayers over the last couple of months.

They visited and chattered all the way to Highpoint. Carla shared one interesting experience after another about Pastor Ted. Tiffany and Joan were getting to see their pastor in a new light…one they liked. He really was as genuine as he sounded when he spoke on Sundays. They were thankful for the privilege of making this trip with Carla. Listening to her made the trip much more enjoyable.

As they got close to town, Carla giggled and said, "I'm so excited, ladies. I feel like a school girl who has just been asked for a date by the most handsome man in school." Both of the ladies laughed with her and Tiffany teased her about thinking Pastor Ted was so handsome. Both of the ladies with her were glad to see the lines of worry gone from Carla's face. She seemed so much more like herself.

As quickly as the laughter came, the black clouds seemed to push it away. "What if they really did do something to Ted? What if he didn't want to tell me over the phone, but he has been seriously hurt in some way? What if…"

Before she could add another negative thought, Tiffany interrupted her. "Pastor Ted is not the kind of man who would hide the truth. He would not say he was okay unless he was okay. Let's not let the negative thoughts drag us down, Carla." Tiffany felt a little out of place correcting the first lady of her church, but she was also a good friend and good friends are willing to speak up when what they have to say is helpful.

"You're right, Tiffany! Pastor Ted would never do such a thing. He has always been a man of integrity and honesty since the first day I met him. Have I ever told you ladies about the day we met?" Carla asked.

"No, I don't believe you have," Tiffany and Joan answered in unison. They were glad the happy side of Carla was showing again and listened carefully as Carla told them about being on the library steps at college when a handsome man asked for her phone number.

When they entered the city limits of Highpoint, Carla suddenly got very quiet. "I don't like this little town," she said softly, just barely above a whisper.

"I can understand why," Tiffany responded. "They didn't exactly make you feel welcome when you were here before." Then she asked, "Carla, do you remember how to get to the sheriff's office. I assume that's where we need to go."

Carla gave her directions and the three ladies drove the last few blocks in complete silence. They were all lost in their own individual thoughts.

After Ted and Ben had given their statements to the FBI, they were escorted from the cabin toward the silver *Lexus*. They had taken only a few steps when a red car turned into the driveway behind them. Both men turned to see who it was. Ben recognized them at once. "It's Harvey and Sergeant Blight," he told Pastor Ted. "I have a feeling they had a lot to do with our being found."

They stood at the side of the driveway as the driver pulled the car toward the other side far enough to allow another car to pass if it was necessary. When Harvey and Sergeant Blight got out of the car, the four men greeted each other with a hug. They were only given a couple of minutes to exchange information. Then the investigator and the sergeant were taken into the cabin while Ted and Ben resumed their walk to the silver *Lexus*.

When the door to the fancy car was opened, the two men climbed into the back seat. It was luxurious with leather seats and all the options you could ever hope for in a vehicle. Mr. Teague got in the passenger's side and a man neither of them had met yet got behind the wheel.

Mr. Teague took care of the introductions. "Gentlemen, this is Jim Crane. He is my supervisor. Mr. Crane has been in charge of this entire operation. He is the one who is most responsible for you being set free from your captors." Then he turned to Mr. Crane and introduced him first to Ted and then to Ben.

Ted expressed his appreciation to Mr. Crane, "Thank you, sir, for all your work in helping me get out of that cabin. No one can imagine how good freedom feels until it is taken from him."

"I wasn't locked in that tiny room as long as the pastor was, but it was long enough to make me glad to be free," added Ben.

"We are just glad everything turned out like it did," Agent Teague replied, as memories of several cases that didn't end up like this one flashed through his mind.

Before Mr. Crane could pull away from his parking place, Ted noticed a familiar figure coming toward the car. When he saw who it was, he wondered why he was not in the SUVs that took all the other men away, but he didn't say anything. If he had learned anything from being in this area, it was to expect the unexpected.

"Hello, Pastor Ted," the man said. "My name isn't really Hank. I'm Geoff Mills. I am a special undercover agent with the FBI. I want to thank you for our conversations in the cabin back there. I'm not really as bad as I let on, but I did need to hear some of the things you had to say. I'm going to do my best to get my family in church when I get back home. I'm sorry I couldn't let you know who I was, but I couldn't risk blowing my cover."

"Thanks, Hank…uh…I mean, Geoff," Ted responded. "I hope I didn't give God a bad name by the way I acted. It was a pretty tough experience for me, and I wasn't real pleased with myself at times."

"You did fine, Pastor. Don't sell yourself short. You let me see that a man can be a Christian during tough times as well as good times. Thanks again for talking with me. I still have my Bible and I promise to read it," Geoff said before he stood up and made his way into the lake house.

Mr. Crane put the *Lexus* in gear and backed from behind the house. As they turned from the driveway onto Log Mountain Road, Ben and Ted noticed a group of about seven motorcycle riders fly down the road. "I suppose they are some of your men as well," Ben stated what he figured was obvious.

"Of course," Mr. Teague responded. "How do you think we kept you from shooting your pastor and then taking your own life?"

His comment left Ted deep in thought. He wondered how they could have known what the plan was. They must have had the cabin wired so they could listen to whatever was being said. Slowly it dawned on Ted that God was aware of what was going on in that cabin, too. God had not forgotten him. He knew what was happening. In fact, He was in full control of the situation the entire time. God had men in place to protect him in ways Ted was only beginning to see now. A tear ran down his face as he thought about the love of God.

Ted turned toward the window as if he wanted to see something outside, but he didn't see a thing. His eyes were closed in prayer. "God, I am so sorry for doubting you," he confessed. "Of all people I should have known that you had not abandoned me. I should have held on to my faith. Please forgive me for my weakness. Thank you for protecting me and thank you for being so patient with me. I'm embarrassed to call myself a pastor. I'm not sure You will still want to use me, but I can assure you of this: I have a much better understanding of how You work now. I want You to know that I'm available if You still want me. If You can use me, I'm willing to do whatever You ask."

A deep, deep peace came over Ted. It was in that moment that he realized again that God does not expect absolute perfection from his children. He had preached that message many times, but now he truly believed it. He knew that God loved him and was pleased with him. Ted was very grateful that God had been present the whole time he was hidden away in the cabin in the woods.

The men had barely gone a couple of miles down the road before Ben spoke up, "Mr. Crane, I have to ask you something. I realize that you may not be able to give me an answer, but I have to ask. Would you by any chance be the man who tried to run me off the road when I first came up to these mountains?"

Mr. Crane looked a little embarrassed. "I guess I'm the culprit," he admitted. "But I followed you long enough to know that you were in perfect command of your car. I really wasn't trying to run you off the road. I just wanted to discourage you from continuing your investigation. I was afraid you might blow our entire operation if I let you keep snooping around. I'm extremely sorry that I had to resort to such risky tactics."

"Apology accepted," Ben replied. "You sure had me fooled though. I thought you were in partnership with the sheriff."

"Well, don't feel so bad," Mr. Crane said. "The sheriff did, too. At least he thought Mr. Ron Richards was." Mr. Crane didn't elaborate any further and Ben knew not to ask any more questions.

The four men rode in silence for a moment or two before Mr. Crane added, "You are a great investigator, Mr. Albright. You came very close to uncovering all the facts in this case on your own. I'm sorry we had to stop you when we did."

At that moment Ben realized that the F.B.I. had more than one man who had infiltrated the ranks of the criminals who had just been arrested. Then he said with a slight chuckle in his voice, "That's okay, Mr. Crane, but I do wish you had not arranged to have me hit so hard. My head is still sore."

Mr. Crane apologized again for the way he had treated Ben and then got quiet. In fact the men rode the rest of the way into the town of Highpoint in silence and went straight to the police station. The sheriff met them at the door when they pulled up in front of the building.

Neither Ben nor Ted had noticed that a second car had traveled along with them. Two agents got out of the car as soon as it arrived. The agents entered the jail and placed a third deputy under arrest. That left the sheriff with only one deputy. The men assured Sheriff Bixley that they would assist him until he could get new deputies trained and on the streets.

When Ted and Ben entered the jail, they were escorted to the sheriff's office and told to wait there. Through the open door they could hear Mr. Crane and Sheriff Bixley in conversation.

"I want you to get in touch with Judge Cox," Mr. Crane instructed the sheriff. "Tell him to do everything he can to set a bond for Ted Black. Tell him it would be too dangerous to put him in a cell with the rest of these men. They blame him for what happened to them. He didn't have anything to do with it, but they would probably try to harm him in some way if he was put in a cell with them."

Ted cringed at the thought of being locked in a cell with the men who had treated him so harshly. He never wanted to be around those men again unless he had an opportunity to tell them about God's love. If he were given that chance, God would give him the courage to tell the men that God loves them and that He wants to forgive them for all the wrong things they had done in their lives. For a moment he began to imagine standing before the men with a message of hope for them. The conversation going on outside the sheriff's office caught his attention again, however. He couldn't help but hope that Judge Cox would listen to Mr. Crane's request.

"I'll try to get hold of him," the sheriff replied. "I'm not sure he can set a bond that quickly for a murder suspect, though."

"Do your best to convince him, Sheriff. If you can't, then request permission to hold Pastor Black in a different jail until the bond can be set. I cannot let this man be placed in such a dangerous place. Now, give him a call, so we know what is going to happen," Mr. Crane insisted.

When Sheriff Bixley called Judge Cox, they exchanged small talk for a couple of minutes. Then the sheriff told him how the FBI had found Ted Black, the man who had been charged with the murder of Marla Harris. He also told him about the other men who had been arrested, including three of his own deputies. Then he asked Judge Cox to set bond for Ted so he would not have to be placed in the same cell with the men who might try to harm him. Judge Cox did not like being asked for favors, but recognized the seriousness of the situation and agreed to have a bond hearing the next day. The judge reluctantly agreed to allow the prisoner to be held in the jail of a nearby town as long as he was kept under careful observation.

"That's the best I could do," the sheriff told Mr. Crane.

"Then Ted Black will remain in the custody of the FBI until tomorrow morning, Sheriff," Mr. Crane informed the sheriff. "I will not leave him here in this cell, but will take him to Clinton and have him housed there until tomorrow."

"Can you do that?" Sheriff Bixley wanted to know.

"Not only can I, but that is exactly what I am going to do," replied Mr. Crane. He sounded so stern and authoritative that the usually gruff and impatient sheriff was timid in his response.

"Have him here by eight o'clock in the morning, then," said the sheriff.

"I will. We are going to wait right here until his wife arrives however. That's the least consideration we can show to a man who has been separated from his family from the day of his arrest," Mr. Crain said as he glared at the sheriff so intently that it caused Sheriff Bixley to squirm.

The sheriff was suddenly aware that Mr. Crane probably knew how he had treated Pastor Black from the moment he was arrested. As he contemplated the implications of that, he felt a wave of fear sweep over him.

Mr. Crane was speaking again and his voice brought the sheriff back to the present moment. "Mr. Teague and I will personally drive Pastor Black to Clinton. Will you alert the sheriff there? Tell him we will be there sometime in the next two or three hours. Let me know what he has to say." Mr. Crane still sounded very much in command of the entire situation. "While you call the sheriff in Clinton, I will tell Pastor Black what is going to happen to him."

Sheriff Bixley started entering numbers into the phone at the front desk, while Mr. Crane went into the sheriff's office. As soon as he entered the room, he spoke to Ted, "Pastor Black, I personally do not believe that you had anything to do with the murder of the young lady you are accused of murdering, but my opinions do not matter at this point. You have been arrested for murder and must be kept in custody until a bond hearing is held and bond is determined. Sheriff Bixley has arranged for Judge Cox to hold that hearing tomorrow. Until then you will remain in the custody of the FBI. It would be too dangerous to keep you here with the men who are being housed in this jail right now. I have arranged to have you held in the jail in Clinton until tomorrow morning."

Ted wanted to interrupt so he could tell the FBI agent that his wife was on her way to Highpoint right now and should be there in a short time. Before he could say a word, however, the agent continued, "I know that your wife is on her way here. I'm going to wait until you have a few minutes with her before we make our way to Clinton. I don't know what arrangements you made with her, but she might want to spend the night here in Highpoint so she can be present for the hearing tomorrow morning. I have a feeling you will be released if you can make bail. Of course I cannot guarantee that, but that is my best guess."

Before Ted could respond, Mr. Crane turned to Ben and said, "Mr. Albright, you are free to go any time you wish. You have not been charged with any crime and are not being held for any reason. I'll have one of my men take you to your car when you are ready to leave. By the way, Mr. Albright, Uncle Harry is free to go as well," Mr. Crane said with a chuckle.

Ben laughed a courteous laugh. Ted was sure he could detect some redness in the private investigator's cheeks.

"Speaking of cars," Ted spoke up. "What happened to my car? It was at the cabin for a few days and then it disappeared."

"The men who were holding you felt like it was too big a clue for anyone who might be looking for you. The man who owns the cleaning service took it to his house. We will be taking possession of it soon, but cannot release it yet. The cleaning service also has your books and other items from the lake house as well. Those items are being picked up right now. They will have to be looked at by the prosecuting attorney to see if they contain any evidence that would be helpful to the state's investigation. Of course, none of the evidence would be any good anyway since the items have been compromised for weeks now. Anyone could have planted anything in them by now. As soon as the authorities have an opportunity to examine them, they will be released to you. I would guess that will take a week or so. If you are released tomorrow, Pastor, will you have transportation?" Mr. Crane suddenly wanted to know.

"Yes, my wife is bringing our other car," Ted answered the question. For the first time since he was arrested, Ted felt like an officer of the law was interested in his welfare instead of trying to pin something on him.

Mr. Crane excused himself and left the office. Ted and Ben could tell by the parts of the conversation they could hear that Mr. Crane was telling the sheriff that his office had been under investigation for several months. He told him about the corruption of the three deputies they had arrested. He informed the sheriff that the deputies had done many things without his knowledge. They had told people they were acting on behalf of the sheriff. It had taken the FBI a long time to get to the bottom of the corruption case. After they did, Sheriff Bixley was no longer a suspect. Neither was his remaining deputy. They did tell him there were some procedures and policies that he needed to change and correct, such as holding a suspect without the benefit of a lawyer of his choice and especially without notifying his family. Apparently the sheriff claimed he was unaware of much of what had happened. Ted could not help but wonder. The sheriff was certainly aware of his attempts to tell his story at the crime scene, and he was aware of his desire to call his family. He had heard Ted beg for his own lawyer, too. The conversation between Mr. Crane and Sheriff Bixley continued, but Ted and Ben were no longer able to hear what was being said because someone closed the door to the office.

"The ladies should be here anytime," Ben observed as he tried to get Pastor Ted's mind on something more positive. "Joan said she is riding up here with Carla and Tiffany so we would not have two cars here. When they get here, Joan and I will excuse ourselves after a few minutes. I will be here tomorrow for the hearing however. I believe God is still at work just like he was back at the cabin earlier. I'm quite sure you will be going home tomorrow."

"Home...that word even sounds good," Ted observed thoughtfully. Then he tried to take care of some business that he knew needed to be addressed. "Ben, I can't thank you enough for what you have done for Carla and me. I'm so sorry that you were injured as you looked for me. When I get back home, I'll settle up with you about your fee. I know there is no way I could really repay you, but I do want to pay you whatever is customary in a case like this."

"Well, we'll have plenty of time to discuss things like that. Right now, you don't need to be concerned with such things. You have a special lady coming who needs your undivided attention," Ben said.

As if on cue, the front door of the jail opened and three ladies entered cautiously. "May I help you ladies," a deputy said in a cheerful voice. Carla could not help but notice the contrast from the last time she entered this place. She noticed two men in deep conversation a few feet from her, but neither of them seemed to notice the ladies enter the jail. "They are apparently discussing important business," Carla thought.

"Yes, I'm Tiffany Lee, this is Carla Black, and this is Joan Albright," Tiffany spoke up. "We are looking for Pastor Ted Black and Mr. Ben Albright. We were told on the phone that we would be able to find them here."

"You've come to the right place," the deputy said. "The men are in Sheriff Bixley's office. If you will wait a minute, I'll make sure it is okay for you to see them." The deputy walked over to the two men in conversation and spoke so softly Tiffany could not hear what was being said. He soon returned and said, "The sheriff has given permission for you to visit the men. If you will follow me, I'll take you to them."

Ted and Ben stood up as soon as the door opened. They watched as three of the most beautiful ladies in the world came through the door. At least that is what they looked like to Ted and Ben. As soon as Carla saw Ted, she ran to him and wrapped her arms around him. He took her into his arms with such gentleness and love that she felt like she could stay there forever. Her tears were drenching his shirt, but she was sure he didn't mind. A few of his tears fell into her hair as well. After they embraced for what seemed like a long time, she looked up at him. His lips pressed against her lips in a kiss that seemed to dissolve all the loneliness and questions of the last few weeks. The kiss lingered much longer than most of their kisses.

A similar embrace was taking place between Ben and Joan so Tiffany slipped quietly from the room, pulled the door closed, and stood there as if to protect the sacredness of what was taking place behind the door.

After a few minutes Ben and Joan left the room, leaving Carla alone with Ted for the first time in what seemed like months to Carla. She ran her fingers over his face, admiring the handsome man that he was. She commented about his looking like he had lost weight. He caressed her arms, holding her at arm's length for a moment as if to drink in her beauty. Then he pulled her to him again, and they locked in another passionate embrace. For a few moments, neither of them dared speak. They wanted to savor the moment as long as possible.

Finally, Ted spoke tenderly, "I love you, Carla. I was so afraid I would never see you again. It is so wonderful to have you in my arms. I hope we never have to be apart again…at least not like we have been. I need you so much. I have a lot of making up to do to you. I've put you though a lot."

Before he could go on, Carla spoke with such a loving voice that Ted thought he could listen to it forever. "I love you too, Ted. I never thought anything so tragic could happen. I know you had nothing to do with causing it. Don't worry about making anything up to me. Just come home with me and be my husband. We will face whatever happens together."

Again they kissed. Ted felt like he could never get enough of those sweet assurances of love. Carla agreed with his assessment of their few minutes together. Finally, Ted remembered Tiffany. He invited her into the room. Ben and Joan had already left to go get Ben's car. Ted gave the ladies a brief summary of what had happened to him since the conversation he had with Carla the night before he was arrested.

Tiffany was as shocked by the unfair treatment Ted had received as Carla was. She kept saying, "They can't do that. That's not right. How can they get away with that?"

After what seemed like only a few minutes, but was actually thirty minutes, Mr. Crane knocked lightly on the door. When he poked his head in, Ted told the ladies who he was. "We'll have to be going in five minutes, Pastor Black," Mr. Crane said. Ted thought he could detect a hint of regret in the agent's voice.

"I'm going to give you love birds that time to be together," Tiffany said as she left the room.

When they were alone again, Ted asked Carla to get permission to bring in a change of clothes for him and gave her instructions about where to stay overnight. He also told her where to be at eight in the morning. Carla listened as closely as she could, but her mind was on Ted more than what she needed to do. She knew she and Tiffany could handle things if necessary.

She looked at Ted as if to say, "There are more important things to do right now." Ted caught the meaning of her look and pulled her to him. They were holding each other in another loving embrace when Mr. Crane knocked on the door again.

Ted invited Mr. Crane in and then asked him if Carla could bring him a change of clothes. He explained that he had not been allowed to change what he was wearing for several days. Mr. Crane asked Carla to bring the clothes to him so he could inspect them first. Then he told Ted, "You wait right here until I return with your clothes."

When he came back, he was carrying a blue blazer, grey pants, white shirt, red striped tie, socks and dress shoes. Ted never thought a sports outfit could look so good. Mr. Crane told Ted to change his clothes before he left the sheriff's office. He stepped outside and waited while Ted quickly changed his clothes. When Mr. Crane came back into the office, he put the old clothes into a black trash bag which he carried with him.

As Ted stepped out of the jail and headed for the *Lexus*, a crusty old man shuffled up to him. Ted had to take a second look, but then he recognized the old man as the man who had been in this very jail with him a long time ago.

"How are you, my friend?" Ted inquired.

"Name's Smith," the old man replied. "I was in jail with you when you was first arrested. And I seen them men kidnap you in the middle of the night. If you need somebody to testify for you when you go to court, I'm available."

"Thank you, Mr. Smith," Ted said. "I just might need you to do that. How can I get in touch with you if I do?"

"Call Rosie at this number," Mr. Smith said as he slipped a piece of paper to Ted. "She always knows how to get in touch with me. It's best if you can give me a couple of days notice. I stay pretty busy," Mr. Smith said.

Ted thanked him again, stuffed the note in his pocket and got in the back seat of the silver *Lexus*. Mr. Crain and Mr. Teague got into the front seats of the vehicle. Mr. Teague asked to see the note and scribbled its content on a notepad he pulled from his coat pocket. Mr. Crane started the car and they were soon on their way to Clinton.

CHAPTER SEVENTEEN

Ted walked into the meeting with the leadership board of his church the first evening after he returned to Little Rock from Highpoint. Judge Cox had been very gracious and released him with the lowest possible bond. Tiffany had ridden home with Ben and Joan following the bond hearing. That allowed Ted and Carla to make the hour and a half trek together. They had a lot of catching up to do and thoroughly enjoyed the drive back to the big city.

At Pastor Ted's request, Tiffany had arranged the meeting and had everyone in place before the pastor arrived. That way he could share his story with everyone at the same time instead of repeating it over and over to each member individually.

As Ted entered the room, Mr. Jeffries stood to his feet and spoke on behalf of the board, "Pastor Ted, welcome home. We are so happy God has brought you back to us. Before you begin with whatever you want to share with us, let me report to you about one item this board considered while you were away. It is my pleasure to tell you that we have unanimously voted to pay you for the entire time you were gone. We know you were kept from us due to circumstances beyond your control. We love you, Pastor Ted, and want to make sure that you will not suffer any financial hardship because of what has happened."

"Thank you, Mr. Jeffries. And thanks to the rest of you as well. You have been most kind and very patient while I was gone. I greatly appreciate your expression of love, but you may want to reconsider your action after you hear what I am about to share with you," Ted stated with a heavy heart.

The members of the board looked at each other with puzzled expressions on their faces. Some wondered if he was getting ready to resign. Others thought he might be preparing to ask for even more time off. Only Tiffany, whose eyes were filled with tears, was fully aware of the disturbing news Pastor Ted was going to share with them.

Ted squared his shoulders and began his report, "About two weeks after I arrived at the cabin near Highpoint, I found a body floating in the water at the edge of Greers Ferry Lake. Since my cell phone battery was dead, I decided to try to tie a rope to the body to secure it to the shore while I went to report it to the sheriff. Two men came along as I was trying to accomplish that task. They thought I was the one who had killed the young lady. They called the sheriff, and I was arrested for the murder of a young woman I had never seen before that moment."

An audible gasp escaped from the lips of two or three of the board members. Ted could not tell if they were shocked by his finding a body or by his arrest or both. It didn't matter. He had even more disturbing news to share with them.

"I was taken to the jail, but was not permitted to contact anyone, not even Carla. I was assigned a lawyer if that is what you could call the man." Ted could tell that the board was having trouble absorbing all that he was saying, but he continued anyway. "During my second night in the jail I was kidnapped and carried to a cabin in the woods where I have been all this time. I was not able to contact anyone, nor could anyone find me. Ben Albright, whom most of you know, was on my trail when he was kidnapped as well and was placed in a room with me. Together we were about to be murdered in what would have been staged to look like a murder-suicide, but undercover FBI agents interfered with the plan. Without our knowledge the FBI was investigating the sheriff's department in Highpoint and eventually rescued us from our captivity. Of course I have omitted many details, but that is the brief version of what happened."

There was obvious relief on the faces of the leadership board when he reported his rescue, but their faces grew tight again with his next comment. "In spite of everything that has happened, I remain under arrest for the murder of the lady in the lake. This morning I was released on bond. I had nothing to do with the murder, of course, and remain confident that I will be set free. However, the news media will be reporting what has happened. As you know, they often make it sound worse than it really is. As you might expect, Hillside Community Church could receive some bad publicity from this." Ted's voice broke a little before his next comment, but he quickly regained his composure and said, "I am willing to offer you my resignation tonight if you think it would be best for the church. I have worked among you for many years and would not want to do anything that would hurt any of you nor anyone in our Hillside family."

Ted could tell that the board was struggling with the news he had just shared with them, so he said, "I want to answer any questions you may have and then give you an opportunity to discuss it without me being present. I will go to my office. You can send someone to get me when you have made a decision."

There were many questions asked. Most of them had to do with details about the arrest and the rescue. Ted was grateful when a lull in the questioning finally came. He placed Mr. Jeffries in charge of the discussion that would follow, excused himself, and then made his way to his office so the board could have a thorough discussion.

After Ted left the room, Mr. Jeffries spoke in a quiet voice that betrayed the heaviness of his heart. "I don't think we have a lot to discuss, Ladies and Gentlemen. Our pastor is going through the most difficult time in his life. He certainly doesn't need for us to abandon him. Yes, we can expect some bad publicity, but it will be even worse if he is found innocent and we have bailed out on him. I, for one, think we should give him a vote of confidence and ask him to stay on as our pastor."

Tiffany was somewhat surprised, but very pleased, by what Mr. Jeffries had to say. She was the next to speak. "I agree with Mr. Jeffries. None of us can possibly believe that Pastor Ted is capable of harming anyone, let alone murdering anyone. But I do think we should ask him to share the news with the congregation. Our worst enemy right now will be the spread of rumors. We have to do everything we can to keep that from happening. Perhaps the best way to do that will be to have the pastor speak about it himself."

"As far as the involvement of the church leadership team in responding to all this, I think we should limit interviews to you, Tiffany," Joe Hawkins inserted. "If we all speak to the media, we might get some things confused. You have remained the closest to the Blacks during this time. We could ask them to keep you aware of whatever is happening. Would you be willing to be our spokesperson?" he asked.

"Well, yes, I would be willing to do it, but I think that should be the responsibility of Mr. Jeffries," Tiffany responded. "He has always been our leader."

"But you are much more eloquent and think much better on your feet than I do," Mr. Jeffries objected. "I think the church would be better served if you would take the lead in this matter."

"Will we lose very many people because of this?" John Ingles asked.

"There is no way to know that," Stan Tucker answered. "Some people might be skeptical about coming to a church where a murder suspect is preaching. Others will admire us for standing behind our pastor. I don't think we can make our decision because of what might happen however. We need to do what we think is right."

There were a few more comments offered before Mrs. Majors spoke up. She had remained quiet up to this point. "I think we need to take this matter before the Lord. We need to seek His direction in this. It is possible for us to allow our affection for the pastor to affect our decision as much our fear of the negative publicity we might receive. Until we know God's direction, we are only acting on our own. We have prayed for God's guidance before. We should not stop doing that now."

Everyone was in agreement with Mrs. Majors and spent considerable time seeking God's will in the hardest decision they would ever have to face.

When they finished praying, George Barrett offered his opinion. "I believe that a man is innocent until he is proven guilty. As of now, no one has proven Pastor Ted guilty of anything except loving us enough to sacrifice his job to spare us from a difficult time. I move that we ask Pastor Ted Black to remain as our pastor."

The motion passed unanimously as did a motion to ask Pastor Ted to address the matter with the entire congregation on Sunday and a motion to limit church interviews to Tiffany Lee.

When Pastor Ted was asked to return to the meeting, Mr. Jeffries shared the unanimous action of the board with the pastor. Expressions of love and support were offered from each member of the board to their leader before they all left the meeting room. Pastor Ted was exhausted when he went home that night but was glad he served such a loving and supportive group of people. Already he was beginning to pray for the service on Sunday.

Hillside Community Church was buzzing with activity the following Sunday morning. Tiffany Lee spent most of the Bible Study Hour giving interviews to the reporters present. All four major networks in town had at least one reporter in attendance and cameras were set up in multiple locations. Everyone had been told that Pastor Ted Black would address the charges that were brought against him. The auditorium was so full that chairs had to be brought in to provide seating for the people. Many visitors were present. Everyone wanted to hear what the pastor had to say.

A hush fell over the congregation as the pastor rose to his feet. Pastor Ted had never felt a greater peace than he did that morning. "Most of you are here today because you want to hear what I have to say about the charge of murder I am facing," he began. He proceeded to tell them as many of the details about his arrest and his subsequent kidnapping as he could. Of course he denied any involvement in what had happened and declared his innocence. People were spellbound by what he had to say about his rescue. They seemed pleased to learn that the leadership board had voted to ask him to remain as pastor. A few even clapped their hands.

After Ted finished his report regarding the details of what had happened to him, he told everyone present that he wanted to share with them the most important lesson he had learned while he was held in captivity. With genuine humility he confessed that he had questioned God and His love during this time. He described the times of prayer when he asked God why He wasn't working to help him like he had promised to do. He admitted that he had not been as strong in his faith as he had believed he would be at such times.

Then Pastor Ted added, "I am sure many of you have had times in your lives when you have doubted the love of God. Maybe you haven't been arrested or kidnapped, but you have wondered why God has not stepped in to help you. You have complained about His lack of involvement in the details of your lives." People all across the audience admitted to themselves that they had, indeed, wondered why God had failed to act in their behalf.

Pastor Ted then shared with them about one of the guards who just happened to be an FBI undercover agent. He told them about the white dog that had led Ben to the cabin in the woods. He told them about the motorcycle riders who showed up at just the right time and about finding a removable knot that gave him contact outside of his confining room.

Pastor Ted concluded by saying, "You see, my friends, when our lives are in God's hands, He is at work taking care of us when we don't even realize it. He works in ways we cannot even imagine. In fact He is at work all the time. We may not be able to see how He is working at the time. But, let me assure you: He is at work. I can say with a newly-found confidence, God loves you and will never abandon you. I encourage you to hold on to your faith. One day you will see the evidence of His presence you have longed to see. Slowly you will begin to understand what He has been doing and how He has been working."

Electricity seemed to fill the auditorium that morning. At the close of his message Pastor Ted asked, "If you have been facing difficulties lately that are so intense they have tempted you to question God's love for you, will you please stand?" Scores of people stood to their feet including one of the young reporters who had been assigned to cover the story. Pastor Ted bowed his head and in a simple prayer asked God to help these people to remain faithful until they could see how He was at work caring for them. He commended them into the hands of a loving God. Then He asked God to show them how He was working to bring good into each one of their lives.

When the service ended, Pastor Ted was surrounded by a huge number of reporters and well-wishers. He tried his best to accept the words of encouragement and still find a way to answer the questions people had. It took nearly an hour for him to satisfy everyone's curiosity. When it was finally over, he was drained emotionally, but had a deep sense of God's peace. Deep inside Ted was sure that God was using his tragic experience for the benefit of the church and for the benefit of God's Kingdom. If that happened, the whole experience would seem worth it somehow.

Ted was glad to find Carla waiting in his office when he finally left the crowds behind and made his way there. "Wow! What a lovely sight for my eyes to behold," he said as he walked into the room.

Carla smiled at his weak attempt to act romantic. She told him what an excellent job he had done that morning, and then told him they had been invited him go with the Williams and the Knights, two families from their church, to a restaurant in a nearby town. They would all ride together in the Knights' big SUV so they could visit on the way there.

Ted was glad for the opportunity to be out of the spotlight for a few minutes and hurried to get ready to leave. Hand in hand Carla and Ted made their way to meet their friends in the waiting vehicle.

CHAPTER EIGHTEEN

Every spare moment during the next few weeks was filled with intense meetings with lawyers and reporters. Pastor Ted tried to be patient as he told the lawyers his story over and over. Interviews with reporters were even worse. Most of them wanted to find some kind of negative information that would give them a newsworthy story. Some even tried to manipulate the conversation so Pastor Ted would say something wrong.

Fortunately the pastor also received innumerable phone calls from people who wanted to talk to him about the personal struggles they were having with their faith. Ted was especially interested in those calls since they made him feel like he was using his horrible experience to help others.

When the day of his trial finally arrived, Ted got up very early and put on his best pin-striped suit and dark red necktie. Carla wore the blue dress she considered Ted's favorite. She was a bit nervous and very restless as they drove down the streets of the north Arkansas town toward the Cleburne County courthouse. Ted did his best to assure her that everything was going to be okay. "After all, I'm an innocent man," he said.

"But innocent people have been convicted before," she reminded him.

"I know, Sweetheart," he acknowledged. "But I have God on my side, and I am sure He won't allow such an unfair thing to happen.

Surely He didn't orchestrate my rescue like He did if He was going to allow something to go wrong now."

As they entered the majestic-looking courthouse with its four tall white columns guarding the front door, Ted met his lawyer just inside the courthouse door. He quickly introduced Carla to the well-dressed, dignified-looking man who looked like he was in his late forties. "Carla, this is Derrick Hodges. He is going to defend me today. You have talked to him on the phone several times. Now you have the opportunity to meet him in person. Derrick, this is my lovely wife, Carla. She has been a really big source of strength for me during this whole ordeal."

"Yes, I'm sure she has," Mr. Hodges said politely. "I'm glad to meet you, Mrs. Black," he added as sincerely as he could. It was obvious, however, that his mind was on the trial that would start in just a few minutes. Carla couldn't help but think that it was all happening too quickly. She was just getting used to having Ted back at home, and now there was a chance that he might not being returning with her to the home they had loved for the last several years.

Since Ted and his lawyer had several items to discuss, Carla excused herself and went into the courtroom. As she stepped into the sterile room where justice is supposed to prevail, she shuddered from the thought of what might happen. After surveying the room, she chose a seat in the front row.

When Ted entered the courtroom with his lawyer a few minutes later, he was encouraged by the presence of at least half of his leadership team. They were sitting in the seats just behind Carla. Ben and Joan had come as well. Of course Ben would have to testify. Harvey was also present. Sergeant Blight even came. Mr. Crane was also there to testify. Ted could not help but feel grateful for such a strong showing of support from so many people.

As soon as his eyes fell on Carla in the front row just behind where he would be sitting, Ted noticed that she had on an outfit that made her look stunning. How had he failed to notice her beautiful appearance earlier that morning? Maybe he was a little more nervous than he realized. Anyway, it was so good to know that she was only a few feet away from him. That knowledge gave him a sense of well being, like things were the way they should be.

The tedious process of selecting jurors began. Two hours later the last juror was sworn in and the trial began. Opening remarks were given by both lawyers. Ted thought his lawyer won that battle easily, but he knew speeches were not enough to sway a jury. Evidence was needed. Ted wondered what evidence the prosecution could possibly have. He also hoped his lawyer could explain, refute, or clarify any charges the prosecution would present.

Mr. Hodges told him that the fact that the rope he was using when he was arrested had not been saturated with water showed that it could not have held any kind of weight to the body while it was submerged in the water. Since it was obvious that the body had been in the water for some time, the rope did not provide credible evidence that supported the prosecution's theory. That rope could not possibly have made the marks on the body, either. There was reason to believe that those marks had been caused by something much larger than the small rope Ted had in his hands at the time of his arrest.

Another piece of evidence that confirmed Ted's story was his cell phone. It had been tested by the one uncorrupted deputy in the sheriff's office when he first arrived at the jail. It was found to have a dead battery, just like he had told the game wardens and the sheriff. Ted's lawyer had also focused a lot of his investigation on the two men who happened to catch Ted tying the rope on the body.

Ted's thoughts were interrupted by the start of testimony for the prosecution. As Ted sat there listening to the testimony, he began to pray for God to direct the jury to the correct verdict. Thankfully he no longer doubted God. Since he knew the value of prayer, he interceded for each jury member. He asked God to help them listen carefully. He asked Him to give them the wisdom and courage necessary to make the right decision. He also asked God to bless each one of their families.

When Sheriff Bixley was cross-examined, Ted's lawyer made him look like an incompetent, arrogant and totally inept officer of the law. Ted almost felt sorry for the man, but realized that he had brought many of his problems on himself. He should have seen some of the things that were happening right under his nose.

Derrick Hodges was a very skilled trial lawyer. Ted was glad the lawyer was on his side. He was somewhat surprised, however, when Mr. Hodges reminded Sheriff Bixley that law enforcement officers were as bound by the laws concerning perjury as other people are. The statement only made sense when the lawyer asked the sheriff, "Did you thoroughly investigate this case or did you jump to a hasty conclusion based on what you were told by the two game wardens, who just happened to be friends of yours? They were your friends, weren't they, Sheriff Bixley?"

"Well, Mr. Hodges, as a matter of fact the game wardens are friends of mine. They are good, young men," the sheriff said. Then he squirmed in his seat for a few seconds before stating, "I thought I had caught the man who did this awful crime red-handed."

Ted's lawyer didn't let the sheriff get by with not answering the question about jumping to a hasty conclusion. He kept asking the sheriff about it until he finally admitted in a soft voice, "I might have been a little hasty with my opinion and probably could have done a better job with this investigation."

"Sheriff Bixley, how much of the investigation was carried out by the three deputies who are now under arrest for corruption?" Mr. Hodges asked as he glared at the sheriff.

"They carried out all of the follow-up investigation," Sheriff Bixley admitted. "I left it with them while I drove the suspect into town to the jail." It was obvious that the sheriff was glad he could put most of the responsibility on someone else.

Mr. Hodges reminded the sheriff about perjury again before he proceeded. "Did you even listen to the defendant tell his side of the story, Sheriff Bixley?"

"Mr. Black got to tell his side of the story when we got to the police station," the sheriff said with an air of satisfaction.

Then Mr. Hodges asked, "Did you already have your mind made up that he was guilty before you even allowed him to share his version of what happened?"

The sheriff really began to squirm in his seat at that point. Ted hoped Mr. Crane and Sergeant Blight could see what was happening. He was sure they would both enjoy the theatrics in the witness chair. After being instructed by the judge to answer the question, Sheriff Bixley said, "Well, I guess so."

"Is that a yes or no, Sheriff?" asked Mr. Hodges, sounding irritated and impatient. "I'm a little unclear."

"Yes, I had already made up my mind. No, I did not seriously consider Pastor Black's side of the story, nor did I try to verify what he told me." Sheriff Bixley had a sick look on his face by the time he left the witness stand.

Mr. Hodges told the judge that he thought there was enough evidence that this case had been handled inappropriately to warrant an immediate dismissal of the charges. The judge was not convinced at this point, however, but he did scribble some notes on the legal pad he had on his desk.

The younger of the two game wardens did a reasonably good job at reporting what he observed that day. Ted thought he looked extremely young to be involved in a trial like this. He wondered about the young man's background and about his relationship with God. Deep inside he felt a strong desire to have a conversation about spiritual matters with the man. He knew that opportunity would probably never come, but he felt the desire increase as the morning passed by.

The game warden's statement that Ted was standing in the edge of the water wrapping a rope around the leg of the victim was the most damaging piece of evidence offered so far. It was damaging in one way, but it was also helpful in another. Mr. Hodges called attention to that by asking the game warden if he was sure Pastor Black was wrapping the rope around the leg of the victim and was not taking if off her leg. The young man confirmed his statement that Ted was definitely trying to put the rope on the leg of the victim. He voluntarily stated that he and his partner had watched Ted for several minutes before they said anything to him.

When asked why he and his friend were in the area, Jeff, the young warden, said, "I was just following orders. Bob told me to stay with him that day in case he needed me." Then he added, "I was just doing what my superior told me to do. That's what a man is supposed to do when he is at work, isn't it?"

Ted noticed that Mr. Hodges ignored Jeff's question. He was sure, however, that his lawyer would be able to explain what really happened on that day. It seemed strange that the day could seem to be such a distant memory now. Deep inside Ted hoped Mr. Hodges could share Ted's explanation clearly enough to convince the jury that he was just an innocent man trying his best to do what he could to secure the body to a tree so he could contact the sheriff. That really was the truth. Hopefully the jury would be able to recognize it as the truth. Ted knew all too well that the same information could be viewed in different ways by different people. He had witnessed that in church work many times.

When Bob, the older of the two game wardens began to testify, he kept trying to add more information to his story than was really present at the time he discovered the pastor with the body. He also mentioned derogatory things he claimed to have heard about Ted. Mr. Hodges objected every time any hearsay was offered. The objections were sustained.

When Mr. Hodges was permitted to cross-examine Bob, he focused on the relationship Bob had with Marla Harris, the victim. Bob admitted that she had been his girlfriend, but said they had broken up about two weeks before Ted's arrest. The lawyer also wanted to know why the young man kept adding additional information to the story. "Are you trying to mislead this jury," he asked in an accusing tone?

The prosecution quickly objected and the judged sustained the objection and then instructed the jury to disregard the question.

When Mr. Hodges wanted to know why Bob and his partner just happened to be in the area, Bob could only give vague answers. He certainly didn't give any explanation that seemed to be feasible. "Did you have reason to believe that my client might find a body in the water that day?" the lawyer wanted to know.

"Of course not," Bob answered. "I didn't know there was a body in the water until I saw Mr. Black taking that rope off her leg."

"Are you sure he was taking the rope off her leg, Bob?" Mr. Hodges asked. "This court has already determined that Pastor Black was trying to tie a rope to the leg. What makes you think he was taking the rope off?"

"Well, I...I...I guess I just assumed he was untying the rope," Bob admitted.

"Let me ask you, Bob. Was the rope saturated with water or was it relatively dry?" Ted's lawyer asked.

"I'm not sure, but I think it was dry," Bob said in a soft voice that let everyone know he realized he had just gotten caught trying to put his own spin on the facts.

Mr. Hodges shocked Ted and everyone else in the courtroom when he stepped out on a limb and said, "Bob, did you have anything to do with the murder of Marla Harris?"

"Objection," yelled the prosecutor, but the judge allowed the question.

"No, I didn't murder anybody," Bob answered in a voice that cracked, making him sound like a boy whose voice was changing.

"Do you know Brian Ansley?" Mr. Hodges wanted to know.

"Yes, he is my best friend" Bob replied.

"Did he help you take Miss Harris' body out into the lake in a boat? Did he help you secure the body to some kind of heavy weight and throw it overboard into Greers Ferry Lake?" Mr. Hodges again implicated Bob in the murder with his questions.

"I don't even own a boat. How could I have taken her body out into the lake and thrown it in?" Bob asked the lawyer a question he thought would disarm the lawyer.

"That's right, Bob, you don't own a boat, but how many days a year are you out on the waters of Greers Ferry Lake in a boat owned by the State Game and Fish Commission?" Ted's lawyer wanted to know.

"I don't know. Maybe fifty or sixty times a year," Bob said quietly.

"So you really would have had plenty of opportunities to take a body out into the lake and throw it into the water if you wanted to, wouldn't you, Bob?" Mr. Hodges asked.

"Your honor, I object to this whole line of questioning," the prosecutor said. "Mr. Black is the one on trial here, not this young man."

"Overruled," responded the judge, but he did call Mr. Hodges to the bench and warned him about trying to play Perry Mason.

"Your Honor, I'm not trying to play Perry Mason," Mr. Hodges said. "I believe this man, or someone known by him, killed Marla Harris. I believe he had a hand in her death in some way. I believe I can show that he had reason to kill Miss Harris or, at least, had the motivation to commit such a crime. I respectfully ask that I be permitted to continue questioning this witness, Your Honor?"

The judge was convinced and allowed Mr. Hodges to resume his interrogation. Every time Mr. Hodges mentioned Marla Harris or asked Bob if he was involved in her death, Bob turned white.

"Do you know the difference between a crime of passion and how that differs from premeditated murder?" Mr. Hodges wanted to know.

"No," Bob said. It was obvious he was trying to show little interest in what Mr. Hodges had asked, but the expression on his face betrayed his interest.

"Maybe you ought to find out, young man," Mr. Hodges said. Then he dismissed the game warden, but reserved the right to call Bob back to the stand if the facts of the case made it necessary.

The coroner, the paramedics who came to the scene that day, and a couple of other witnesses for the prosecution came forward and gave their testimony. It was mostly technical and required very little time. The prosecution rested its case without introducing any additional evidence.

Hope began to build inside Ted's mind as he prepared himself to hear from the witnesses who were present to speak in his behalf. Before Mr. Hodges had the opportunity to call any witnesses, however, the judge dismissed the court for a lunch break. He spoke in a monotone voice as he instructed everyone to be back in the courtroom and ready to resume by 2:00 p.m.

Ted's lawyer accompanied Ted and Carla to lunch, but Ted barely touched the sandwich he ordered. Carla had no appetite either. Both of them realized how different their lives would be if, for some reason, Ted were found to be guilty. As they ate, Mr. Hodges did his best to prepare Ted for the time he would spend on the witness stand. He knew Ted was used to speaking publicly, but he also knew what nerves could do to a person when they were grilled by professionals. He sure didn't want to take any chances. He wanted to make sure his client knew what to expect.

When they got back to the courtroom that afternoon, Ted noticed that the prosecutor had not yet arrived. A minute or two after Ted's lawyer came into the room, a court official came over and spoke with him. Mr. Hodges told Ted that he had to meet with the judge about something and assured him that he would be back before anything began. He told Ted that had no idea what the judge wanted, but said he would soon find out. Then he whispered something he had not said in any previous meeting. "Pastor, I would suggest that you breathe a prayer while I am in this meeting."

Ted wondered what in the world he meant by that. Was something going wrong? Had some new evidence come to light? Was a conviction likely? Was his life in jeopardy? He started to turn so he could look at Carla, but decided he needed to follow his lawyer's advice. Right there in the courtroom Ted closed his eyes and began to ask God to be in control of whatever was happening right now. He also asked for a sense of calmness and for a new assurance of God's presence.

Carla sensed the unrest in Ted's spirit. If she had learned one thing in the thirty years they had been married, she had learned to tell when her husband was concerned about something. Carla had no idea what had happened, but she knew it had robbed Ted of the peace he had enjoyed up to that moment. She leaned forward and tried to touch his arm two or three times, but her arm was not long enough.

Finally, Carla stood to her feet and stepped over to Ted. She put her hand gently on his shoulder, leaned down and spoke softly in his ear, "I don't know what has you concerned, Sweetheart, but I want you to know I love you. I also want to remind you that you are in the hands of a loving God." Then she delivered a messaged she thought he needed to hear by repeating the very words Ted had spoken to her earlier in the day. "He didn't orchestrate your rescue like He did just to allow something to go wrong now," she said.

Ted recognized the message as his own, but somehow it seemed more like an assurance from God now. He looked up to Carla, smiled tenderly, and said, "I love you, too, Honey. Thanks for the reminder. I needed to hear it. For a moment my faith was in danger of wavering again, but I feel a new level of confidence now. You are a great partner to me. You always know what I need to hear."

Carla could tell Ted's words were sincere by the peaceful look that spread across his face. It replaced the troubled look that held him a few moments earlier. She patted his shoulder a time or two and looked deep into his eyes before she made her way back to her seat on the front row.

As soon as Carla was seated, the prosecutor came into the courtroom followed closely by Ted's lawyer. As they took their places, Mr. Hodges leaned over to speak to Ted. Before he could say anything, however, the bailiff spoke, "Will everyone please rise? The Honorable Judge Glen Cox, presiding, in the case of the State verses Ted Black."

As they were standing to their feet and Judge Cox was entering the courtroom, Mr. Hodges whispered to Ted, "It was just some procedural things, Pastor Ted. Don't worry about a thing."

Ted breathed a sigh of relief, but he was still glad to sit down when permission was given. His knees felt a little weak. Silently he asked God for the courage he would need for the afternoon session. "I don't want to question You again, Lord. Please keep me strong in my faith. Help me to overcome Satan's attacks," he prayed.

When the afternoon proceedings began, a parade of witnesses took the stand testifying about Ted's spotless integrity and his compassion toward others. Ted was humbled by what they said, but was grateful they felt the way they did.

When Ben Albright, the private investigator, shared his findings, the judge kept writing things down on his notepad. Ted couldn't help but wonder what the judge was writing. Judge Cox seemed especially interested in the information he shared about the holes in the ground and the fingerprint in the cabin. His testimony was lengthy, and the cross-examination took even longer. Ben never wavered in his testimony however. It was obvious to Ted that Ben had testified many times before.

Ted was shocked when his lawyer called Saul Mitchell to the stand. He was one of the men arrested the day Ted and Ben were set free by the F.B.I. Ted wondered why he was being asked to witness for the defense. He didn't have to wait long to find out.

The questions Mr. Hodges asked were routine until he asked, "Mr. Mitchell, did you take any possessions belonging to Pastor Ted Black from a cabin located on Lot 53 on Log Mountain Road?"

Mr. Mitchell had the look of a child who had been caught with his hand in the cookie jar as he looked around the courtroom. "Absolutely not!" he snorted.

"Then why were his clothes, his books, his computer, his wallet, his keys and all of his other belongings found in your place of business?" Mr. Hodges wanted to know.

"I don't know. Maybe Paul, my twin brother, put them there." Saul replied in a defiant tone.

"Mr. Mitchell, let me remind you that you are under oath. This court has heard testimony that your fingerprint was found in the cabin. It was not the fingerprint of your brother. This court has also heard testimony that you were hired to clean the cabin a couple of days after the arrest of Pastor Black. Now, let me ask you again, 'Why were the possessions of Pastor Ted Black found in your place of business?'" Mr. Hodges glared at the man on the stand with such intensity that it made Mr. Mitchell shift from one position to another.

Mr. Mitchell looked around the courtroom as if he was looking for someone to give him an answer. Finally he answered, "All right, I did take them, but I did it because the sheriff wanted me to store them for him. I was just doing what the sheriff asked me to do."

"Was it the sheriff, Mr. Mitchell, or was it one of his deputies who asked you?" Mr. Hodges asked.

Again Mr. Mitchell shifted his body in the chair before he answered. Finally, Mr. Mitchell admitted, "Well, I never actually spoke to the sheriff, himself. But one of his deputies told me the sheriff wanted me to store the items until Mr. Black was located. It really doesn't matter who I talked to, does it? As far as I was concerned, it was the sheriff who asked me. I was just doing what I was hired to do."

"Yes, I'm sure you were, Mr. Mitchell." Mr. Hodges said with a tone that indicated that he was quite sure there was more to it than that. The he asked, "And did he also ask you to store Pastor Black's car?"

Again Mr. Mitchell looked guilty. "Well, yes, as a matter of fact, he did," he replied.

"And where did you store that car?" Mr. Hodges wanted to know.

"I put it in safe keeping," Mr. Mitchell said smugly.

"Was it being safely kept in a barn on your property, Mr. Mitchell? Was it safely kept there for weeks? Did you move it there because you were afraid someone would see it beside the cabin where you had Pastor Black locked in a room for about a month?" Mr. Hodges asked a series of questions before he paused long enough for Mr. Mitchell to answer.

"Now, wait a minute! I didn't lock Pastor Black in any room. I didn't have anything to do with that. Yes, I had his car and yes, I kept it in my barn, but I was only doing what I was told the sheriff wanted me to do," Mr. Mitchell looked sincere as he passionately tried to explain his actions.

"Mr. Mitchell, when did you first find out that Pastor Black was in the cabin hidden in the woods off Log Mountain Road?" the lawyer asked.

"Just a few days before the F.B.I. found him in the back of the deputy's car," Mr. Mitchell replied, trying to sound convincing.

"Mr. Mitchell, I remind you again. You are under oath. Do you know what can happen to someone who says something that is not true when he is under oath?" Mr. Hodges sounded like a patient teacher who was trying very hard to help a student learn a very difficult lesson.

"Yes, I know what can happen," Mr. Mitchell answered in a defeated tone. "I learned about the preacher being in the cabin when they asked me to pick up his car and store it at my house." Mr. Mitchell sounded irritated by being asked to tell the truth.

"Who asked you to move the car, Mr. Mitchell?"

"The deputy," Mr. Mitchell said, suddenly dropping his voice.

Mr. Hodges and Mr. Mitchell continued to spar for several more minutes as Mr. Hodges slowly introduced more and more details about the time Pastor Black spent locked in a cabin in the woods.

After several other witnesses made their way to the stand, Mr. Hodges rose to his feet and asked Judge Cox if he and the prosecutor could approach the bench. Permission was granted, so the two men made their way forward.

"I have reason to believe that one of the primary witnesses for the defense will be on the stand for an extended time, Your Honor. Since we don't have much time left today, I respectfully ask you to adjourn for the day, so we can start hearing that testimony tomorrow morning. If the prosecutor doesn't object, would you grant that privilege, Your Honor?" Mr. Hodges was careful to give the judge all the respect he could.

"Well, it is getting kind of late," Judge Cox said. He turned to the prosecutor and said, "Unless you object, Mr. Birch, I am going to grant this request. It is only thirty minutes before we would adjourn anyway."

"I have no objection, Your Honor," Mr. Birch said.

When the judge informed those in the courtroom that they would adjourn until the next day, Ted had mixed feelings. He was tired and emotionally drained from the proceedings of a very long day, but he was also eager to get this thing over. He was sure that he and Carla would spend a long, restless night before the next day dawned.

Ted took Carla's hand and they slowly made their way out of the courtroom. They accepted the invitation from some of the members of their church and accompanied them to dinner. Neither could eat much, however, and they sure didn't feel much like talking. Ted smiled inwardly as he thought about the irony of a man who made his living taking not wanting to talk.

The people they were with kept trying to encourage them. "Your lawyer is killing the prosecution! There is no way you will be convicted, Pastor. You are going to be a free man by this time tomorrow. You just wait and see," said Mr. Jeffries, sounding more confident than Ted had ever heard before. One benefit from this whole ordeal, if it turned out the way it should, might be a stronger relationship between Mr. Jeffries and himself.

Ted wanted to respond to Mr. Jeffries' comments, but could not think of a word that sounded intelligent at the moment. He just smiled politely and said, "Thank you, Mr. Jeffries. I sure hope you are right."

As soon as they could without appearing antisocial, Ted and Carla excused themselves and left the group. They quickly made their way to their motel room. They had a lot to discuss before they tried to go to sleep.

CHAPTER NINETEEN

When his alarm went off the next morning, Ted realized that he had slept very well. One glance at Carla told him that she had not enjoyed the night nearly as much as he had. He didn't mention her appearance however. He simply took her in his arms and said, "Thank you, Honey, for standing beside me all these years. You are the best gift God has ever given me. I love you more than you could possibly know." He leaned toward her and pressed his lips on hers. Their hug lingered a few extra moments before they both busied themselves with the task of getting ready for the day.

Neither could manage to eat much breakfast that morning, so they made their way to the Cleburne County Court House. As they walked up the steps to the stately building, Mr. Hodges fell into stride with them. They made their way through security and walked toward the courtroom as Mr. Hodges talked with Ted about his appearance on the stand. Reporters were trying to ask questions and cameras were flashing, but the two men kept walking toward the courtroom, completely ignoring the reporter's questions and their many requests for interviews.

Carla tagged along a few steps behind the men. Worry was etched into her brow. She wondered if this might be the day when her husband would be falsely convicted of murder. A litany of questions began to rush through her mind. Was last night the last night they would spend together for many years? How would she be able to explain it to the congregation if he was convicted? How would she be able to support herself once Ted's salary was no longer coming in? Would she have any friends left? What should she do first if Ted was not allowed to go home with her?

Slowly Carla made her way to the same seat where she had been sitting the day before. As she walked toward the seat, it seemed like it was an almost impossible assignment just to place one foot in front of the other. No one else was in the courtroom except Ted and his lawyer.

Quietly Carla bowed her head and began praying, "Dear Lord, please don't let this jury convict my husband for something he didn't do. You know how much I depend upon him. I simply don't know what I would do without him. Please, God, let my husband and I continue serving you in our church. I'm doing my best to trust you, but my faith is so weak at the moment. Help me to be stronger than I am right now. Help me to trust You more than I ever have. I really need Your help at this moment."

She continued to plead with God for several more minutes and then finally prayed a prayer of surrender. "Lord, I place my husband and the outcome of this trial into Your hands. I put our future and everything I am so worried about under Your control. You have always taken care of us. I know You will take care of us now. I trust You, Lord, and I ask for Your help in the name of Jesus, my Savior and Lord. Amen."

Her simple prayer of surrender caused a flood of peace like she had never previously experienced to wash over Carla. She felt as if she were standing in a waterfall with a cascade of God's peace running across her body from the top of her head to the bottom of her feet.

When Carla raised her head after praying, Ted was standing before her. He looked handsome in his dark blue suit and light blue tie. For a moment she thought he looked like an angel. She noticed that his tie was slightly crooked so she reached up and straightened it as she said with a weak smile creeping across her face, "Well, don't you look handsome, Rev. Ted Black?"

"I doubt that," Ted said. "Honey, I know this has been hard on you, but God is in control. He is going to help us get through this.

I feel a strange sense of confidence today. Very early this morning, God reminded me of the instructions Jesus gave when He sent the disciples to start their ministry. Listen to what He told them, Honey. I looked it up when I got here. It's in Matthew 10:19-20. *When they arrest you, do not worry about what to say or how to say it. At that time you will be given what to say, for it will not be you speaking, but the Spirit of your Father speaking through you.* He is going to help me on the witness stand today, Carla. I'm sure of it, and I am just as sure the outcome will be the correct one. Please try to keep from worrying, Carla. God is going to be in control today."

"Is it showing that much, Ted?" Carla asked. "Yes, I was pretty low this morning, but I just had some time with God, too. I feel much better now. In fact, I am experiencing the most peace I have felt since the day before you disappeared. I believe God is giving us just what we need for today. Don't you, Honey?"

"I'm sure He is, Sweetheart," Ted replied softly as he squeezed her hand. "I have to get back to my seat now. I love you."

"I love you, too, Ted." Carla managed to say before a couple of tears fell from her eyes and dripped to the shiny, wooden floor of the courtroom.

Ted took his place beside his lawyer and the men were soon engaged in an intense conversation. Neither man seemed to be aware of the rest of the courtroom as people made their way into the room that morning. Several people came up to speak to Carla before they made their way into the seats a little ways behind her.

Tiffany Lee walked into Carla's row, however, and sat down beside her. "You look like you could use a friend this morning, Carla. Do you mind if I sit with you?" she asked.

"That would be wonderful," Carla said honestly. She was glad to have Tiffany with her, and soon began to tell her about the wonderful sense of peace she was experiencing. Tiffany was thrilled that God had given such peace. She only wished she felt the same level of assurance deep in her heart. A nagging question kept forcing its way into her mind. Could Pastor Ted have done such a dastardly deed?

As she sat beside her friend, Carla looked at the décor of the room for the first time. She noticed many details, like the luxurious drapes that covered the windows and the deep, rich tones of the wood in the furniture. It was an impressive room. She had not even noticed its beauty the day before. "Isn't God's peace wonderful?" she thought to herself. "When you are at peace with Him, you can see things you do not see at other times." Deep inside she hoped that Tiffany was enjoying the same peace she was.

Mr. Birch, the prosecutor, rushed into the courtroom obviously concerned about something. He nodded toward Ted's lawyer. Before the men could speak, however, the bailiff asked everyone to rise and Judge Cox made his way to the bench.

"I believe that you were ready to bring one of your primary witnesses to the stand, Mr. Hodges," Judge Cox said, as if there had been no overnight break.

"That's right, Your Honor," Mr. Hodges replied. "The Defense would like to call the Reverend Ted Black to the stand."

At least four reporters grabbed their notepads and all six members of the leadership board of Hillside Community Church bowed their heads simultaneously. Ted rose from his chair beside his counsel and walked confidently to the witness stand. Carla looked admiringly at her husband. She still thought he was one of the most handsome men she had ever known. Carla didn't feel the need to pray. She was now as sure of God's help as Ted was. Both of them seemed to be held in a capsule of God's peace.

Step by step Mr. Hodges led Ted through the time he was at the lake house. Ted talked about the enjoyment of the first two weeks he was there. He told about finding a body near where he went to read each day. He told about his cell phone with the dead battery and about trying to tie the body to a tree to make sure it didn't drift away while he went to report what he had found. He told about the details of his arrest. Judge Cox wrote furiously at times during the testimony.

Ted told about his first night in the jail. He told the jury about the old man in the cell with him and about seeing him the night he was kidnapped from the jail. He told about the men dressed in black who took him from the jail to a hidden cabin in the woods where he spent many long…and sometimes tortured…days. No, he wasn't physically tortured, but he was tortured deep within because he doubted God's love and concern for him. To Ted this was the worst torture a person could endure.

With a smile Ted told about finding a loose knothole, through which he was able to make at least a visual contact with the outside world. He told about Buddy, the white dog, who came around at least twice at just the right time. He happily reported receiving a Bible from Hank and about the conversations they had.

Ted told about the confusing day when Ben was brought into his room and thrown on the bed. He told about his concern for his friend as he sat by the side of his bed until he regained consciousness. With tears in his eyes he told about how close his friend had been to being "forced to shoot his pastor" before "ending his own life." Only a group of motorcycles kept them from losing their lives that day according to Ted's report.

By the time Ted told about his rescue by the Federal Bureau of Investigation, tears were sliding down the faces of his Leadership Board. They had not realized how much their pastor had suffered while he was held against his will. When Ted told about the F.B.I. agents who had protected him during such dangerous times, He gave God credit for using the F.B.I. and went on to testify about the way God can use any means necessary to accomplish His will and to protect His children. Everyone in the courtroom was spellbound. Not a word of objection was uttered.

Ted concluded his testimony by describing what it was like to see Carla after so many days of fear and uncertainty. As he described seeing her for the first time, a tear made its way down his cheek. He told about holding her in his arms and looking into her eyes. One could sense the fact that several on the jury were choking back tears as well. Ted paid tribute to his wife and said that she had suffered as much or more than he had during this entire time. He publicly thanked her for standing by his side during the worst days of his life.

By the time Mr. Birch, the prosecutor, began his cross-examination, everyone in the courtroom was held in the grip of a man whose peace and assurance saturated the room. Mr. Birch tried to question some of details of the story Ted had given without much success. Instead of getting him confused, it merely gave Ted another opportunity to share about his own personal growth. It also gave him the chance to talk about the marvelous, and sometimes mysterious, way God works. Without intending to, Ted made the authorities look much more like the guilty party than he could ever be.

After only a short time, Mr. Birch gave up. He could not break this man's confidence. Nor could he get him confused about any of the facts in his story. Every time he tried to create some doubt about what happened, he ended up giving Rev. Black more time to convince the jury of his spotless integrity. Mr. Birch soon realized that he had witnessed much more than a man's testimony. He didn't know how to explain it, but he was convinced that Ted had told the truth and nothing but the truth. Mr. Birch told the judge that had no further questions and Ted was allowed to return to his place beside his lawyer.

"Wow!" Ted's lawyer whispered. "I've been practicing law for a long time, and I have never seen a display like that. It was almost like someone was speaking through you, Ted. You swayed the judge, the jury, and the entire courtroom. Why, I even think Mr. Birch was touched by your performance."

"It was no performance, Mr. Hodge," Ted corrected his lawyer. "I was merely sharing what God placed in my mouth to share. I give Him praise for whatever took place. I can truthfully say someone was speaking through me. Remind me after the trial is over and I'll explain what I mean."

Before Ted could say another word, Judge Cox asked Mr. Hodge if he had other witnesses. He did and proceeded to call Old Man Smith, Mr. Crane, and a few other important witnesses. They verified the story Ted had told while he was on the stand.

About four o'clock in the afternoon the lawyers made their closing statements. Mr. Birch sounded apologetic for the actions of the police in the way they handled this case, and insisted that the jury not judge the police. They were to judge Ted Black instead. His summary of what supposedly happened that day had no evidence to support it and sounded rather hallow and unconvincing.

Mr. Hodge, on the other hand, sounded confident and sure of his account of what really happened. He underscored the fact that the state had nothing but a far-fetched theory.

"The facts don't add up, Ladies and Gentlemen," Mr. Hodge concluded. "It is obvious that someone else did this crime and got their buddies to help them try to cover it up. It will only be a matter of time before the true killer is discovered and justice will then be served. Until then, let us not make an awful mistake by convicting an innocent man. Let's not send a man who has done so much good for so many people to jail because an irritated sheriff rushed to judgment before he bothered to find the facts. I'm asking you to do what you know deep inside you should do. Declare this pastor not guilty so he can resume his ministry to others. Thank you, Ladies and Gentlemen, I know you will do what is right."

Judge Cox then instructed the jury regarding its deliberations and dismissed them to follow the bailiff to the jury room.

After the judge left the courtroom, Ted stood to his feet and walked over to Carla. Instead of inviting her to leave the courtroom with him, however, he sat down in the chair on the opposite side of her from Tiffany. One by one the leaders of Hillside Community Church came to where Ted and Carla were sitting. Individually they assured him of their support. A few said they were proud of him. More than one declared that it was evident God was in the courtroom that day. Without exception they expressed their love for him. Then they did something that surprised both Ted and Carla. They made a circle around them and committed them into the care of a powerful and strong God. It was a very tender and special moment.

As his leaders lifted him to God, Ted decided he needed to take Carla out of town for a few days of rest and recuperation once this was all over. When the leaders walked away, He presented the idea to Carla. He asked her to accompany him for a few days atop Mount Magazine, one of their favorite places to visit. She was thrilled at the possibility of getting away from the spotlight for a few days, and immediately agreed to his plan. In that moment neither of them considered the possibility that Ted might not be set free.

About an hour later word circulated that the jury had reached a decision. The courtroom began to fill up again. Ted took his place beside Mr. Hodges. Tiffany sat beside Carla. Another lady from the church made her way to the other side of Carla. Tension was mounting in the room, but Carla and Ted revealed nothing on their faces but complete peace. Neither seemed worried or anxious. Both were resigned to the outcome.

When Judge Cox asked the foreman of the jury if the jury had reached a decision, the ladies on either side of Carla clasped her hands in theirs. Each tried in her own way to will the jury to announce a not-guilty verdict. The foreman of the jury rose to his feet and spoke with confidence, "We, the jury in the case of the State verses Ted Black, find the Reverend Ted Black, not guilty of the murder of Marla Harris."

Ted and Carla simultaneously whispered, "Thank you, Lord." Tiffany and several other spectators dabbed their eyes with tissues. Mr. Hodges shook Ted's hand.

As soon as Judge Cox dismissed the courtroom and left the room, Ted went to Carla and held her in his arms for several minutes. The couple was surrounded by well-wishers, but everyone showed amazing restraint. They waited until the couple turned to face them. Slaps on the back and assurances of love and support came from nearly everyone in the courtroom that day. Mr. Birch even uttered to himself, "Best case I ever lost."

As soon as Ted and Carla walked out of the courthouse, they were immediately surrounded by reporters and cameras. Every station in Little Rock had a team of reporters present. Patiently Ted answered question after question from the crowd of reporters. He showed the same confidence that he had shown in the courtroom.

When the questions finally ended and the reporters began putting things away, Ted looked across the lawn toward the buildings straight in front of him. When he did, he couldn't believe his eyes. Walking on the sidewalk in front of a building across the street was a big white dog.

"Buddy," Ted whispered, as he tried to push past the people around him so he could go see the dog. A tall man stood up right in front of him blocking his view. By the time he got around the man, the dog was gone. Ted looked in all directions. He even ran across the street and searched the side streets, but there was no white dog in sight.

As Ted walked back across the street, his mind filled with memories of an earlier time when a white dog was a part of his life. A smile spread across his face as he looked toward the sky and said, "Thank you, God, for sending Buddy." Then he took Carla by the hand and led her to their car. As soon as they buckled their seatbelts, they praised God for His deliverance, and drove back to Little Rock.

A Word from the Author

During my years as a pastor, I have heard more than one person complain that God doesn't answer their prayers. They can usually share long lists of petitions that bought no apparent results. When answers did not come for extended periods of time, some were ready to throw their hands up and abandon their faith. This temptation to set one's faith aside increases dramatically when the petitions are connected to tragic events.

When God's answers do come, people still struggle with His timing. They think He should have answered in a positive way as soon as the petition was made. They are sure things would have been better if God would have adjusted His timing to fit what they have determined would have been best. It is increasingly difficult for these questioners to hold on to their faith when the answer seems to be delayed for extended periods of time.

It is for these people that I have written this book. Hopefully the struggles Pastor Ted and his wife experienced when answers to their prayers were delayed will help readers of the book to understand that no one is exempt from such questions. I pray that those who feel like it does no good to pray will be able to see that apparent delays can actually be opportunities for God to accomplish things that might not otherwise happen. Certainly I hope they will learn how valuable it is to cling to one's faith no matter how intense the struggles become.

The idea for this book came when I was granted a sabbatical leave from my responsibilities as the lead pastor of First Church of the Nazarene in Little Rock, Arkansas. I chose to spend that time in a borrowed, redwood cabin located on the bank of Greers Ferry Lake, a 40,000 acre recreational lake located about seventy-five miles north of Little Rock. The owners of the cabin affectionately call it "The Lake House."

While I was there, I read feverishly, spending many hours sitting in a lawn chair near the lake. I also took daily walks and was accompanied on many of those walks by a big, white dog. Since I didn't know the name of the dog, I called him "Buddy." Other details from the thirty days I spent at the Lake House appear in the book. Of course most of the details are purely fictional. I will leave it to the reader to decide which details are fictional and which are real. I will say, however, that, to the best of my knowledge, there is no Highpoint, Arkansas, nor is there a Sheriff Bill Bixley. There was no FBI probe, nor is there a Hillside Community Church in Little Rock. Those details only exist in my mind, but they could describe people, churches, and communities almost anywhere. In fact, many of the fictional details could have happened anywhere at any time.

It is my prayer that your faith will have been strengthened by reading this book. Please remember these words from the Apostle Paul as you make your journey through life, *"And we know that in all things God works for the good of those who love him, who have been called according to his purpose."* (Romans 8:28 NIV) Perhaps you will discover the strength to trust God during your struggles even when it looks like He is not answering or is, at best, delaying His answer.